SNAP

BELINDA BAUER

LARGE
PRINT

First published in Great Britain 2018
by
Bantam Press
an imprint of Transworld Publishers

First Isis Edition
published 2018
by arrangement with
Transworld Publishers
Penguin Random House

This book is a work of fiction and, except in the case of
historical fact, any resemblance to actual persons, living
or dead, is purely coincidental.

A catalogue record for this book is available
from the British Library.

ISBN 978–1–78541–606–4 (hb)
ISBN 978–1–78541–612–5 (pb)

Published by
F. A. Thorpe (Publishing)
Anstey, Leicestershire

Set by Words & Graphics Ltd.
Anstey, Leicestershire
Printed and bound in Great Britain by
T. J. International Ltd., Padstow, Cornwall

This book is printed on acid-free paper

For my wonderful agent, Jane Gregory.
Happy thirtieth birthday!

There are two kinds of people in the world.
Those who think it could never happen to them.
And those who know it will . . .

20 August 1998

It was so hot in the car that the seats smelled as though they were melting. Jack was in shorts, and every time he moved his legs they sounded like Sellotape.

The windows were down, but no air moved; only small bugs whirred, with a sound like dry paper. Overhead hung a single frayed cloud, while an invisible jet drew a chalky line across the bright blue sky.

Sweat trickled down the back of Jack's neck, and he cracked open the door.

"Don't!" said Joy. "Mum said stay!"

"I *am* staying," he said. "Just trying to get cool."

It was a quiet afternoon and there wasn't much traffic, but every time a car passed, the old Toyota shook a little.

When a lorry passed, it shook a lot.

"Shut the door!" said Joy.

Jack shut the door and made a tutting sound. Joy was a drama queen. Nine years old and always bursting into tears or song or laughter. She usually got her own way.

"How long now?" she whined.

Jack looked at his watch. He'd got it last birthday when he'd turned eleven.

He'd asked for a PlayStation.

"Twenty minutes," he said.

That was a lie. It was nearly an hour since the car had coughed and jerked and rolled to a crunchy halt on the hard shoulder of the southbound M5 motorway. That made it over half an hour since their mother had left them here to walk to an emergency phone.

Stay in the car. I won't be long.

Well, she *was* being long — and Jack got that niggle of irritation he always felt when his mother was not his father. Dad would have known what was wrong with the car. He wouldn't have sat turning the key over and over until the battery ran flat. He would have had a mobile, and not had to walk up the road to find an emergency phone like a caveman.

Merry grizzled and wriggled against the straps of her car seat, the sun on her face making her restless.

Joy leaned over and put her dummy back in.

"Shit, it's hot," said Jack.

"You said shit," said Joy. "I'm telling." But she didn't say it with her usual conviction. It was too hot for conviction.

Baking hot.

For a while, they played "I Spy". S for Sky and R for Road and F for Field, until they exhausted the limited supply of real stuff and started on stupid things like YUF for Your Ugly Face.

"Shut up!" said Joy.

Jack was going to say *YOU shut up!* But then he decided not to, because he was the oldest and he was in charge. Mum had said so . . .

2

Jack's in charge.

. . . so instead he spied D for Dust and looked up the road and tried to guess how far the phone might be, and how fast his mother had walked there with her slow, pregnant waddle, and how long she had stayed on the phone. He didn't know any of the answers but he felt instinctively that she had been gone for too long.

She'd pulled over in the shade of a short row of conifers, but their shadows had shortened to nothing.

He squinted into the vicious sun.

If he just looked away, and then back again, he would see her come around the bend. He imagined it. He willed it to happen.

If he just looked away.

And then back again.

Slowly.

She would be there.

She would be there . . .

She wasn't there.

"Where is she?" said Joy and kicked the back of the seat. "She said ten minutes and she's been ten hours!"

In the front seat, Merry started to cry.

"Look what you did!" Jack hung over the seat and fussed over Merry and gave her the bottle, but she only had one suck of water and then pushed the teat out of her mouth so she could go on grizzling.

"She hates you," said Joy with smug satisfaction, and so Jack sat down again and let her have a go, but it turned out that Merry hated everybody, and cried and cried.

And cried.

Merry was two but still did a lot of crying. Jack didn't like her much.

"Maybe she needs a new nappy," said Joy warily. "There's one in the bag."

"She'll stop in a minute," said Jack. He wasn't doing a nappy.

Neither was Joy; she didn't mention the nappy again — just bit her lip and frowned at the bend in the road.

"Where is she?" she said again — but this time in a voice that was so small and scared that Jack had to do something or he'd get scared too.

Scareder.

"Let's go and meet her," he said suddenly.

"How?"

"Just walk," said Jack. "It's not far. Mum said so."

"If it's not far, why isn't she back?"

Jack ignored the question and opened the door.

"Won't she be angry we didn't stay like she told us?"

"No. She'll be pleased we went to find her."

Joy's eyes became big and round. "Is she lost?"

"No!"

Her bottom lip trembled. "Are *we* lost?"

"No! Nobody's lost! I'm just hot and bored and want to walk about a bit, that's all. You can come with me or you can stay here."

"I don't want to stay here," said Joy quickly.

"Then come," said Jack.

"What about Merry?"

"She can walk."

"She won't, though."

"We'll carry her then."

"She's too heavy."

"I'll carry her."

"What about the cars?" Joy said at the sparkling flashes that whooshed past. There weren't many, but they were fast. "It's too dangerous," she added softly.

That was what their mother had said when they had wanted to go with her to the phone.

It's too dangerous.

"Come on," said Jack. "Everything will be OK. I promise."

Joy carried the baby bag, and Jack carried the baby.

She refused to walk, of course.

The breathless air twitched in the wake of each car, then flopped down dead in the dust again.

They walked right up close to the crash barrier. The strip of wavy steel was much bigger than it looked from a speeding car — elbow-high, and nearly down to the cuff of Jack's blue soccer shorts. The ground on the other side of the barrier was covered with long brittle grass. It fell steeply away into scrub and small trees, and then bottomed out. Beyond that were hedges and beyond the hedges were fields. Grass. A few sheep. Mostly the fields were empty, and the nearest barns were far away — little brick toys with corrugated roofs.

The hard shoulder was wide, but it wasn't empty. It always looked that way from the car, so Jack was surprised to see that it was actually full of things. Coke cans and workmen's gloves and bits of plastic pipe and soft toys — a random collection, united by having been squashed flat and covered with the same fine, grey dust.

"What if a car stops?" said Joy. "Should we get in?"

"Of course not," he snorted. Everyone knew that getting in a stranger's car was a good way to get murdered.

Joy knew it too, and seemed reassured that her brother wasn't taking any chances.

Jack turned to look back at their car. It sparkled in the blinding light but already seemed a long way away — as if it were a boat sinking in a deep ocean, and once it was gone they would never be able to reach it again.

Or maybe *they* were sinking . . .

Merry was heavy, and all the heavier for being fractious and whiny. Her face was red and screwed up and she wriggled like a lead worm in Jack's arms.

"The sun's in her face," he said. "Is there a hat in the bag?"

They stopped and Joy put the bag on the ground so she could look in it.

"No. Only a bib." She held it up to him, squinting in the white-hot sun. The bib was yellow with a blue duck on it. Jack draped it over Merry's head and she calmed down a bit.

They walked on.

"My feet hurt." Joy was wearing silly pink flip-flops with a plastic flower between her first two toes.

"Not far now," said Jack, although he had no idea how far it was to anywhere. It was just something his father said. He glanced over his shoulder; their car had disappeared around the bend.

They were completely alone.

Jack wished Dad were here. He could have carried Merry and Joy and the baby bag.

Easily.

His arms ached, so he put Merry down and tried to make her walk, but she still wouldn't, even though she could. She hung back and stiffened up, so he couldn't drag her along.

He wanted to smack her.

Instead he blew out his cheeks and wiped the sweat off his forehead with the back of his hand, then hoisted her up again and went on.

A lorry horn blared as it roared past, and the bib blew off Merry's head and fluttered over the crash barrier.

"Oh!"

Joy stood on her toes to reach over the barrier for it, but another car went by and the bib leapt off the tops of the stiff yellow grass and floated down the steep slope.

"Leave it!" said Jack.

"But it's the one with the duck!"

Jack kept walking and, after a moment, Joy caught up with him. She kept looking back at the bright spot of bib.

"I wish I had an ice cream," she said.

Jack ignored her but he wished he had an ice cream too. A lolly would do. His mouth was so dry. He wondered whether it was possible to die of thirst in the middle of the lush Devonshire countryside.

It felt possible.

He hated his mother. He hated her. Why couldn't they have gone with her? Why did she say she wouldn't be long when she was long?

When they found her, he wouldn't speak to her. That would show her! He should just slide down the bank right here, find a gate in a hedge, walk to a farmhouse, get a drink and a phone.

Call Daddy.

Let him be in charge.

Let her worry when she got back to the car and found them gone . . .

But he didn't do any of that.

They reached a scrubby little apple tree and lingered for a moment in its latticed shade. Jack put Merry down with a groan. Immediately she plumped down on the cushion of her nappy among the small, bright fruit that had spilled across the hard shoulder.

"Don't put her on the ground," said Joy. "It's filthy!"

"I don't care. She weighs a ton."

"So does this bag." Joy dropped it and picked an apple off the tree. It was red, but when she nibbled it, it was hard and sour and she spat it on to the tarmac. Instead she suckled water from Merry's bottle, then offered it to Jack. They took turns until it was all gone.

"We should have saved some for Merry," said Joy.

"Too late now," said Jack.

Cars passed. Nobody stopped.

"Let's go," said Jack.

"I don't want to," said Joy. "It's too hot."

"We have to. We're not going to find Mum by sitting around here."

Joy squinted up the road. It was long and straight and there was no sign of their mother or anybody else on the hard shoulder — only a shimmering lake, like a desert mirage.

"I want to go back."

Jack took the key out of his pocket and held it out. "OK," he said, "here's the key."

Joy didn't take it. She looked around at the bend that now hid the car, then sighed and said, "The bag is soooo heavy."

"Leave it then. Just bring a nappy so Mum can change her."

That's what they did. Joy took out a nappy and Jack jammed the baby bag carefully into the narrow gap where the apple tree almost touched the crash barrier, so that nobody could see it but they could find it again when they all got back to the car.

Then he picked up Merry and they carried on walking.

On the opposite carriageway a blue car slowed down in the fast lane and the driver stared at them. Jack looked away, his heart fluttering with groundless fear, until the car's engine faded away.

Merry wriggled on his hip and started to bawl again — "Mama! Mama!" — her chubby arms and splayed fingers reaching out towards the car that was already too far behind them to return to.

"Mama's not there," said Jack. "She's this way. We're going to find her."

Merry's bawling faded slowly until finally she put her arms around his neck and her cheek on his shoulder, and emitted a low, gravelly drone that pulsed to the rhythm of his footsteps.

Joy stopped and said, "What's that?"

Up ahead, three crows pecked and hopped over a bloody lump.

"I don't know."

"Is it something dead?"

"I don't know."

But it was something dead. As they got closer they could hear the flies.

It was a dead fox — squashed flat, but not yet covered in dust — its slick pink guts bulging from a tear in the orange fur. The crows were fighting over its eyes.

Jack couldn't look. He swallowed the disgust in his throat, while Joy waved her arms at the crows. They flapped away — but only a few feet — then hopped back again.

"Yaaa!" she shouted. "Yaaaaaaa!"

But the crows laughed and lurched around her like a cruel gang.

She rushed at them.

"JOY!"

Jack grabbed her arm and a car split the air with its angry horn as it swerved to miss her.

Joy looked at him — her eyes huge in her white face, her mouth an "O" of shock.

Then they both laughed. High and cackling, like the crows. It wasn't funny laughter, but they kept on anyway, like playing laughter chicken, long after the mirth had run out and their faces started to ache.

Then Jack pointed over Joy's shoulder.

"There's the phone!"

A hundred yards away was a small orange lollipop.

They hurried away from the dead fox with new urgency. Jack walked so fast that it was almost jogging. Joy took hold of the back of his T-shirt, as if she were scared she might be uncoupled from their little train and left behind. Jack's arms ached and sweat burned his eyes. Merry's dangling feet kicked his thighs and Joy's tugging unbalanced him, but he didn't slow down. Not until they were thirty or forty yards from the phone. Then he started to look around for his mother — over the barrier and down the grass slope. And even further, into the trees and the hedges and the fields beyond, his desperate eyes sought clues.

Maybe she had fallen, or was waiting on the other side of the barrier. Maybe she was watching them approach now, and waving. Waiting for them to see her. When he saw her, he would wave back. He would speak to her. Of course he would! Everything bad would be forgotten! He was excited by the anticipation of relief.

"Where is she?" said Joy.

Jack ignored her.

"Jack?"

"Sssh."

He hurried on, frowning. Ten yards from the phone, he stopped.

The orange receiver was dangling from the box. It hung down, just touching the tops of the yellow grass, motionless on its twisted wire.

Jack got a very bad feeling.

It was all wrong.

11

All, all wrong.

Joy moved. She let go of Jack's shirt and brushed past him. "It's broken," she said, and reached for the phone.

"Don't touch it!" he yelled, and she burst into tears.

They walked another quarter-mile through the stifling air.

Still nobody stopped.

Nobody wanted to get involved.

People in cars — families! — with air-con and mobile phones and Coca-Colas drove past them, while Joy sobbed quietly and Jack kept carrying Merry.

Kept walking, although he couldn't feel his legs.

Or his heart.

It wasn't until they were halfway up the slip-road that a car finally slowed and then ground to a halt on the gravel ahead of them.

They stopped, trembling and tear-stained, and exhausted by heat and by fear.

There was a long, hot blink of arid time.

Then the car door creaked open, and a policeman stepped out.

2001

Catherine While woke with a start and the feeling — the certainty — that somebody was in the house.

"Adam?"

Adam wasn't there. He was in Chesterfield. Catherine knew that because only yesterday he'd sent her a postcard of the bus station with an ironic doodle on it.

And yet she called out again.

"Adam?"

Nothing. Just that creepy feeling that she was not alone. The streetlamp outside the window flickered and went out, leaving her momentarily blind.

It felt . . . planned.

"Adam?" she whispered into the blackness.

"Prrrrrp!"

Catherine squeaked as the cat landed on her legs.

"Get off, Chips!"

She sat up with a grunt and a series of awkward wiggles under the weight of her occupied belly, and shooed the cat off the bed.

"Don't panic," she told her tummy firmly. "It's only the cat."

Adam had had a second cat, called Fish, who had been squashed by a car before they'd met. Catherine had made a sympathetic face, of course, but secretly she had been relieved to hear it. One cat was more than enough to worry about sitting on the baby's face. Chips was a fluffy white rag-doll, with fetching blue eyes, but Catherine wasn't a cat person. That didn't make her a dog person, mind — she'd never had a pet of any description, not even a goldfish — but in the two years she and Adam had been together, she'd learned enough to know she definitely wasn't a cat person.

He was. He was all over the cat, and the cat — and its hair — was all over him. Catherine was sure that cats had their place in the grand scheme of things — but she was equally sure that that place wasn't shitting in a box in a corner of the kitchen.

Or jumping on her bed.

She must have left the bedroom door ajar last night, and Chips had seen his chance to reassert his right as a cat to lie on his minion's pillow, and to piddle freely in his sock drawer.

Catherine hissed, and Chips stepped haughtily out of the room with a look over his shoulder that said, *I'll remember this.*

"Do your worst," said Catherine defiantly, and lay back on her pillow.

At least Chips had brought her back from her fright.

Catherine clasped her hands over her stomach — amazed and amused by how far away it was from what she'd always thought of as her body. The first few months had been nothing really — a bit of a turn, of

14

the sort that might quickly disappear after a few weeks on an exercise bike. Then the bulge had become big enough to celebrate by leaning back and sticking it out — like carrying a potted plant in from the garden. Now, seven months in, getting out of a chair felt more like hoisting a bag of compost on to a trolley at B&Q.

She couldn't wait for the day when the baby was laid on her breast, red and screwed up and bawling . . .

I'll never let anything hurt you!

The vehement promise was not something Catherine had ever formulated or decided. It came unbidden and at random times, straight from her heart, in the same way she imagined the baby would come from her womb — in a rush of emotion that brought tears to her eyes and steel to her spine.

She wiped her eyes on the heel of her hand and sighed and cursed Chips. She was going to need all the sleep she could get quite soon, and resented missing out on even a wink.

Dr Samuels had told her to create the utmost serenity for herself and her unborn child.

Utmost serenity.

The doctor had actually used those words and Catherine had actually laughed at them. But the longer her pregnancy went on, the more she could see the value of utmost serenity, and she had started to meditate and light candles, and to read trashy novels in the bath. She had foot massages and kale smoothies and went to weekly antenatal classes, where she rolled around on her back like a stuck beetle while Adam helped her to breathe and to push and to giggle helplessly in supposed readiness for what was to come.

Catherine decided to read herself back to sleep. She had a tempting To Be Read pile, but her hormones kept drawing her compulsively to *The Big Book of Baby Names*. It was silly really; she and Adam both preferred traditional names, and the book was full of ridiculous ones. Plus, they'd sort of settled already on Alice for a girl and Frank for a boy, for her grandmother and his father. But while she knew she was never going to call her baby Bunker or Crimpelene, Catherine felt duty bound not to overlook even a remote possibility.

She turned to switch on the lamp, but stopped with her hand in mid air.

There was a noise.

She couldn't identify quite what or where it was, but it sounded like somebody trying not to make a sound.

Somebody in the house.

Catherine's neck prickled with ancient warning.

She was thirty-one and had lived alone all her adult life until she'd moved in with Adam nearly two years before. When you lived alone, and you heard a noise in the night, you didn't cower under the bedclothes and wait for your fate to saunter up the stairs and down the hallway. When you lived alone, you got up and grabbed the torch, the bat, the hairspray, and you sneaked downstairs to confront . . .

The dishwasher.

Which was the only thing that had ever made a noise loud enough to wake her.

But she hadn't set the dishwasher . . .

Catherine wasn't as well prepared as she used to be — and was a lot more pregnant than she'd ever been. But there was nobody here but her. And so, with a muffled grunt, she swung her legs out of bed and rocked to her feet.

She crept on to the landing and picked up the vase from the bookshelf. It was chunky Swedish glass and she'd never liked it. Throwing it at an intruder would kill two birds with one stone.

She took a deep breath, then snapped on the landing light and yelled, "Whoever's there had better get the hell out of this house! I've called the police and I'm armed!"

She started down the stairs, holding the vase at shoulder height, feeling both terrified and idiotic. At the bottom she stopped and listened again.

Nothing.

Had she been mistaken? It wouldn't be the first time. Being alone in a house made every noise louder. Scarier. If she'd been sure, she'd have called the police, and she hadn't — even though the phone was right next to Adam's side of the bed . . .

She adjusted the vase in her right hand, and moved cautiously from room to room. She gained courage with each doorway she passed through. The lounge and the dining room and the kitchen.

There was nobody there.

Catherine put the vase down on the kitchen table next to her camera and phone, and blew out her cheeks in relief — glad to be wrong.

Then she stared at her camera and phone. She didn't remember leaving them on the table. Why would she? And Adam's laptop was beside them, when it was always on the desk in the study —

Son of a bitch!

Catherine understood in a flash. The items were on the table next to the back door so that the burglar could pick them up on his way out!

Breathless with panic, she checked the door. It was unlocked! She had locked it, she was sure of that. The intruder must have left through it when she'd shouted — not even stopping to grab his loot!

Quickly she locked it again, and then pressed herself desperately against the cold glass — cupping her hands around her face to see into the night.

Then she sucked in her breath as a liquid black shape detached itself from the shadow of the house and flitted through the shrubbery and over the fence, like oil.

"I see you!" she shouted. "I see you, you bastard!"

Her heart hammered but the words gave her strength.

And then it was over.

He was there and he was gone.

She was scared and she was safe.

It was over, and the patch of condensation her shout had left on the glass shrunk slowly away to nothing.

Catherine stepped back from the door. Her legs shook, and she sat down and put a trembling hand on her belly.

Her mind flitted through the events — darting back and forth between cause and consequence, and what was and what might have been, until it finally started to settle and function at a more normal rate.

She was OK.

They were OK.

Nothing bad had happened. Nothing had been taken.

Those were the most important things. The basics.

But there was more. She also hadn't panicked. She hadn't screamed. She hadn't hidden under the bed. She hadn't had to be rescued by a man. She'd been brave and she'd been clever.

Catherine had almost forgotten what independence felt like, and she went back upstairs with a tiny grain of pride starting to swell in her chest.

She went into the bedroom and closed the door firmly behind her and let out an enormous sigh of relief. Then she turned to the bed and her stomach clenched so hard that the baby kicked back.

The bedside lamp was on.

It hadn't been on. Her hand had stopped in mid air, remember? She *knew* she hadn't turned it on.

And in the little pool of light, there was a knife.

Not a kitchen knife.

A *real* knife.

Catherine moved without walking.

She looked down on the knife.

A bright blade — serrated on one edge, curved on the other to a cruel point; the handle inlaid with pearly clouds reflected in a petrol sea of . . .

Abalone.

The word surfaced from the deep ocean of her mind and felt right, even though she wasn't sure what abalone was. The pale shell was so serene, so beautiful, that surely the blade could not be as brutal as it looked? As if from a great distance, Catherine watched her own hand reach out and touch a brief finger to the point.

She gasped as electricity raced up her arm and neck to the top of her head. Tears sprang to her eyes and a tiny red ball swelled from the pad of her forefinger and sat there shining like a ruby in a Swiss watch.

She put her finger in her mouth with a shudder.

And noticed the birthday card.

Flowers in a bucket. *To my Daughter on your Special Day.* Her mother chose the worst cards. A week after her birthday Catherine had bundled it up with all her others and put them in a drawer in the spare room.

And yet, here it was, next to her bed . . .

She felt disorientated, as if this were a dream, or a time warp.

She opened the card.

Her mother's scratchy signature had been roughly crossed out and on the blank side of the card was scrawled a new message . . .

I could have killed you.

August 1998

It had been a week.

A week when nobody spoke above a whisper, apart from Merry, who cried as often and as loudly as she liked, until a neighbour they called Auntie, but wasn't, came and took her away, "Just until Eileen comes home."

When she'd gone, the quiet house got *so quiet* that the silence itself was nearly a noise.

Jack and Joy didn't go to school. It wasn't as much fun as it sounded. They played cards, or watched cartoons with the sound down, between the silhouettes of policemen who wandered in and out like clumsy ghosts. The head policeman had a moustache as big as a cowboy's. "Call me Ralph," he told them, but they called him nothing — just watched him go in and out of the kitchen with papers and pictures, to say secret things to their father.

When they were hungry, they ate cereal straight from the packet. When they were thirsty, they drank from the tap. When they were tired, they leaned against each other on the sofa like penguins in a snowstorm and slept awkward, restless sleeps where they dreamed of hot, dusty tarmac and of nobody stopping.

Nobody getting involved.

Now and then, their father would look up as if he had just remembered them and say, "Are you two all right?" and Jack and Joy would both nod furiously, because he was very busy with the police and with the papers, and because if they said they were *not* all right, maybe another Auntie they didn't even know would come and take them away like Merry.

The newspapers came through the door every morning in a series of thuds, like dead birds falling out of the sky and on to the mat.

Every paper, every day.

Their father sat at the kitchen table, obsessively reading and rereading every word anyone knew or had guessed about his wife's disappearance — bent close to the pages to glean more meaning, his lips moving and his fingers darkening with newsprint. He wouldn't throw a single paper away in case he'd missed something, and kept every copy in a pile that grew shockingly fast.

Jack and Joy weren't supposed to read the papers, but they sneaked a peek now and then when their father was upstairs, discovering in random snatches that the search for their mother was still going on and that the police were looking for clues but not finding any.

Uncle Bill came from Ireland, with his ugly wife, Una. She pretended to like children, while he sat in the kitchen and watched their father heave piles of papers from one side of the room to the other, pointing at pages, explaining his theory of what might have happened to his wife.

Theories.

He had several and Jack was sick of hearing them. All were relayed in shaky little word-bursts not at all like his father's man-voice. And all involved a mistake, a misunderstanding, a miscommunication that would seem obvious once Eileen came home and explained where she'd been all this time, and everything would be all right.

Jack hummed loudly so he didn't have to hear his father sounding so pathetic.

"Shut up," said Joy.

Jack hummed louder.

They couldn't go outside because of all the reporters who knocked on the door and stood on the corner near the pub, or sat in cars parked up and down the street.

Waiting.

"What are they waiting for?" said Joy, as they played cards on her bedroom carpet.

"I don't know," said Jack, although he thought he did — and thought she must too.

But she got off the carpet and opened the bedroom window and shouted down at them, "*What are you waiting for?*"

Nobody told her. But the next day her picture was on the front of all the papers that came through the door.

The headline was "ABANDONED JOY".

It tortured Jack.

Maybe his mother really had abandoned them on the hard shoulder. Maybe he was too noisy and Joy was too irritating and Merry was too shitty for her to take any more. Maybe she'd never even called for help from the orange phone. Maybe she'd just got sick of him and Joy bickering in the back, and had pulled over and walked round the bend, and stuck out her thumb and hitched a ride to a whole new life. A richer husband, a better car, and the new baby, who would be getting all the toys and hugs instead of him and Joy and Merry.

If he tried hard enough for long enough, Jack could get angry enough not to care if his mother *ever* came home.

But even at those times, he secretly wished that she would.

Three Years Later

Catherine sat with the phone in her hand until morning. Twice she had dialled Adam's number and twice she had hung up before it could ring.

Once she had started to call the police, but never reached the third nine.

Now she just sat on the edge of the bed, with Chips pressed against her thigh for warmth.

She was desperate to hear Adam's voice. Had run through their conversation in her head a hundred times in the past few hours.

"*Hello?*" he'd say gruffly, and she'd say a small *hello*, and then she'd burst into tears.

She knew she would, however hard she tried not to. Just thinking of it made her well up. And then his voice would change to that soft one she knew so well ... "*Catherine? ...*" — the way it had when she'd announced she was pregnant. He'd been so happy! He'd immediately made her lie, giggling and protesting, on the sofa with tea, toast and the remote control, while he'd rushed out and bought chicken soup and multivitamins and all the things that a new baby might need from an all-night garage. These had included a pack of disposable nappies, age 12–18 months, six jars of Heinz banana pudding, and a remote-controlled train that blew bubbles from its stack. Two days later he'd signed up for a St John Ambulance course in Baby First Aid, and had traded in his Golf for a repulsive pea-green Volvo with Side Impact Protection System and automatic child locks . . .

She couldn't tell him.

Couldn't tell him that while he'd done everything in his power to protect her and the baby, she'd bumbled about the house, making silly threats, with only a vase to defend herself and their unborn child against a knife-wielding invader.

That she'd let in!

She'd left the bathroom window open so that Chips wouldn't bother her if he wanted to go out, even though Adam had told her not to.

But it's so hot! her brain always whined when he said it. *And it's so small and so high! Nobody could get in there.*

But somebody *had* got in. The air freshener had been knocked on to its side and — if she cocked her head right — she could see a smudged footprint on the white-tiled sill. Piecing it together in the long dark hours, Catherine guessed the burglar had got in there and headed straight downstairs, where he'd collected the obvious things and unlocked the back door to make sure he wouldn't be trapped.

Then he'd come back upstairs . . .

26

He must have been right behind her while she was standing at the top of the stairs, waving the vase and shouting empty threats.

Catherine shivered.

She hadn't been brave, she'd been reckless. She could see that now.

It must be baby brain! People had told her that pregnancy could lead to irrational decisions, illogical choices, and Catherine had dismissed it as misogynist nonsense.

But now she saw that she'd been as stupid as a stupid blonde in a horror film who wouldn't turn the stupid lights on.

She'd put herself at risk, and — even worse — she'd put their baby at risk.

How could she tell Adam that?

She couldn't. She wouldn't. He'd be furious — and justifiably so. Her utmost serenity would be *over*, and it would be all worry and guilt and heightened security while Adam wrapped her in cotton wool until she choked . . .

The panic rose in her.

9—9—

She stopped dialling again. Thought it through once more.

What could the police do? The burglar hadn't taken anything. Hadn't broken anything. She hadn't even *seen* him. If she called the police she'd have to relive the whole thing — parade her stupidity for the whole world to see — for nothing. The police rarely caught burglars. Everybody knew that. The *Gazette* was full of crimes the police couldn't solve. One burglar had been at large for so long they'd even given him a nickname: Goldilocks — because he slept in the beds and ate the food in the houses he broke into. And if the police couldn't catch *him*, Catherine doubted they'd be working overtime to catch the man who'd knocked over her air freshener.

Calling the police would get her nothing but embarrassment. Embarrassment and hoo-hah.

That's what her mother would call it. *Hoo-hah*. Fuss and nonsense.

Catherine tossed the phone aside and hugged her belly. "We don't need hoo-hah, do we, Crimpelene?"

She sighed at her bad luck. She wasn't even supposed to *be* here! She and Adam were supposed to be away for the weekend in Sidmouth, celebrating their anniversary. But rent was due and they were saving up so hard for the baby, and when the opportunity for overtime had come up, they'd cancelled.

Even so, it was adding insult to injury to be burgled and threatened, when she should have been waking up to breakfast in bed overlooking the sea.

She looked through the window now as if the view might surprise her with a miracle, but all she saw was Mr Kent's house on the other side of the cul-de-sac, washed with a pink glow from the rising sun.

Although it wasn't the ocean, the view made her feel better. The night had been bad. But the night was *over*, and the dawn painted her fear a new, less scary colour.

I could have killed you.

Yes, she thought, *but you didn't, did you?*

That was the comforting truth.

The intruder hadn't killed her. Even when she'd been wavering at the top of the stairs, fat and unbalanced, with a vase wobbling in her hand. Even when a gentle nudge would have sent her plummeting to the hallway . . . he *still* hadn't killed her. Had done his best to *avoid* her, before escaping the way he'd come in.

In fact, *she*'d scared *him* out of the house!

Maybe he'd just wanted to scare her back . . .

Catherine blinked.

That felt plausible. The burglar, thwarted by her noisy bluster, had made his own spiteful gesture in return. Left the knife and the threat, knowing he'd stolen her security, if not her valuables.

It was logical.

Likely . . .

And that was how Catherine started to think of it. How she *decided* to think of it. Empty bravado. Signifying nothing. And if it was nothing, then nobody needed to know. Nothing had to change. It would be best for her and — more importantly — best for the baby.

Utmost serenity.

And so Catherine While didn't call her husband to tell him of the burglary. And she also didn't call the police.

Instead she covered the shimmering knife with a tissue and picked it up gingerly, holding it at arm's length, as if it might go off in her hand.

Then she pushed it to the very back of her bra drawer, and burned the birthday card in the kitchen sink.

August 1998

Missing Eileen's Last Call for Help.

Jack's breath stopped in his throat with a soft click and the dangling orange phone on the twisted wire came back to him with all the sick terror of that moment.

Don't touch it! . . .

The headline was above a weird story that ran down the page in short, ragged lines, like a poem — but Jack didn't need to read the story to know what it meant.

His mother *had* called for help. She'd held that orange phone. She'd been *right there* . . . How long before they had arrived?

Ages?

Moments?

Jack's heart twisted with regret. If only he'd gone after her sooner! If only he'd walked faster! If only he hadn't played stupid "I Spy", or had to carry Merry, or stopped under the apple tree! They would have caught up with her, and she wouldn't have disappeared.

He was in charge! He could have saved her!

If only . . .

He took a deep, shaky breath.

Hello?

The word floated off the page at him and Jack could hear his mother say it as clearly as if she were standing at his shoulder.

Hello?
What's your emergency?
Oh. Hello. My car's broken down.
What's your name please, Ma'am?
Mrs Eileen Bright.
OK, Mrs Bright, and where is the car now?
On the hard shoulder.
Is it parked safely off the carriageway?
Yes.
Are you alone?
My children are with me.
Are they still in the car?
Yes.
Can you get them out and move them to the other side of the crash barrier away from the traffic? I'll wait for you.
Um, no. I can't. They're not here with me. The car's back down the road. It was too dangerous to walk up the road with them all. Merry's only a baby, you see? And I didn't know how far it would be. But they're safe.

Jack hitched in a shocked breath.
Safe? How could she say that? How could she say they were safe? They *weren't* safe! She didn't know how

unsafe they'd been! How Joy's flip-flops had hurt her, or how Merry had cried, or how his arms had almost fallen *right off* with the effort of carrying her. Or about the fox and the crows and the car that had nearly hit them!

Or how nobody had stopped. Nobody had got involved.

Anger lit a match in Jack's belly. She didn't care about them! How could she? She'd left them! Joy was abandoned. They *all* were!

A creak overhead and Jack held his breath at the ceiling, then read on fast . . .

OK, Mrs Bright, is the car to the north or the south of your location?

Umm, let's see [laughs]. We were going to Exeter —

[Sound of a car pulling over]

Oh, somebody's stopping to help now . . . Hi . . .

[Sound of muffled voices. Eileen Bright. Unidentified male.]

Mrs Bright?

[Silence]

Hello, Mrs Bright?

[Silence]

Mrs Bright. Are you there?

[Silence]

[Sound of car driving off]

Jack stared blankly at the last line.

Sound of car driving off.

He didn't want the story to end like that. He even turned the page, in the dumb hope that it went on somewhere else but, of course, it didn't.

Sound of car driving off.

With his mother inside it?

He didn't know.

Apparently nobody knew.

But *everybody* knew that getting into a stranger's car was a good way to get murdered . . .

There was a knock at the front door. He pushed the paper into the pile and scuttled back to the sofa.

Low voices in the hallway. It was Call-Me-Ralph, and with him was a jolly-looking young policewoman, who smiled at Jack and said her name was Pam, and asked if she could sit next to him on the sofa.

Jack didn't want her to sit next to him, but she did anyway, while Call-Me-Ralph followed his father into the kitchen with a higgledy-piggledy pile of papers under his arm. Folders and forms and photos, and a plastic evidence bag.

Jack felt a sudden rat-ball of fear and fury squeeze his throat in a tight, writhing lump. His cheeks blazed and his ears went all underwater.

In a horrible dream he got up, but Pam caught his wrist and held it hard enough so that he knew she wasn't going to let go without a fight.

"Let me go," he said, through gritted teeth. "Let me go."

Then they both flinched as behind the kitchen door his father wailed like a butchered dog.

And Jack knew . . . he *knew*! And he *hated* them all for letting him guess what he didn't want to know.

"Let me *go*!" he cried, and twisted and jerked his arm and broke Pam's hold. He ran out of the room and drummed upstairs.

Joy was in her bedroom playing Snap with her doll. She looked up at him and said, "What's all the shouting?"

He couldn't speak. He couldn't say. He just stood.

"You want to play?" she said.

Jack didn't want to play. But he also didn't have the words to tell her that their mother was dead.

Instead, he sat slowly down on the scratchy blue carpet and watched Joy fumble the cards back together, so that they could start at the beginning again.

2001

Catherine kept busy all day long.

She renewed the car insurance. She put in a half-load of washing and assuaged her eco-guilt by turning the temperature down to 30. She planned a menu. Janet and Rhod were coming over on Friday but she wasn't going to push the boat out. They were level-two friends — inviteable but not investable. She'd worked with Jan at the estate agency, but Rhod was just part of a couples package that was likely to be upgraded at some point in the future. Catherine had only met him once. He did something dull in an office — even Jan wasn't sure what.

Catherine thought she'd do risotto. It was easy, yet somehow people were always impressed. So she had to buy the right rice. And lamb's lettuce and feta and butternut squash and pomegranate seeds. She'd get it all on Friday morning so it would be fresh.

Or maybe she'd practise first to avoid another dinner-party disaster like the one Adam always called the Great Pork Fiasco. Dinner on that occasion had been pulled pork. She'd got it a bit wrong and it was like shoelaces, but Adam had saved the night by making a joke of it so that nobody had felt obliged to clear their plate.

Adam never minded her kitchen misadventures. He would shrug and finish every bit and say, *You'll get it right next time*. At Christmas he'd bought her a cookery book, with an Ann Summers gift voucher marking the page on pulled pork.

After that she'd got it right.

After that they'd got *everything* right . . .

Catherine patted her tummy and smiled and looked at the clock. It must be nearly lunchtime.

It was half past ten.

She called her mother.

"Oh, hello!" said Helen Pitt. "To what do I owe *this* honour?"

It was her default greeting — designed to provoke guilt in her daughter. But instead of her usual irritation, Catherine felt a sentimental little welling-up at the sound of her mother's voice.

Delayed shock, she imagined. Silly, really.

"I know," she said. "It's been a while."

"Months!"

It *had* been months. But her mother was an easy woman to avoid. She was impatient, self-absorbed and judgemental. She disapproved of Adam because he'd been in debt when they'd married, but had cut him no slack for working all the hours God sent to pay it off since then.

Once she'd told Catherine that she'd left her own husband because he moved his lips while reading.

"Drove me absolutely crazy!" she'd said with a melodramatic wave of her arm. "Irretrievable breakdown!"

Whether the reason was true or not, the breakdown *had* been irretrievable, and Catherine's father had removed himself to a safe distance — Canada, in fact — before he could apparently feel confident of a bit of peace and quiet. So Catherine had grown up with only one parent — and often suspected that it may not have been the better one.

Almost unconsciously she touched her bump, reassuring the baby that it would always have two parents who loved it very much.

"How are you, Mum?"

"My hands are fat," her mother grumbled. She had arthritis, which meant that sometimes she experienced the agony of her diamond rings not fitting. She complained to the doctor about it constantly; she'd paid good money for those rings and somehow felt that the NHS simply didn't want her wearing them — socialist cartel that it was.

Catherine made a sympathetic noise for the fat fingers and changed the subject.

"How was Palma?"

"All right," said her mother. "Although I don't know why it has to be so *hot* there."

Catherine ignored the discontent.

"Weren't you going somewhere?" said Helen vaguely.

"We were going to Sidmouth this weekend for our anniversary, but we had to cancel at the last minute. We'll go after the baby's born."

"Why did you have to cancel?"

"Adam took a job up north."

"Hm," said Helen darkly. "Let's hope that's all he's got up north."

Bitch!

Catherine refused to rise to the bait.

Finally her mother asked, "How are you?" Better late than never.

"Good," said Catherine tightly.

"When's it due?"

She knew when it was due. Catherine had marked it on the calendar on her mother's fridge.

"Eight weeks now."

"You peeing all the time?"

"All the time."

"Bloody awful, isn't it?"

Catherine shrugged. "It won't last for ever."

She wondered whether she should tell her mother about the burglary. She was a woman, after all — and a mother, albeit a poor one — and it would alleviate the guilty burden of silence. At least her mother would never tell Adam —

"I'm going shopping," said Helen suddenly. "Shall I bring you in a fish pie?"

"No thanks, Mum, I'm not eating fish while I'm pregnant."

Helen snorted. "You and your fads!"

"It's not a fad. I want the baby to be healthy, that's all."

"Fish pies are healthy! There's no fat in them, it's all fish! And lovely puff pastry."

Her mother thought pastry was a food group.

"Thanks, but fish contains mercury."

"Really!" Helen snorted. "You'd think nobody had ever had a baby before!"

"Look, Mum, everyone's different. I've never had a go at you for smoking while you were pregnant with me, have I?"

"Why would you?" said Helen breezily. "You were perfectly healthy."

"I weighed six pounds."

"That was normal in those days."

"Because everybody smoked!"

"My God, Catherine, stop making a fuss! People have been having babies for thousands of years without all this hoo-hah about fish and cigarettes."

"Oh, for God's sake!" Catherine hung up, incandescent. And then, as quickly as it had flared, her anger fizzled out to nothing and she laughed instead.

The call had certainly taken her mind off the break-in! And even if she'd told her mother about it, she shouldn't have expected any sympathy from her. After all, people had been getting murdered for thousands of years without all this hoo-hah about knives and death threats . . .

The next day, when Adam came home, Catherine didn't tell him — for the very same reason.

Hoo-hah.

Jack found his mother.

He was on the hard shoulder and she was there too, in her white summer maternity dress, keeping pace with him on the opposite side of the barrier, pressing through the long yellow grass in the blazing heat.

"Come back over this side," he said.

I can't, she said. *I'm too fat.*

So he stopped to help her, but he wasn't allowed to touch her hand, he was only allowed to throw her a long ribbon striped in red and white, like a barber's pole. He kept throwing it, and she kept missing it. He would have to go over and help her. He climbed the barrier, hissing through his teeth as the steel scorched his hands and his bare thighs.

But he was too late.

Always.

Even as he straddled the hot, sharp metal, his mother slipped and stumbled and slid a little way down the bank on her knees.

Mum!

She laughed up at him, pretending it was funny, but it wasn't funny.

Then she slid some more, and grabbed two handfuls of brittle grass to stop herself. The grass broke. But she kept on grabbing it and grabbing it, and it kept on breaking and breaking, and she slid down the bank in tufty jerks with her fists full of bundles of dry yellow stalks until she disappeared into the scrub far below . . .

Jack woke with his heart beating so hard he could hear it.

It wasn't real! He wasn't there! He was here, safe in bed, and the pillow under his cheek smelled of childhood. Like gym ropes and sparklers, and Marmite sandwiches in warm Tupperware.

If he turned, he'd see last night's underpants draped across the hairpin bend of his Scalextric track — the Monza edition. Ferrari v. Lamborghini. He always drove the Ferrari; Joy always got the Lambo. When she wasn't around, he straightened and cleaned the brushes on the Ferrari so they made the best possible contact with the track.

He always won, and victory smelled like burning wire.

The sweat cooled on his forehead as his breathing evened out.

Soon Mum would call him for breakfast and he'd pretend not to hear.

Pretend he was still sleeping.

He closed his eyes. An extra few minutes before school . . .

Jack? Ja-a-a-ack!

Jack slowly opened his eyes and frowned at the Artex ceiling with its design of repeating fans.

There was no point. No matter how hard he tried, he could never pretend she was there.

Dreams died, but the nightmare of reality went on. Sometimes it was difficult for him to tell one from the other, as the past and its tattered variations haunted him whether awake or asleep. Sometimes Jack's memories were so dark that he couldn't make them out — and didn't want to try.

He sat up slowly and rubbed his face. The thin white latex gloves snagged on the soft blond prickles on his cheeks.

Beard.

He didn't want one, but he looked forward to shaving it off.

He swung his legs out of bed, still in his clothes. Still in his shoes.

He stood up — three years taller now, but they hadn't counted for much: he was still just a skinny kid, with ragged blond hair and no arse in his jeans. Without the stubble, he could have been twelve. With it, he looked like a twelve-year-old with stubble.

Only his eyes were older.

Much older.

Jack Bright's eyes were narrow as a smoker's and pale grey, as if all the colour had been cried out of them. They were divided by a single deep frown line that belonged to a man in his fifties with the cares of the world on his shoulders.

He opened the drawers of the chest one by one and picked out random items of clothing. A vest. Some knickers. Socks. A child's T-shirt . . . He put them in a backpack and closed the drawers.

There was a framed photo on top of the cluttered chest. Jack picked it up. A boy and a girl at a zoo, laughing into the sun. Ice creams in cones melting down chubby fingers, while a resigned lemur stared mournfully from the cage behind them.

Jack remembered days like that. At least, he thought he did. Sometimes his memories felt like stories he'd once been told of a parallel boy with another life.

He dropped the photograph on to the carpet, and stamped on it.

Once.

Twice.

Then he ground his heel into it until nothing could be seen of the shattered children.

He reached up and tore the dinosaur lampshade off the swaying flex, then picked up a hammer from the bedside table and set about the toys — rampaging through the room, knocking heads off dolls and crushing pink plastic underfoot.

He took a kitchen knife and plunged it into the mattress, slashing and tearing the bed and the bedding until the room was a snow globe of feathery, foamy white.

Then he pulled his hoodie tight around his cheeks and over his mouth, and jogged loosely down the stairs, hammer in hand.

The lounge had been tastefully decorated in creams and pale blues, and the TV was still on from the night before.

Everybody Loves Raymond.

Jack hit the screen so hard that the hammer got stuck and he had to jerk it out of the hole in Raymond's face. The television swayed violently on its stand as the image flickered into a neon rainbow and then failed with an electrical fizz.

Jack jumped up and down on the coffee table until it snapped and folded drunkenly in half. He beat the family's pictures off the walls, then hunted down their ornaments — smashing heirlooms and childish pottery to powder and shards.

He stood for a moment, his chest heaving from the rush of destruction, then stabbed at the cushions of the sofa and chairs — jerking the blade through the fabric, so that foam and kapok bulged obscenely from the tears and nothing could be saved, nothing repaired, nothing recovered.

A lesson in loss.

He moved on to the kitchen, where a discoloured puddle had spread across the floor from the open door of the fridge freezer. At one end of the table were the remains of a meal. Pasta with salad. The pan sat unwashed on the hob. He put it in the washing machine, then tossed in the plate and the cutlery and the leftovers, and set the machine to spin.

Jack picked up his stuff. A video camera, a jewellery box, and a PlayStation and games. He slid them all into his backpack, along with the hammer, a packet of spaghetti, and six shiny red apples from a bowl.

Then he left through the back door, vaulted over the garden fence, and walked quickly away from the ruined house.

Nobody saw him.

Nobody cared.

Nobody wanted to get involved.

It was a spectacular day for murder.

The wide West Country sky was blue and gorgeous. It hummed with bees and smelled of hay.

Detective Chief Inspector John Marvel scowled and pulled down the blind.

The sky stung his eyes. Of course, it was the same sky as in London, but at least there you couldn't see so much of the bloody stuff. Marvel didn't know what was worse: too much sky above or too much green beneath. He'd been born and bred in the city, and was suspicious of both.

But he was here now. Exiled by pen-pushers who didn't understand that when it came to murder, sometimes you had to bend the rules to get your man.

Sometimes to breaking point.

And sometimes you *still* didn't get your man.

That was the harsh reality. But nobody seemed to understand reality any more — not even the police.

Policing was changing. Now it was all about stats and paperwork and degrees and equality, and good old-fashioned coppers like him, who worked on contacts and hunches and sheer hard-won *experience*, were on the endangered list with targets on their arses.

Marvel had finally been forced out by a single unfortunate incident that had resulted in the death of a suspect fleeing custody. Not his fault, really, but he'd been picked off anyway. He wasn't mortally wounded, but he'd been winged hard enough to knock him off course, from heading a murder team in Lewisham to heading nowhere in darkest Somerset.

Fuck it, Marvel thought for the hundredth time. *It's not for ever.*

He'd be out in the cold for a bit. Have to prove himself to a bunch of bloody yokels as penance for his supposed transgression. And as soon as something came up in another metropolitan force, he'd be off.

In the meantime, he had rented a two-bedroom house in Taunton. It was tiny in the way that only modern houses could be — with space for all mod cons but no room for character. You could have a dishwasher or an alcove, but not both. The Lego-trained architect had tried to inject some personality into the neighbourhood by aligning each carbon-copy house at a different angle on its handkerchief plot, but that only made the place look untidy, rather than interesting.

Marvel didn't care. It was a place to shower and to sleep. He'd only brought three pieces of furniture with him — a brand-new bed, a sagging blue corduroy sofa, and a big TV with six surround-sound Acoustic Energy speakers. He'd taken hours to set up the speakers just the way he liked them, so that a ripple of applause at Lord's seemed to go all the way around the room.

It was almost like being there.

Debbie had kept the furniture, but Marvel didn't miss it. Or her. What was there to miss? There was a microwave in the kitchen and a Burger King at the bottom of the road.

He missed the dog a bit, which did surprise him.

His shirts and suits and shoes filled a fifth of the built-in wardrobe, and his socks rolled about in a single drawer.

Marvel wasn't one for knick-knacks but he did have an ashtray shaped like lungs. He was planning to quit, but, until then, he kept it within easy reach on the arm of the sofa.

At one point he'd thought he might buy a table, but then realized that the laminate floor was flat, and even better for laying out files and crime-scene photos, when you didn't have a dog or children to mess them up.

There was a knock at the front door and Marvel picked up his jacket. It was his first day on the job and they were sending a man to drive him until he learned the lie of the land.

He paused with his hand on the doorknob.

Stuck to the wall next to the door with a single tab of tape was a photograph. A little girl on a BMX bike. Goofy teeth and a sprinkling of summer freckles; bobbed brown hair caught behind one sticky-out ear . . .

John Marvel took a deep breath.

Then he opened the door and went to work.

Marvel resolved to learn the lie of the land asap, because DC Parrott was a terrible driver — light on the accelerator and heavy on the brakes, which made for a slow and jerky ride. Toby Parrott was extremely thin — or wore a uniform that was extremely big. Marvel couldn't quite make up his mind which it was, but he reckoned he could stick a milk bottle down the back of the man's collar without chilling his neck. He also had a very large, beaky nose, but hadn't even smiled when Marvel had called him Polly.

Bollocks to him, thought Marvel. He'd made the joke and wasn't going to unmake it just because Parrott was a humourless prick. Back in London, Parrott would have liked it or lumped it.

They left Taunton and headed down the M5, flanked by rolling hills dotted with cows, then turned on to a dual carriageway that rose and fell and twisted and turned through seven more miles of green, before descending steeply into Tiverton.

Taunton was a hick town, but at least it *was* a town, with gum-stuck pavements and recognizable shops, and the homely reek of diesel fumes. Tiverton was at the bottom of a crater made of countryside, and it seemed to Marvel that there was not a single place from where you couldn't see a hedge and at least a couple of sheep.

He had been there once before.

Well, not there, but somewhere just as bad. A childhood holiday in Cornwall? He wasn't sure. He just remembered being sick in the back of the car all the live-long way, and then having little to do for two long weeks other than bicker with his brother.

It was hot, and Parrott said the air-con was broken, so Marvel put the window down and grimaced.

"Smells like cowshit," he said.

"That's because it is cowshit," said Parrott stiffly.

Marvel put the window up and they drove the rest of the way in hot silence.

Detective Sergeant Reynolds was a very clever man.

And that was official.

His IQ score was 138 on the Stanford-Binet scale. And he'd been under the weather on the day he'd taken the test — as he never tired of telling his mother. Bit of a sniffle, he would say, and then let a modest shrug indicate: *Otherwise, who knows . . .?*

Reynolds loved being a police officer. He'd always had a finely honed sense of right and wrong, and felt it his duty not to waste it. It wasn't a complicated thing: he was right and everybody else was wrong. Luckily, he was clever enough to know that his always being right was unlikely to find favour with all those who were correspondingly always wrong. He was usually able to overcome any Dunning-Kruger types with his people skills, his sense of humour and his humility.

Everybody liked him.

If they were smart enough . . .

Now Reynolds ducked down and squinted into the wing mirror of the unmarked Ford Focus. It was a scorching day, and Reynolds knew that most officers would be in shirtsleeves, but his mother always said that shirtsleeves were for factory workers at the seaside, so he was wearing a lightweight pale grey suit, a red silk tie with sharp white stripes, and black shoes that were so shiny they were almost patent.

He examined his face in the mirror, and touched his thick brown hair with two tentative fingers. The new DCI was arriving today, and Reynolds wanted to look his best.

Then he walked across the street and knocked on the door of a mid-terrace house. While he waited for an answer, he touched his hair again, with the very tips of his fingers, just to make sure that all was well with the world.

A sinewy, red-faced man in shorts and sandals opened the door.

"Mr Passmore? Detective Sergeant Reynolds."

The house was a mess. A gigantic TV lay face-down on the carpet, while three sunburnt children stared at it from the sofa, as if it might right itself at any moment and resume normal service.

Mr Passmore pointed at it. "Nearly new, that was. Only had it a couple of months. I've got the receipts for everything. If it helps to identify them."

"I'm sure it will," said Reynolds, although he seriously doubted they would ever achieve the luxury of recovering any of the items in order to make a match. He didn't tell Mr Passmore that most burglaries were only investigated in the most perfunctory way. It wasn't that nobody cared — only that nobody cared to pay for the time it took, and the lousy return on investment in terms of convictions. Of course, they would do their best with what they had, but it was more to show willing to the taxpayers than in any real hope of tracing the perpetrator or recovering stolen goods.

Every now and then somebody would come home to find a junkie swaying in the middle of their living room with a microwave oven in his arms, and call the police. The junkie would cough to twenty or thirty other burglaries that could be taken into consideration for sentencing purposes. And then those burglaries would be marked "solved" and they would all feel better about themselves.

Everybody else just got a crime reference number to give the insurance company, and bought new stuff. Reynolds didn't like it, but it was a fact of life. When it came to burglary, he considered it his realistic role to provide the two "Rs" — Recording and Reassurance. The third "R" — Recovery — was something that only happened on TV.

And yet Reynolds had driven all the way from Taunton to Tiverton this morning for this burglary . . .

"Did they go upstairs?" he ventured.

Before Mr Passmore could answer, a voice behind him said, "Perverts."

Reynolds turned. The kitchen doorway was filled with a woman he assumed was Mrs Passmore. She was a hefty blonde and the sunburn on her face was interrupted by white circles around both eyes where she'd apparently worn very good sunglasses all holiday long, like a reverse panda.

"Perverts," she said again. "In our bed. Disgusting. We'll have to get rid of the bedding, the mattress, the lot."

Reynolds nodded and wrote carefully in his book. *GOLDILOCKS?*

"Could I see?"

Mr Passmore led him back through the front room to the hallway. As he did, he waved an angry arm at the suitcases still standing at the bottom of the stairs. "You don't expect to come home from holiday to this."

"Indeed you don't," said Reynolds sympathetically. "Are you insured?"

"Yeah," the man scowled. "But you know what those bastards are like. Always looking for ways not to pay you."

"Well, you've done the right thing leaving everything as it was for us to see, Mr Passmore. I'll be giving you a crime reference number for the insurance claim."

"Thanks." Passmore nodded, slightly less maroon.

The second "R" ticked off, Reynolds went upstairs.

In the master bedroom, he hit paydirt. The bed had obviously been slept in. The duvet had been pushed aside, all the pillows were on the floor. Reynolds took out his notebook again and, with a triumphant flourish, crossed out the question mark after *GOLDILOCKS*.

A wedding photo of Mrs Passmore — forty pounds and three shades lighter — was smashed on the bedside table.

"Fucking hell!"

Reynolds winced at the expletive. He stepped quickly on to the landing and leaned over the bannister in time to see a stocky, middle-aged man kick a child's pink suitcase across the hallway.

"Excuse me!" said Reynolds sternly. "This is a crime scene!"

The man glared up at him. "You Reynolds?"

"Yes."

"You ever hear of clear passage? I nearly broke my bloody neck!"

Reynolds paused, and then said warily, "DCI Marvel?"

By way of an answer, the man scowled. "Where's the body?"

Reynolds hurried down the stairs. "Sir," he hissed in soft warning, "there are children in the front room."

Marvel lowered his voice. "Dead children?"

"No, sir."

"Then why are you telling me about them?" boomed Marvel. "Where's the bloody body?"

"There is no body, sir. It's a burglary."

"A what?" Marvel blinked at him.

He was shorter than Reynolds, and fatter. And infinitely scruffier. But there was something in his eyes — a piggy cunning — that put Reynolds on the back foot.

Mr Passmore opened the door to the front room and Reynolds spoke quickly, before Marvel could.

"Detective Chief Inspector Marvel, this is Mr Passmore. He and his family got home from Portugal today. They found their house broken into and several items of value missing, and other things damaged."

Mr Passmore stepped out of the way so Marvel could see the big TV. He straddled the set and lifted it up so they could get a good look at the victim.

"See?" he said. "Smashed."

He let it drop to the rug once more.

"But that TV's broken," complained the smallest of the children — a blonde girl with blistered lips.

"That's right," snapped her father. "Some b — bad man's come in and broke it. Smashed. Only got it two months ago."

Marvel ignored him and his TV and addressed Reynolds. "I'm a homicide detective," he said. "When I'm rushed to the scene of a crime, I expect a murder victim, not a broken TV and a shit on the rug."

He stormed out.

Mr Passmore turned to Reynolds with a look of confused disgust on his face.

Reynolds cleared his throat weakly. "Some burglars do . . . that," he said, then hurried after Marvel, who was already halfway across the road, striding towards the car, against which DC Parrott was leaning with his hands in his pockets.

"Devon and Cornwall asked for our help, sir," he told Marvel's back. Then he glanced at Parrott and lowered his voice diplomatically. "This perpetrator's been running rings around them for a year and they don't want to look . . . inefficient."

"Why?" said Marvel. "Because they *are* inefficient? You don't waste a homicide detective on a fucking B&E!"

Marvel waved Parrott towards the driver's seat, opened the passenger door and lit up a cigarette.

"Very true, sir," said Reynolds. "But everyone mucks in when we don't have enough murders to go round."

Marvel turned and squinted at him. "What do you mean, not enough murders?"

Reynolds gave a little shrug. "Well, we get our fair share, of course, but sometimes there's . . . you know . . . a lull . . ."

"A lull?"

"Yes, sir," said Reynolds. "A lull."

Marvel looked completely stumped by the idea of a lull in the murder rate and, while he was adjusting, Reynolds pressed home his advantage.

"And this is not just any old burglary, sir. You must have seen it in the papers. They call him Goldilocks."

"Never heard of him," said Marvel. "What papers?"

"*Tiverton Gazette*," Parrott piped up. "Front page."

"God's sake!" said Marvel, and looked up and down the road, as if searching for someone with whom to share the disdain, but there was nobody.

He sighed and pinched his nose and said "*Shit*" under his breath, then gave Reynolds a glare that was furious and yet so resigned that Reynolds felt it was incumbent upon him to recognize the concession.

"I understand it's beneath you, sir," he said soothingly. "But we'd all be very grateful."

DCI Marvel stripped off his suit jacket, balled it up and tossed it into the car.

"Don't be an arse-creeper, Reynolds," he said as he rolled up his shirtsleeves and stomped on his cigarette.

"Yes, sir," said Reynolds, and followed him back across the road.

"Spare change? . . . Spare change?"

The homeless man lived against the buckled wall of the old stone archway between the shops that led to the tiny Tivoli cinema.

He was there all day, whatever the weather, sat on a square of cardboard under a poster for this week's Hollywood blockbuster, with his legs encased in a sleeping bag like a big blue caterpillar.

"Spare change?"

He repeated the words every time feet passed him. Next to him was an old plastic ice-cream tub for money. Jack had seen him take the good coins out, to make people feel sorry for him. To make them give him more money.

More free money.

"Spare change?"

People walked past.

"Spare change?"

Jack walked past. He kicked the tub so hard that it skittered noisily off the walls of the archway, while the coppers rolled and tinkled across the pavement. The man shrunk from him, shoulders hunched, a protective arm raised at the side of his head.

"Oi!" somebody yelled. "None of that here!"

An ancient farmer in market-day tweeds. Jack ignored him.

"Get a fucking job!" he threw over his shoulder as he headed for home.

From the outside, you couldn't tell that the house had died. From the outside, it was as neat and normal as a house could be that was squeezed into the middle of a short terrace next to a busy road.

The narrow strip of grass outside the door was always mown. A good lawn was the first line of defence. People saw the outside of the house being cared for and assumed that everything inside was cared for too.

The lawnmower was the best thing Jack had ever stolen. He'd got it from a garage that was bigger than their whole house up near Blundell's School, and had walked it home through the streets with a noisy rattle — but without any excuse as to why he had it, or where he might be going. So every time a car or a person had approached, he'd simply let go of the lawnmower and walked on without it.

What you doing with that mower, mate?

Not mine, mate. Just standing there when I come past.

But nobody *had* stopped him.

Nobody ever did.

He had nicked a litre of black gloss paint from HomeFayre and painted the front door.

He washed the windows.

He weeded the path.

He mowed the lawn.

And — like magic — people seemed to forget they were there.

But *inside* . . .

The door got stuck halfway, and Jack had to edge around it.

"*Shit.*"

There was a stack of newspapers behind the door. It wasn't big, but that wasn't the point. The hallway had to be kept clear. *Had* to. In case of visitors. It rarely happened, but if it did, everything must look . . . normal.

"Joy!" he shouted. "*Joy!*"

He kicked the stack angrily, then bent and hoisted it awkwardly into his arms —

Like Merry

– and walked into the living room.

After the house had died, it had been buried — slowly but relentlessly — under a mountain of newspapers.

All the papers, every day. His father had started them and they had never stopped. Over the years, they had been stacked into wavering walls that formed haphazard passageways as high as Jack's head and barely wide enough to walk through. They hid the real walls, blocked light from the windows and sucked it from the overhead bulbs so that it never found the floor — and mice and spiders made their homes there in the darkness.

Jack knew it was Joy, working at night when he was out. Moving walls and shifting stacks to maintain some crazy notion of home and family. Their mother was *in* the papers, and their father would not throw them out, and so Joy wouldn't throw them out. And so they kept coming. Forty pounds a week they cost him! Jack used to sneak them out of the house and dump them in the recycling bins outside Tesco, but one time Joy had seen him doing it and had chased him down the street, making a scene.

The place smelled of mould and must and mouse piss. Jack was so used to it that he barely noticed it any more except on the warmest of summer days, when the air outside was so fresh that coming indoors made him cough.

He had disconnected the gas fire, and it had disappeared overnight. There was little visible furniture in the house, although he knew it was still there, somewhere underneath. The only place to sit in the sitting room now was one cushion of the sofa, which Merry and Jack tried to keep clear by taking it in turns to sit there, hemmed in by news, so that Joy couldn't fill it with more.

Jack couldn't remember the last time he'd seen the television.

Upstairs, the bath and his bed were thick with mountains of news, and Merry slept in a nest she'd made of shredded paper, like a hamster.

Sometimes a clearing mysteriously appeared — in front of a window, or at the top of the stairs — but there never seemed to be any reason for it, and a day or a week later it would shrink and close and become another wall or a passageway, and be consigned to uncertain memory. For a long time there had been a roundel of blue carpet in Joy's room where they had once played cards, but even that had finally turned from a space into a pillar of papers.

Jack turned on the living-room light but it made little difference except to illuminate the headlines on the very tops of the piles.

He dumped the stack of papers on the head-high wall that bisected the lounge and stole the daylight. "There's papers in the hallway again, Joy. Don't say I didn't warn you."

There was the smallest sound behind the wall. It could have been a mouse. There were enough of them. Jack had got traps and sometimes one screamed in the night.

It wasn't a mouse though.

He edged through the corridor to the kitchen. To the table — the original source of the river of news that had flooded this room too, reducing it to a canyon between the piles on the groaning table and the cubbyholes containing the sink, the fridge, the washing machine and the cooker. When the papers had started to slide on to the hotplates Jack had taken the fuse out of the switch between meals so that nobody could burn the house down. Eventually he'd just left it out, and stolen a microwave instead, which now sat on the stove.

The paper canyon in the kitchen ended at the half-glazed back door, making the whole house into a dingy alimentary canal. Merry had cleared one end of a bench and was eating cornflakes from a bowl in her lap, with her bare feet resting on the gnarled shell of a large tortoise.

Merry had grown into a wan, pinched-looking child, with her brother's pale eyes and hair the colour of smog. She wore Hello Kitty pyjamas as faded as she was and two sizes too small, so that her pale shins stuck out like sticks.

"Hi," she said.

Jack said nothing. He put the spaghetti in the cupboard and the apples in the fridge, then checked through the stacks of newspapers, looking at the dates. He found a pile he wanted and sat cross-legged on the floor, pulling the first one into his lap.

Merry ate her cornflakes while he turned the pages. They were brittle at the edges — yellow and foxed — and every page he turned sounded like the wings of small bugs whirring through the hot summer air . . .

Small bugs

Small bugs

Next to his ear, Merry's spoon clinked against her bowl.

"Could you be a bit more noisy?"

She said nothing, just clinked and clinked until the cornflakes were gone, and then drank the milk from the bowl. There was nowhere to set it down because the table was piled almost to the ceiling with newspapers, so she just held it in her lap — her foot swinging gently beside Jack's arm.

"Did you buy me a book?"

"I got you some clothes."

Merry sighed. She was five, but a master of the sigh.

Jack scowled up at her. "What?"

Merry rolled her eyes.

"Read one of your other books."

"I read them all."

"Read them again."

"I read them all again. I read them loads."

She had, he knew. Merry was a demon for books. A home-schooling inspector had once called her "gifted" and been so dazzled by her that he hadn't noticed Jack's spelling or Joy's clumsy maths.

Jack waved a brief arm around the room. "Read the papers."

Merry pulled a face. "I read them all the time. I want to read a *real* story."

"I'll get you a book tomorrow."

"What one?"

"I don't know."

"Why don't you know?"

"I just don't."

"Can you get me one with vampires?"

"Jesus, Merry! I don't know!"

Jack went back to the papers. Back to the small bugs. Back to the hard shoulder. He could almost feel the heat through his shoes . . .

"What you looking for?"

"Stuff."

"What stuff?"

"Stuff about Mum."

"But *what* stuff?"

"Stuff you're too young to remember."

Merry frowned and pursed her lips. Then she tapped the tortoise with her toe and said, "Donald's older than anyone. He would remember."

Jack snorted. Then hissed with annoyance. Someone had cut a story out of the page, leaving only an L-shaped hole.

He went on to the next paper.

Then the next.

And the next.

There were more square holes than stories about his mother.

"There's a new old lady in Mrs Coyle's house," said Merry. "She's got glasses and a whirly bench."

Jack looked at her sharply. "Did you talk to her?"

"No."

"You know what to say."

"I'm not stupid," said Merry.

Jack turned a page and saw his mother's name.

Eileen.

DAD's PLEA TO MUM-TO-BE EILEEN

Angry embers spat and popped inside him. The papers always called her "mum-to-be". But she was a mum-who-already-was.

Everyone had forgotten him and Joy and Merry.

He scanned the story. There was nothing in it he didn't know. There was a photo of his mother, small and blurry, blonde hair, blue eyes. Smiling.

Alone.

Jack hated that photo but it was the only one the papers ever seemed to use, even though he remembered his father handing over a whole bundle of family photos to the police. Photos he'd never seen again. Photos of them riding bicycles and standing in paddling pools and on days out to places he couldn't even remember now.

But there had been one of them all together . . . The sea beyond them and their hair in their eyes — blown there by the North Devon wind, where they'd once rented a tumbledown cottage near a haunted house that hung off a cliff . . .

For a little while the photo had been on the fridge, and then it had been replaced — by a gas bill or a school report or one of Joy's drawings of a cat.

Something.

And now it was lost, and he wished he could find it. He thought one of the papers *must* have used that photo instead of this nasty little one of his mother, all alone . . .

Merry leaned a bony elbow on his shoulder and he winced.

"I remember Mummy."

"No you don't." He twisted away from her.

"I do," she insisted. "She looked just like that."

"What? Small and blurry?"

"Yes," said Merry defiantly.

Jack let it go. Merry didn't remember their mother. Not the way he did. And Joy, perhaps, although Joy was nuts, so it was hard to know what was left inside her head.

The other photo with the story showed his father behind a long table and a microphone.

Crying, of course.

He closed the paper angrily and pulled a different copy on to his lap.

Merry put her little feet on his back and wiggled her toes. "I'm giving you a massage."

He turned the pages.

Small bugs

Small bugs

"When I grow up I'm going to be a massager."

Jack said nothing, and after a few moments Merry sighed and slid off the bench and stood on a pile of papers so she could rinse out her bowl and her spoon in the sink, then put them on another pile to dry.

The paltry light in the kitchen dimmed further as she pressed her forehead against the back door.

"Can I go outside?"

Small bugs

"Jack?"

"What?"

"Can I go in the garden?"

"What time is it?"

Merry squinted at her watch. It was a child's old Timex, with red markings for "past" and blue for "to" times.

"Twenty past ten."

"Then, no."

"Why?"

"You know why."

Merry sighed on to the glass and wrote her name in her breath.

"Well, what *can* I do?"

Silence.

"What *can* I do?"

"You can get out of the bloody light."

Merry leaned to one side and said, "Keep your hair on!" She must have read that in some book, and it obviously amused her because she was using it all the time now.

"I'm going to pick the lock," she announced, and pushed a small finger into the empty keyhole and rattled the handle, but Jack looked up at her with such menace that she let go as if it were hot, and stepped away from the door and edged past him and sat down again.

She pulled a random newspaper from a pile.

"SHRIMPMAN WAS 'ANGEL OF DEATH'," she read loudly. "What's a shrimpman? Is it like a fisherman?"

"*Ship*man," said Jack, and stood up.

"A sailor?"

"It's his name. He's a doctor who killed a bunch of old people."

"Why?"

"Crazy, I suppose."

Merry studied the photo of the bearded, bespectacled man in a zip-up cardigan.

"He doesn't *look* crazy," she said.

"Nobody does," said Jack.

"Then how can you tell?"

"You can't," he said.

There was a long, troubled silence.

"But you can tell *vampires* though," Merry finally said. "Because of the teeth."

"Yeah," shrugged Jack. "But only when they smile."

"What's wrong with *you*?"

They were on a bench by the canal, and Smooth Louis Bridge was shaving his legs.

Jack jiggled the baby buggy and squinted angrily into the sun. "Nothing."

"Face like fourpence," said Louis, running the knife up his shin.

Smooth Louis was nearly hairless. What he couldn't shave, he plucked — openly and unashamedly. He had short black hair on his head, but no brows or discernible stubble, and always carried a pair of small pink tweezers with him, the way other young men carried cash and condoms.

He wore cargo shorts even in the depth of winter, for access to his knees, and his hands were rarely still. His long fingers played a constant tune on his own body. He ran them in an unconscious circuit along his brow, his jaw, across his shoulder and up his arm, down his thigh, his knee, his shin, and back to his face.

Checking for bristles.

If he found one he'd pluck it — there and then, without breaking conversational stride.

"Whatever," he said. "What do you want?"

"One fifty?"

Louis sucked air through his teeth like a bad plumber over a broken boiler.

Jack ignored it. It was habit, that was all. One fifty was a fair price, and Louis was a fair bloke. He wasn't worried.

Tiverton was not a metropolis but it was big enough to sustain a reasonable subclass of petty thieves and burglars, and two full-time fences — Louis Bridge and his estranged father, Mr Bridge.

Although he was only twenty-three, Louis had inherited the family business two years before, after his mother was tragically incarcerated.

BRIDGE FENCING.

That was the sign outside the timber yard. It made all the boys laugh, but Bridge Fencing was legal — and profitable enough to raise no suspicions if a person were careful. And Louis Bridge was very, *very* careful. He had been to prison once, in his old burgling days, and had sworn never to go again. "You know what this is?" he would say, tapping the side of his own nose. "Cleanest nose in the West Country."

It wasn't true.

Louis wasn't the oldest sibling of five, but he was far and away the most crooked. On a sliding crooked scale, it was Louis, Shawn, Tammy, Victor, Calvin. Louis was sharp and ambitious, and his mother had left him in charge of both fencing operations because Victor was too lazy, Tammy too crazy and Shawn too fond of heroin.

Louis's twin brother Calvin was the white sheep of the family. At nineteen he had run away and joined the police. It made things awkward between them, of course, but Louis still loved his brother and each turned a blind eye to the other's unfortunate career choices, and once a year they went camping together on Exmoor.

However, Mr Bridge wouldn't speak to Louis because of it. He already didn't speak to Calvin for betraying the family — even though he himself had abandoned the whole lot of them when they were children and set up house with another woman.

The Bridge family was full of cock-eyed principles and shifting alliances.

The baby stirred as if he might wake, and Jack jiggled the buggy some more.

The baby wasn't his. It was Louis's baby.

Baz. The Bazster. Bazman. Baz Baby Bunting.

All Louis's boys took their turn looking after Baz. If you weren't ready to do that, you weren't ready to do business with Louis.

Jack didn't mind. Baz was no bother, except you had to remember not to swear around him. Much of the time he was in the buggy, and if he wasn't, Louis clipped an extendable dog lead to a belt loop on his tiny jeans, which made babysitting not unlike flying a chubby kite — reeling him in for orange squash, or yanking him off a collision course with drowning or dog poo.

Louis's girlfriend, Lorraine, had a proper job, and didn't see why they should pay for childcare when Louis was at home all day.

So Jack jiggled the buggy.

He liked it here by the canal. It was quiet and smelled good, and sometimes there was a kingfisher skimming the surface of the water like a brilliant pebble.

On the opposite towpath a large skewbald horse dragged a narrowboat so slowly that the water bent rather than rippled around the bow, and left a wake of lazy humps instead of waves. The horse was called Diamond, and the man who walked at his shoulder was Stan.

They knew Stan, but he didn't acknowledge them.

Somebody might see.

"One sixty-five," said Louis.

"What?" Jack was miles away. Hadn't heard him.

"One seventy then," said Louis, plucking pinkly at his knee. "As it's you."

Jack laughed and they shook on it.

Louis didn't give him the money, and Jack didn't give him the stuff. That wasn't the way Louis worked. He never touched the goods or carried more than a few quid. When they parted, he would walk away and get one of his boys to leave the money in a place, and Jack would pick up the money and leave the stuff in that same place.

Then on his way back from the lock, Stan would pick up the stuff and — with Diamond clopping alongside him — take it to Louis at another place.

Not his home. Not the timber yard.

Jack never asked where. That was Louis's business, not his.

It was all about trust.

Jack watched Louis shave. Hairs too short to bend before the blade popped off his leg like sparks.

"Sharp," said Jack.

Louis twisted the knife in the sun to make it glint. "Jay Fisher," he said. "My proudest possession — apart from the Bazster, of course. Cost a fortune but it'll last for ever."

And back to his shin . . .

His was an obsession so weird that people gave him funny looks in the street. But Jack didn't care how odd he was.

Because Smooth Louis Bridge had saved his life . . .

One morning — two years after his mother had left them — his father had gone to the shop for milk, and never come home.

They'd waited for the milk for a week.

Nobody missed them. They'd never been back to school after their mother's death, just as their father had never been back to work. Arthur Bright had called it home schooling, but that was a grand term for not watching television between nine and three. And while the few neighbours in their short row had been kind in the immediate aftermath of their mother's death, two years down the line they had returned to their own lives, their own troubles. The children had their father, after all — which was more than many could say in this day and age.

With his father gone, it was the hard shoulder all over again. Jack was in charge, only this time he was frozen — not knowing whether to stay in the house or go out to find help.

The priority was still to keep Merry from crying . . .

He'd told her they were in an experiment and, for the first two days, it was almost like fun. Merry coloured in Donald's shell with felt tips, while Jack read out loud to her about the Viet Cong. Joy, who'd always been the most conscientious student, opened her algebra but then just stared at the door, and chewed her pen so hard that it leaked blue on her lips.

So Jack used what he had left of his pocket money to buy food, and then used Joy's. It wasn't much. By the fourth day, he roamed restlessly about the house, hunting for money and clues, while Joy sat on the sofa and cried.

"Social Services will take us away."

"He'll be back soon," Jack had insisted.

"We'll have to go into care," Joy had wept. "And then we'll all be adopted!"

"Shut up!" Jack had hissed. "Or Merry will hear you."

"What's adopted?" said Merry.

The electricity had run out on the fifth day, the food on the sixth. They'd gone to bed hungry and woken up hungry and Joy was still crying and then Merry started, and Jack didn't know what to do.

Mrs Coyle next door might have lent him a tenner — but now that Joy had mentioned adoption, Jack didn't want anyone to know that their father hadn't come home, in case that actually happened. The only relative they knew they had was Uncle Bill in Ireland, and they

74

all agreed that they'd rather live in a box than with Auntie Una — even Merry, who'd never met her.

On the seventh day, there was a knock at the door and Joy hissed, "Social Services!" And the three of them had crawled under the living-room window and cowered behind the newspapers that were already piling up around the walls. Joy had held a finger to Merry's lips, and Merry had brushed it away and whispered loudly, "I'm not talking!"

A few minutes after they hadn't answered the door, the little window over their heads had rattled and scraped and then somehow opened, and — to their utter astonishment — a young man with no eyebrows had slithered through the crack. He'd stopped when he'd found himself face to face with the three frightened children looking up at him, and hung there, folded in the middle and with his legs still outside the house.

"Ahoy there!" he'd saluted, and they'd all giggled.

Within minutes of dropping hands-first into the front room, Louis Bridge had bypassed the meter and got the lights back on. Then he'd left and come back with cheeseburgers.

While they had filled their bellies to drum skins, Smooth Louis had searched the house with a burglar's eye and found an envelope with three hundred pounds in it in the toe of a tennis shoe in their father's wardrobe, and a folder containing household bills and bank statements. He'd spent an hour running through what needed to be paid every month, and made a list for Jack.

"We've taken care of the electric," he'd said, as if Jack had somehow been involved in that cleverness. "You think you can handle the rest?"

"No," Jack had told him bluntly. "I'm thirteen."

"So what?"

"So, what can I do?"

Louis had looked him up and down for a minute, then said, "Plenty."

And that's when he had started to teach Jack how to get into houses and stay out of prison.

First — the basics: stay thin, wear gloves, secure your exit first, and always be ready with a lie and a smile. Then he'd taught him the ins and outs of the business of breaking and entering. Locks. Hinges. Catches. Flashings. PVC *v.* wooden windows. Phillips *v.* Velux star points. Which tools to carry so you couldn't be done for going equipped; the best order of a search; what sold; what didn't; who to trust (him) and who not to trust (everybody else) — and the basics of criminal law.

"My brother's a copper," he'd said once with pride. "I know all the tricks of the trade."

Jack had been brilliant at it from the start. Burglar was not a job he'd ever aspired to but he took it as seriously as if he'd signed for a Premiership football team. He was small and wiry and stole all the right food to keep himself that way. Fruit and veg and brown rice and chicken. He stole books on nutrition. When the opportunity arose, he stole organic. He did light weights, and stretched industriously, until he could touch his knee with his nose, and the back of his head with his heel.

He stole enough to put money away for emergencies, until there was a secret bag with nearly two thousand pounds in it on top of the wardrobe in his room.

Burglary was like magic to Jack. Like conjuring money.

And food. And clothes and books . . .

He always knew it wasn't *right*, but his anger made it feel *fair*.

Jack had never asked Louis why he'd decided to help them instead of rob them blind, he was only grateful for it. So, at a time in his life when he hadn't trusted anyone, Jack had chosen to trust Smooth Louis Bridge — thief, fence . . .

And liar.

"Hey, Louis," Jack said tentatively. "You ever been inside?"

Louis stopped shaving and squinted at him.

"Why?"

"No reason," shrugged Jack. "Just asking."

Louis frowned. "Once," he said, then turned back to his leg and continued to scrape sparks from his skin.

"What happened?"

"The cops happened," he snapped. Then he shook his head and Jack thought that was all he was going to say. But after a moment he went on, "I was up for B&E for the first time as an adult. Before that it had just been slap-on-the-wrist stuff, but I knew this time I could go inside, so I did a deal." He shook his head and snorted at his own stupidity. "I thought, give them something really tasty so I'd have a bit of leverage to plead it down, y'know? So I did, and they said thank you very much and took it and gobbled it up for dinner . . . and then they had me for afters anyway."

Jack's eyes widened.

"Four months inside. Just like that." Louis clicked his fingers, and nodded sombrely. "Don't ever trust a copper, mate, whatever they promise you — those greedy bar stewards will always get you for *something*."

Baz grizzled but Louis continued to stare at Jack until he nodded his understanding of cops.

"You all right to jiggle him?" said Jack. "I got to go to HomeFayre."

"Nah, he needs to run around a bit or he'll be up all night and Lorr will kill me." He got up and lifted the toddler out of the buggy. "All right, Baz mate? How you doing?"

Baz screwed up his face and dropped his head on to his father's shoulder.

Louis rubbed Baz's back, then took a scrap of paper from the tiny pocket of his son's fat-with-nappy jeans and handed it to Jack.

"Shawn says they're in Thailand till Saturday."

"Cheers, mate."

"You remember what I said."

"I will."

Louis set Baz on the ground and clipped the dog lead to his belt loop. The little boy yawned and looked around — then made a beeline for the canal.

Jack almost didn't ask. "What did you give them?"

"Who?"

"The cops. What tasty thing did you give them?"

Louis gave a bitter laugh. "My old man."

Jack laughed too. Then he walked away towards Gold Street. Before he turned the corner, he looked back to watch as Louis expertly applied drag to the line to slow Baz down and bring him around in an arc, like a marlin.

HomeFayre sold everything, but its USP was chaos.

The window display was not unconventional for a small market town — casseroles, school supplies and sheep wormer — but HomeFayre customers must ideally have been born and bred in Tiverton to have any grasp of its random stock and bizarre layout, which had been created by a creeping annexation of neighbouring shops over many years. Immediately inside the door, the floor sloped steeply up to the back of the shop more than fifty yards away, and branched out sideways up and down the street, behind the doors and windows of other shops, like a big fat cuckoo tree.

The bell on the door rang behind Jack and he leaned into the carpeted hill and climbed past greetings cards and frying pans, board games and lampshades, magic wands and thermal socks and litter bins, all the way to the back of the shop, where the floor and the ceiling threatened to meet, and tall regulars ducked, while tall tourists bumped their heads and smiled ruefully because it was all part of the charm.

There — fully twenty feet above street level and under a wall of quiet clocks — Jack picked up a box of latex gloves, turned, and started his descent to the till.

There were several routes down, and he took a different one. Sewing thread, fake flowers, car oil, icing bags, they passed him faster and faster as he picked up speed . . .

Just before hair accessories he stopped, with some difficulty. Then he backed up the hill a little to look at a shelf full of photo frames — each with the same fake family smiling happily behind the glass: a girl, a boy, and a beach ball. Always a beach ball.

Jack ran a narrow eye down the row of frames.

He picked up two to compare them, then put one back.

He only paid for the gloves.

Then he remembered he'd warned Joy, so he walked up to the Busy Bee and cancelled the newspapers. Mr Dolan — the already morose newsagent — nearly cried.

In the bedroom he rarely used, Jack edged through the stacks of papers, past the bed piled with news, to the window.

He took the stolen photo frame from his pocket and studied it. The two children and the beach ball were a garish contrast to his own gloomy surroundings. They were so clean! Even their fingernails. Their hair was washed and their teeth were straight and white. He imagined the bedrooms they would have — all the toys and the books and the clean bedding — in homes filled with warmth and light and love.

Jack slid the picture from the frame and crumpled it to the floor. Then he placed the empty frame on the sill.

Somehow, having it there, ready and waiting, gave him hope that he might find the photo to fill it.

He felt better for having it, even though he knew it was childish.

Hope was hard to come by, and even a little bit went a long way . . .

Jack drew back sharply at a movement in Mrs Coyle's garden.

For a year before she'd died, Mrs Coyle had been in a wheelchair and had rarely gone outside. She'd been deaf and cantankerous, and had no interest in getting involved with anything or anybody.

Jack had liked her. He'd done her shopping, and mowed her lawn — always opening with "My dad sent me round" to head off suspicion.

But there was a new neighbour now. Merry had said so, and there she was. Thin but ramrod straight. She wore a straw hat, and carried a trowel in one hand and a black bucket in the other, but wasn't dressed for gardening, in a pale pink shirt, white trousers and sandals.

She didn't do anything with the trowel — just walked to the centre of the patchy lawn and made a slow circle to survey her new domain — and beyond.

As she turned his way, he withdrew even further from the window so that he was in shadow and could not be seen.

But the old woman tilted her face up to the window, as if she knew he was there.

Jack got a tiny rumble of disquiet in his gut.

Even from here, the new neighbour looked nosy.

It was bedtime and Adam was at the back door, calling the cat.

"Chiiiiips! Chiiiii-ips! Come on, Chips!"

Catherine smiled to herself. Chips always made Adam beg. She *never* begged. She called, he came, or she locked him out for the night. Simple. Chips knew that, and always shot in from the garden like a furry white arrow. But he had Adam wrapped around his little claw, and wouldn't come in until his own personal human had been thoroughly humiliated — whistling, wheedling, and shaking the box of treats like Barry Manilow on the maracas.

The phone rang.

"I'll get it," she said, and heaved herself off the sofa at the second attempt.

"Who can *that* be?" she asked the baby, but the baby apparently didn't know.

"Hello?"

Silence on the line.

"Hello?" she said again.

"Chips! Come on, my good Chipper!"

But nothing from the caller.

Catherine opened her mouth to say "Hello" a third time, then slowly shut it again. The silence was too deep, too dark, to be a fault on the line.

Somebody was there. They just weren't talking.

The memory of the night of the knife dripped down the back of her neck, like slow black oil, coating her in slick fear.

Somebody breathed shakily.

Maybe it was her.

Somewhere a long, long way away, Adam shook the box of treats as if he was at the Copacabana.

"What do you want?" whispered Catherine. And when no answer came immediately she said it again, like the start of a panic. "What do you want?"

There was a small intake of breath.

Then nothing. Only the abyss in her ear.

"What do you want?" This time her voice was so low that she wasn't even sure she'd made a sound.

A long, low nothing. Had the person hung up?

And then came a whisper — as quiet as her own — as if he, too, didn't want to be overheard.

"I could've killed you."

Catherine's face went numb. She couldn't feel her mouth.

There was no menace in the voice. It was a statement of fact. No more, no less. But her legs felt like jelly, and she put a hand on the wall to steady herself.

Then the seashell of silence was replaced by something close and technical, and Catherine knew he was gone.

Slowly, she lowered the phone.

Behind her, Adam said, "Who was it?"

She didn't turn around. "What?"

"On the phone?"

"Oh," she said. "Wrong number."

She turned then. Adam had the cat in his arms, all fluffy and smug.

"I hope they apologized," he said. "It's nearly eleven."

"Yes," she said haltingly. "She said she was sorry."

Adam frowned at her. "You OK, Cath?" he said. "You look a bit pale."

She gave a weak smile. "I think I got up too fast."

Adam spilled Chips from his arms and on to the floor. He steered Catherine gently back to the sofa, then knelt on the rug in front of her, looking up into her face anxiously. "Would you like some water? Or tea? I can make tea?"

She nodded. "Yes please, sweetheart. Tea would be lovely."

She wanted him to go into the kitchen — go anywhere — so she wouldn't have to pretend. Wouldn't have to lie to him.

But he stayed. "Are you sure that's all?" he said. "I can call the hospital. Get the bag . . .?"

Her bag had been packed and beside the front door since her fourth month. Back then she could still wear size 12 jeans, and it had seemed surreal that she would ever need it. But now she looked at it every day, just to make sure it was still there. Sometimes she added things, or changed something for a better something.

"It's not the baby," she reassured him. "I just got up too quickly to answer the phone, I think. Went a bit dizzy."

She smiled at him and squeezed his hand. "I'd *love* a cup of tea, please, darling."

His brown eyes searched her own, and so she closed them and leaned carefully back against the cushions.

Adam fetched another, and pushed it gently under the small of her back.

"Better?" he said.

"Thank you," she said.

He kissed her forehead and then her tummy.

Catherine blinked back tears of gratitude. Sometimes he made her feel like a princess and a lover and a cherished child, all at the same time.

And she was lying to him!

As if he'd heard her thoughts, he looked at her seriously. "You would tell me if there was anything wrong, wouldn't you, Cathy?"

She nodded automatically. "Of course!"

But she wouldn't.

Because if she told him about the phone call, she'd have to tell him about the burglary, and then not only would he be angry about the open window and the Swedish vase — he'd also be hurt and angry that she hadn't said anything before now.

Catherine fervently wished that she hadn't kept *anything* from Adam, but now that she'd started down this path, she could see no easy way back from her lies.

She felt as if she were cheating on him.

"I love you," he said, like a dart tipped with guilt.

And for a moment she let him hold her close, even though she wanted to be alone.

Merry checked her little red-and-blue watch. When it said three thirty, she took the back-door key from the hook and rushed out into the garden with Donald in her arms.

She shivered with delight as the sun hit her skin, then put Donald down on the lawn and threw herself headlong on to the warm grass, as if diving into a deep green pool.

She lay flat, cupping her face, with the grass prickling her eyelids and nose as she breathed in the green and the soil and the roots. Then, slowly, she turned on to her side, so that she could listen to the garden.

There was the whisper of the stalks bending and breaking under her cheek, and the dry rub of her own hair against her ear. But once she was still and her breathing had slowed, she could hear the whole world under her head — the tiny sounds of beetles and bugs and — she fancied — earthworms moving through the soil, and the soil moving through them.

Apart from Donald, worms were her favourite animals. Jack had made her a worm hotel out of a shoebox, with little doors and windows cut out and shutters drawn on, and filled half full of soil so that Merry could watch the worms without the shield of grass. She would catch them and accommodate them for a few days, then would check them out of the hotel and send them back to their working lives in the garden, and new guests would arrive.

In a big black notebook she kept a careful felt-tip register of arrivals and departures, and gave them names like Snake and Riggles and Slinky and FootLong. She was pretty sure FootLong was a regular, even though Jack said that was unlikely.

Merry closed her eyes and stretched out her arms in the grass as if embracing the whole planet. She listened to the worms and the beetles with one ear, while the other filled with the soft chirping of birds and the drone of bumblebees coming and going like country-lane traffic.

There was a slow, throaty cough, then a snap and a clank.

A brief silence, then it happened again: *prrrrr*, snap, clank.

Merry raised her head and looked at the fence. Somebody next door was trying to start a lawnmower.

She got up and stood carefully on the brick surround of the cold frame so she could hang there, up to her armpits in fence.

The new neighbour was there — an old woman in unsuitably pale trousers and a pink flowery blouse.

"Hello."

The old woman looked up, but at the wrong place, so Merry waved a helpful arm and said, "Over here."

"Oh," said the woman. "Hello."

"I'm Merry," said Merry.

"Oh," said the old woman. "Good."

"What's your name?"

"Oh," she said again. "Your name is Merry?"

"Yes," said Merry. "I told you."

"Well!" said the old woman. Then she said nothing for a bit — as if she didn't know what there was to say about that.

At last she said, "Merry's a pretty name."

"Is it?" said Merry. She'd never thought about it. It was just what she was called — as much part of her as her fingers or toes. They weren't pretty or ugly, only fingers and toes.

"What's your name?" she repeated.

"Mrs Reynolds."

"Oh," said Merry. Mrs Reynolds wasn't a pretty name or an ugly name, so now she was the one who had nothing to say about names.

Mrs Reynolds pulled the starter on the mower again. It didn't sound like starting. Merry knew because when Jack started their mower for her, it was fast and loud and made her cover her ears. Mrs Reynolds' mower sounded wheezy and ill.

"We have a lawnmower that goes," she said.

Mrs Reynolds said nothing, just pulled the cord again. *Prrrrrr*, snap, clank.

"I mow the lawn," Merry added. "But my brother has to start the lawnmower for me."

"Very good," said Mrs Reynolds, as if there was something wrong with that.

"Do you live there alone?"

"Yes." *Prrrrrr*, snap, clank.

"I live with my brother and sister and my dad. But my dad works away a lot. On an oil rig."

"Oh yes?" said Mrs Reynolds, but she was unscrewing a cap on the mower and peering inside it, and Merry got the feeling she wasn't really listening.

"Yeah," she went on. "So mostly it's just us, alone."

"That's nice," said Mrs Reynolds. "There's petrol in it. And oil. I don't know what's wrong."

Jack would know what was wrong, thought Merry. Jack would fix it in a jiffy. She so wanted to offer up Jack as a lawnmower repairman, but he'd be cross if she did. Jack didn't like to get involved with the neighbours in case they wanted to get involved back. So Merry didn't say anything about the lawnmower. She had things she was allowed to say, and wasn't supposed to deviate.

"I'm home schooled," she said.

"Are you now?" Mrs Reynolds did listen to that. She looked up sharply from the mower at Merry hanging over the fence.

"If your father's away, who home schools you?"

"My brother and sister," said Merry. "I've read loads of books."

"Oh yes?" said Mrs Reynolds suspiciously. "And what's your favourite subject?"

"Vampires."

"Vampires?"

"Yes," nodded Merry. "I know all about them. They suck your blood, but only if you invite them in."

92

Mrs Reynolds frowned, so she explained, "They can't just come in. That's against the rules."

"Well!" said the old woman firmly. Then she put her hands on her narrow hips and glared at the lawnmower before looking back at Merry. "How old are your brother and sister?"

"Twenty," said Merry. "And nineteen."

"Oh," said Mrs Reynolds. "That's very young."

"Not to me," shrugged Merry. Then she said, "Do you still have children?"

"Still?"

"Well, because you're so old."

"I'm sixty-three," said Mrs Reynolds stiffly. "How old are you?"

"Nearly six," said Merry. "So do you? Still have children?"

"I have a son."

"Maybe he can mow the lawn for you."

Mrs Reynolds gave a sigh and said, "Maybe he can," and pushed the mower back into the garden shed and locked it with a padlock, then put the key under a pot on the patio.

"Nobody steals stuff around here," said Merry.

"You can't be too sure," said Mrs Reynolds. Then she straightened up and said, "So. Vampires and what else?"

"Loads," said Merry.

"Such as?" said Mrs Reynolds.

"Ummm . . . the news," said Merry. "I know all the news."

"Really?"

Something in the word made Merry think that Mrs Reynolds thought she was lying, so she screwed up her nose and racked her brain to think of what she'd read in the papers.

"The last ibuk in the world died."

"What's an ibuk?" said Mrs Reynolds.

"A kind of sheep."

Mrs Reynolds frowned, then said, "You mean an ibex."

"Yes, an ibex," said Merry.

"It's a kind of goat," said Mrs Reynolds.

"It doesn't matter anyway," shrugged Merry. "Because a tree fell on it."

"Is that right?" said Mrs Reynolds dubiously.

"Yes, and a sumberine sank under the sea in Russia and they couldn't get them out and they all died."

"A sumberine," said Mrs Reynolds.

"Yeah," Merry ploughed on with a defiant eye. "And I know all about Shipman. He killed a whole bunch of people, but only the old ones."

Mrs Reynolds pursed her lips, and looked about to say one thing, and then seemed to change her mind and said, "Should you be hanging off the fence like that?"

Merry had never thought about it before, but now she looked down at the fence, and at herself, and at her feet balanced on the low brick wall of the cold frame. Everything looked OK to her.

"I think so," she nodded.

Mrs Reynolds put her hands on her hips again. She seemed cross.

94

"Well, as long as you don't break it," she said, and went inside and shut the back door without saying goodbye.

Merry didn't know how she could break the fence. What a stupid thing to say. It was a *fence*!

She hung there for a little while longer, staring at the overgrown mess of the neighbouring garden. Then she climbed carefully down so as not to tread on the glass lid of the cold frame. There were tomatoes in there, and lettuce and spring onions. It was her job to water them and she never missed a day because it got hot in there, even when it wasn't sunny. She knew because Jack had once made her lie down in the cold frame and shut the lid, so she'd know how much the plants needed water.

Now she opened the lid and took out a sweet little cherry tomato and popped it with her small white teeth.

She was allowed because salad was good for you.

She took one in for Joy.

Friday night, and Catherine's risotto was a triumph. All she'd done was stand there and stir it while *The Archers* was on, but Jan went on and on about it as if she'd spit-roasted a unicorn.

"I *must* get this recipe!" she said three different times. "It's just *delicious*."

"It's only rice and elbow grease," Catherine replied, smiling, the first time. The second time she only smiled; the third she ignored, and Jan didn't say it again, although she did question the difference between risotto and paella, which they were all hazy about. They took ages to settle on "fish".

Conversation was awkward. Catherine had enjoyed her job at the estate agency. She'd been good at it, and loved the office banter, but when Jan talked about it now, it just felt meaningless. And the more Jan talked, the thinner her material got, and the more trite it sounded.

"So I said to Mr Bevan, they're *never* going to sell it with that pond in the garden! It's a family house! It's like a red flag with added koi carp!"

Jan laughed, but only Catherine made the effort to smile and agree, if only to keep Rhod from speaking.

Rhod was of average build and height, with small eyes and dull features. He was not an ugly man, but Catherine felt him grow more unattractive as the evening wore on.

For a start, even though she'd only met him once before, and briefly, he'd come through the door and kissed her cheek — and then *rubbed her tummy*, as if she were a rabbit's foot!

"Wonderful news," he'd said, seven months late.

Catherine had forced a smile and dipped away from his hand and tried not to get within an arm's length of him for the rest of the evening.

But even at arm's length, she didn't like him. He blustered to Adam about cars, claiming expertise that only exposed his ignorance; he told them about some idiot at work they didn't know and didn't care about — and then was affronted that they couldn't muster the interest to share his dislike. He'd never tasted risotto like it, and demanded to know Catherine's secret ingredient, then tried to turn "secret ingredient" into a running pregnancy joke that he told every time with a wink or a nudge and a notable absence of reactive laughter.

By eight thirty, he was the Elephant Man, and Catherine couldn't wait for them to go.

The gaps in the conversation grew wider and wider, Jan's attempts to close them grew increasingly desperate, and Adam made no contribution apart from "Pass the salt." Now and then he glanced through the door towards the television, and once spent so long in the bathroom that she just *knew* he was reading in there . . .

Catherine tried at first, but just couldn't be bothered to keep the frothy conversational balls in the air while a far darker truth bubbled within her.

If she opened her mouth, she'd say it. It would all come pouring out.

I don't care about any of this! A man broke into our house! He threatened to kill me!

It almost made her smile to think of how quickly the veneer of dinner-party politeness would crack.

"More wine?" said Adam and she shot him a look that said *no* — then realized Jan had spotted it too.

Catherine reddened.

"Are you OK, Cath?" said Jan, putting her head on one side sympathetically.

Catherine understood the subtext.

Why are you being such a miserable bitch? If you didn't want us here, why invite us?

"Sorry, Jan," she said. "I've been looking forward to this so much, but I'm just exhausted. The baby, you know?"

Nobody could argue with a baby.

"Of course," Jan smiled. "And all that stirring."

All that lying, she meant.

They left straight after coffee, and Catherine hugged Jan at the door because she did feel bad — although not bad enough to beg them to stay.

When Adam had closed the door behind them, Catherine fell into his arms with a groan of relief.

"Thank God!"

He patted her back.

"I'm sorry," she said against his chest. "I just wasn't up for it. Poor Jan. I'll call her tomorrow and apologize. Right now I just want to get into a hot bath and fall asleep."

He patted her back again but said nothing. Catherine looked up at him. "You OK?"

"Fine," he said.

She drew back from him a little. "What's up?"

Adam shrugged. "That Rhod's an arse, isn't he?"

"Total arse," she agreed, and laid her cheek against his chest again. "Even I could tell he doesn't know a thing about cars!"

"And the way he touched your tummy."

"I know," said Catherine. "It's really inappropriate."

"I don't like him," said Adam.

"I don't either," she said. "But Jan never makes it past year two of a relationship, so his time's almost up."

"Good," he said. "I hope we never see him again."

Catherine smiled and detached herself from Adam and started up the stairs.

Before she'd taken three steps, there was a knock on the door.

It was Rhod. He had a flat.

Ugh.

Rhod came back in to call the RAC, while Catherine went outside to sympathize with Jan and look at the tyre.

In the warm summer darkness, she and Jan stood shoulder to shoulder beside the Toyota.

"What a pain," said Catherine.

"Rhod only just put new tyres on it," said Jan. "I'll tell him to take it back and give them hell."

They both looked to see whether Rhod was on his way back to them.

He wasn't.

Silence.

Catherine was loath to invite them back into the house to extend the evening, when that hot bath had seemed *so close*.

"You and Rhod seem happy."

"So far, so good," Jan nodded, and crossed her fingers. "He was nervous tonight, I could tell. He doesn't know a bloody thing about cars!"

They both laughed.

"But he treats me so well," said Jan. "It's a nice change."

"That's great."

"Yes, it is."

"Do you know what he does yet?"

"Not a clue!" said Jan.

Catherine laughed again, and was pleased that they were sharing this moment when she'd been such a poor host all night.

"I'll send you that risotto recipe."

"Oh please do. It really was amazing. It's so hard to get Rhod to eat anything that isn't fried in batter."

Finally Catherine could stall no longer.

"Why don't you come back inside and wait?"

"Are you sure?" said Jan.

"Of course."

As they walked back up the short driveway, Jan said, "Oh no! Did you get a ticket?" She reached across the bonnet of the pea-green Volvo and took a slip of paper from under the wiper. She unfolded it under the orange streetlamp and frowned.

"What is it?"

"Weird." Jan held it out to her and Catherine's heart dropped as she read the familiar scrawl.

Call the Police!

Detective Sergeant Reynolds was beginning to not like John Marvel.

Reynolds was not a judgemental man, so he'd given Marvel the benefit of the doubt at their first meeting. After all, the DCI was a stranger in a strange land, who had just fallen over a pink suitcase. Things were sure to be a little bumpy.

But a week later, and things were still bumpy.

And Reynolds had the distinct impression that they were only going to get bumpier.

For a start, Marvel looked awful. He was overweight and unkempt, with ears that jutted out at different angles, and although he wore a suit, it didn't look like one that belonged to him. He also had hair in his nose. That alone would have been enough to make Reynolds shudder. He believed firmly that hair had no place on a civilized man except on his head. He himself had a Braun trimmer, which he ran obsessively around his nasal cavities every morning. But Marvel had nose hairs a-plenty, and sometimes pinched his nose between his thumb and forefinger — in mid conversation — as if he suspected there might be something dangling from them.

Marvel also stank of cigarettes and drank too much. He wore scuffed brown shoes regardless of the colour of his trousers, and a tie that had not only not been dry-cleaned any time in recent history, but looked as though it had not even been *untied* since Marvel had first looped it over his big lopsided head.

Reynolds could hardly bear to look at its grubby little knot.

He flinched as Marvel snapped his fingers under his nose.

"Wake up, Reynolds!"

Reynolds reddened and Elizabeth Rice winked at him.

Reynolds wasn't sure he liked her either. She was pretty enough, but very unladylike. He'd once seen her run across a car park for no reason.

And a DC shouldn't be winking at a DS unless it was in the line of duty.

He sighed. There were no boundaries any more. Everything was equality and first-name terms.

So Reynolds turned away from Rice without acknowledging the wink.

For her own good.

Marvel had unrolled a large map on the floor.

They were in the empty front room of a small house on a north Tiverton estate — not unlike the one Marvel himself was renting.

They all leaned over the map. There were dozens of red dots marked on the map in felt tip.

"Each of these dots is a Goldilocks crime scene," said Marvel. "Most are around this area. So this is where we're setting the trap."

"What trap?" said Parrott.

Marvel swept an arm around the room like an estate agent. "Welcome to the capture house!"

"What's that?" said Rice.

Marvel grinned a rare grin. "This is the house where we're going to catch Goldilocks."

"How?" said Parrott.

Marvel paused for dramatic effect.

"By giving him everything he wants!"

His team looked at him blankly.

Well, not *his* team, but the team that had been imposed upon him. If he'd been choosing, he wouldn't have chosen Reynolds, for a start — with his shiny shoes and red silk tie.

He also wouldn't have chosen DC Rice. Marvel wasn't in favour of women on the force. He'd only ever seen one good one in action, and was pretty sure she was a lesbian. Rice was too young and too pretty, and would only be a distraction. Not to him, of course — he had sworn off women — but to the rest of the team.

That was completed by Toby Parrott, who'd driven him down on the first day and who — it turned out — had been on the Goldilocks case for almost a year. He had been left on it as a bridge between the old Devon and Cornwall police team and the new one from Avon and Somerset. Parrott did not inspire confidence. He sat scrunched up on his chair with his hands jammed defensively between his knees and his skinny shoulders hunched like someone at his first AA meeting.

Marvel sighed. Team Goldilocks indeed. None of them was just right.

"Come *on*," he said. "This bastard's been running rings round the police for too bloody long! I don't want to waste my life on a shitty little thief, when I've got killers to catch, so pull your fucking fingers out and tell me what he wants!"

He had no killers to catch, of course; however, this was not about truth, but about motivating the troops.

"A bed for the night?" said Rice cautiously.

"Hence Goldilocks," said Reynolds helpfully, but won only a glare from Marvel.

"That's once he's inside," said Marvel. "But I need to know what makes Goldilocks choose *this* house to break into and not the one next door."

"Detached house," said Parrott.

"Good," said Marvel.

"But the Passmores live in a terrace," said Reynolds.

"That's not a Goldilocks job," said Marvel.

Reynolds looked taken aback. "Bed slept in, food stolen, TV and family photographs smashed. It has all the hallmarks."

"No it doesn't," said Marvel in a tone that did not invite debate.

"I'll tell you," he went on. "What this bastard wants is *privacy*. The detached house on an anonymous estate, the small, high bathroom window, the easy access via the kitchen roof, the back garden with trees for cover. All these crime scenes have these things in common, and this house has got them all.

"Now all we have to do is dress it up and make it look lived in. We fill it with all the little easy-to-carry bits he likes to nick, and wait for him to find it."

"And then he comes in and steals all our stuff," frowned Parrott, as if Marvel had overlooked this critical flaw in his own plan.

"That's the whole point," snapped Marvel. "Because *then* . . . he trips a silent alarm and hidden CCTV cameras that we're going to install, so we catch him red-handed and have him on film in glorious Technicolor into the bargain. Cue a nice quick guilty plea, God knows how many other offences taken into consideration, and Bob's your uncle."

Reynolds, Rice and Parrott looked around the empty room.

"It could work," said Reynolds.

"It does work!" snapped Marvel. "I've seen it work."

That wasn't true, but he'd heard that it did.

"Great," said Rice. "When do we start?"

"You and Reynolds start right now."

"Me and DS Reynolds?" she said in surprise.

"DS Reynolds and me," corrected Reynolds, and they all looked at him blankly.

Marvel was talking again. "You two are going to play house here to make it look authentic. You can furnish the place with stuff from the warehouse in Exeter. Doesn't have to be fancy, just real. Then you spend a week or so living here, chatting to neighbours, drinking in the local, coming and going, and then you go off" —

Marvel did air quotes — "on *holiday*, and we wait for Goldilocks to pay us a little visit."

He rubbed his hands together and looked very pleased with himself.

Reynolds said, "Hmmm."

Marvel turned to him. "Something wrong, Reynolds?"

DS Reynolds looked uncomfortable. "Sir, it's just that I know DC Rice has a . . . partner . . . and I don't want there to be any . . . awkwardness . . ."

Marvel snorted and Rice flapped an unconcerned hand. "Oh, Eric won't mind."

"Don't panic, Reynolds," quipped Marvel. "You don't have to shag her."

Toby Parrott laughed, but Rice said, "This is probably a stupid question, sir —"

"Then don't ask it," said Marvel, and he rolled up the map to show that the conversation was at an end.

"Well, I will anyway," shrugged Rice, and Marvel thought, *She's trouble*. "How is Goldilocks going to find the capture house?"

"Leave that to me," he snapped, and Rice nodded and did just that.

Marvel brooded all the way back to Taunton.

Bloody women! he thought. *Always asking questions!*

But it was a good question. And one for which he had no answer.

Yet.

On his dim and distant Cornish holiday, Marvel had gone fishing.

It was the only part of the holiday he remembered with any fondness. He and his father and brother. He recalled standing in the dark recesses of the local fishing shop — the Angling Man — dutifully not touching a jail cell of vertical rods, racks of camouflage waterproofs, and a whole wall pan-tiled with little plastic bags containing alien artefacts whose use he could no more fathom than the meaning of life. Bright baubles and feathers, silvery fake fish, little lead balls and big lead torpedoes, Day-Glo centipedes, a thousand variations on ball-bearings and loops and hooks, and dozens and dozens of reels of bright blue fishing line.

On a battered freezer was a list of bait as long as his ten-year-old arm.

Back home in south London, he'd imagined only worms and a rock to throw them off, but his eyes had been opened that day to the sheer trickery of fish, as the Angling Man grilled his father as to where they were going to be, and what they wanted to catch, and how far the boys could cast a line . . . which had later turned out to be no further than ravenous crabs.

"You'm don't want to be chumming a river, see?" the Angling Man had concluded with a smoker's cackle. And although he'd not understood it at the time, the phrase had stuck in Marvel's head like a West Country burr.

It came back to him now.

You'm don't want to be chumming a river.

108

Marvel was convinced that the capture house was the right bait.

But they would have to cast that bait in the right place if they wanted to catch the right fish.

Jack looked down at Louis's scrap of paper to check the name and address.

Tony and Sara Gomez.

It had been torn from an envelope and there was a Wine Club logo he'd seen before. More than once. Wine Club. P&O Cruises. Boden. Any number of equine catalogues. All selling stuff he'd never be able to afford.

But he knew people who *could*.

At least, he knew their houses . . .

Jack knocked on the door.

Nobody answered, of course, because the people in the Wine Club were in Thailand, but he was all ready to be confused, and then apologetic, about getting the wrong house.

Aww, sorry mate! This estate is so confusing!

But nobody answered the door, and Jack didn't knock again. He glanced around once and then walked boldly down the side of the house and into the back garden, snapping on his latex gloves.

This was the only dodgy moment. If a neighbour saw him and came over, it would be much harder to say he was lost once he'd abandoned the front door.

Nonetheless, he had a lie, all ready to go: *Tony's son borrowed my bike. I've only come to get it back from the shed.*

Jack hoped nobody would challenge him because he was not a liar by nature. Of course, he was not a thief by nature, but he was slim and fit and desperate, which made burglary a viable occupation for him. However, he did not have the gift of the gab like Smooth Louis did, and preferred not to talk if he didn't have to.

He walked down the side of the house, knowing that the bathroom would be over the extended kitchen, which had only a slight slope to its roof. They were all similar, these new houses, and Jack knew them like the back of his hand. He liked knowing what to expect. In the summer the bathroom window was often open, and it if wasn't, that didn't mean he couldn't get in — just that it would take longer. And taking longer was more risky, so he liked an open window.

And there it was . . .

Nobody believed someone could get through a window so small and so high.

Their lack of imagination was his house key.

There were Leylandii in the back garden too. That was always a plus. Thick green foliage hid him from almost any eye prying from the neighbouring homes, even in broad daylight. Which it wasn't.

The guttering was brilliant.

Like any burglar worth his salt, Jack's eyes ran naturally up the wall of any house, following the map of gutters and downpipes, sizing up the dwelling in a single flashbulb moment of forward-planning.

This downpipe ran straight up alongside the kitchen and the bathroom. Once he was on the kitchen roof, Jack only had to shin a few feet up the drainpipe and lean across to pull the window fully open. From there it was a stretch, a brief hang, a wriggle, and he was in.

From leaving the ground, the whole thing took him less than thirty seconds.

He'd have been very unlucky to have been seen. Even more unlucky to have been seen by anybody who was prepared to do anything about it.

Jack vaulted off the sill and over the basin like a Russian gymnast, making a perfect-ten landing on the bathmat. He took a deepbreath and let the smell of the house fill him all the way to his fingertips.

Wright's Coal Tar Soap over citrus Toilet Duck. It smelled like a fire in an orange grove.

Jack liked the smell of the houses. Some had chemical smells, of air fresheners and fake-flower washing powder, but Jack preferred the houses that smelled like a family. Shampoo in the bathroom, clean sheets in the bedrooms, food in the kitchen. Even mud in the utility room and socks in the laundry basket took him back to the way his house had been . . .

Before.

Their house used to smell that way. He was pretty sure it had, or he wouldn't recognize the aromas he found in the houses he burgled. Once, he had sniffed out a bottle of watermelon shampoo they'd all used as children, and had stuffed it into his backpack with hands that shook as if he'd uncovered King Tut's tomb on a Tiverton housing estate. Back home he had washed his hair over the basin because the bath was always full of newspapers, and then hidden the shampoo in the garden so that nobody else could use it.

Merry had found it, of course. Digging for worms. She hadn't said anything, but he hadn't even needed to get close enough to smell her to know what had happened — her hair was that shiny. She'd tried running upstairs, but where was there to go? He'd caught her in a box canyon in the baby's room, and slapped her for taking what wasn't hers.

"I hate you!" she'd shouted over the bannister as he'd stormed downstairs again, sending sheaves of newspaper sliding ahead of his feet, nearly falling. "I hate you and I hope you get run over by a lorry!"

She'd cried then, and he'd felt bad, but that would teach her to take his shampoo . . .

Jack made dinner. He chose carefully from the fridge and cabinets stuffed with cans and packets. Some things he set down next to the back door to take home — dried pulses, oats, salad. There was a free-range chicken in the freezer. There was beer in the fridge, but he never drank. He was scared to drink in case he fell out of a window or something.

Then what would happen to Merry and Joy?

He made an omelette with vegetables, then helped himself to a little pot of trifle from the fridge. Jack rarely ate sweet things, and felt dizzy from the rush.

He put his feet on the coffee table and watched TV. He didn't change the channel. Any channel was good when you couldn't find your own TV. He watched until he caught himself nodding off, then dropped the empty trifle pot and spoon on the carpet and went upstairs.

He showered to get clean, then bathed for fun, floating like flying, as the hot water rose past his ears and then lifted him up off the porcelain as it lapped over the edge and started to gush on to the floor.

He let it run.

He washed his hair and rinsed and repeated well after it had squeaked, just to feel the foam between his fingers.

There were four big fluffy bath towels. He used them all.

In the master bedroom he found a hair dryer. He dried his hair and then just stood in the centre of the room, naked, running the dryer over his damp skin too. Taking his time, enjoying the feeling of warm air moving around him. The uninterrupted square footage of carpet, the soft clean wool under his feet, the view of one side of the room from the other.

The space.

He dressed, feeling warmer.

The kids' names were on their doors in coloured jigsaw pieces. Dan and Sharona.

Sharona's room was a shrine to a boy band called The Troublemakers, whose names were apparently Lance, Ade, Scotty and The Mighty Mick. Jack thought they didn't look at all troublesome. Jack thought he could smash in their faces all by himself, and tore their posters off the walls in shiny strips.

In Dan's room was a bed in the shape of a racing car. Jack had always wanted a racing-car bed. He put his backpack on the floor and laid his hammer on the bedside table, then got into bed without taking off his clothes or his shoes, in case he needed to make a quick getaway.

But the bed wasn't the fun he'd thought it would be. Once he was in it, it just felt like any other bed. Still, the duvet cover was fresh and adorned with Transformers, and Optimus Prime pillowed Jack's head in his soft iron lap.

Jack closed his eyes, and drifted cautiously towards the darkness.

And there — right at the threshold of sleep — he found a hairline moment when everything was OK.

After the weekend, Adam headed back out — this time to Cornwall.

His job on the road had never bothered Catherine before. He went away for three or four days at a time, selling horse feed to farm shops and stable yards, and she lived her life here and looked forward to welcoming him home. She'd always found their nightly phone chats and his funny postcards of crap places enough to feel connected and secure.

Not any more. Now that she knew how false that sense of security had been, she felt wobbly at the thought of Adam leaving, and of the long nights to come.

Of another phone call.

A message . . .

A visit . . .?

"I'll miss you," she said on the driveway.

"I'll miss you too," he said as he slung his bag on to the passenger seat. "Always."

"Have a nice time at the seaside."

"I'll send you a postcard."

"Nothing saucy," she said.

116

"You ruin everything," he scowled, then laughed and held her as close as the baby allowed. "Will you be OK?" he said into her hair.

"Of course," she said, because what was the point of saying anything else? He would only worry about her, and still have to go to work.

"Take good care of our baby."

Guilt pricked Catherine. It was as if he knew! She could almost hear the end of his sentence: *Because you didn't last time.*

You're being paranoid, she told herself. He doesn't know because you didn't tell him.

"I will," she said seriously. "Nothing's more important to me, Adam."

"I know that," he said. "You sure you're OK?"

She made herself smile. "I'll miss you, that's all. With the baby coming so soon, I'm just, you know . . ."

"Hysterical?" he suggested.

"Well," she shrugged, "I *am* a woman."

"True," he nodded wisely, and they both laughed.

"Seriously though, Cath," he said, "I hate leaving you right now. You know you can call me any time, about anything, and I'll just get in the van and drive straight home to you. Be here in a jiffy. From *anywhere*!"

"I know," she said, and felt her face grow warm with shame.

Adam kissed her one last time, got in the van with RED RIBBON EQUINE on the side, and drove slowly away. Catherine stood and waved until he turned the corner and disappeared — then instantly felt lonely.

And colder, as if the bright morning sun had drifted behind a cloud.

She hugged her arms and looked around the cul-de-sac.

Nothing moved. Nobody was putting out the recycling or chivvying the kids along for school.

She hurried inside, but inside didn't feel as safe as it used to and, when she closed the front door, Catherine didn't know whether she was shutting danger out, or in.

With her . . .

She stood for a moment at the front door, listening to the silence of the house growing louder and louder.

She thought she'd bake a cake!

She hadn't baked for ages, but the warm smell of banana loaf was just what she needed to feel cosy and safe.

She talked the baby through every step, feeling more normal with every passing minute, and half an hour later she and the kitchen were covered in flour but there was a cake in the oven, and the sense of having achieved something.

Then she saw the bananas she hadn't put in the loaf.

"Oh shit!"

Baby brain.

She didn't know whether to laugh or cry.

"I blame you!" she scolded her tummy — then looked up sharply.

Something had caught her eye in the garden. Something on the fence? Their garden wasn't big, but had a tall fence around it — six-foot wooden planks —

118

and beyond that was a handkerchief of common ground with trees that crowded their boundary.

What had she seen? She wasn't sure. A big bird, maybe?

No. Bigger than that —

Catherine opened the back door and walked slowly across a lawn still jewelled with dew. The sky was clear and cloudless and the day was already lovely. Even the sound of a lawnmower only served to enrich the experience of summer, rather than sully its peace.

She reached the fence. It was too tall for her to look over. The neighbours' conifers pressed against it in places, pushing the overlapping slats apart a little.

She walked beside the fence, stepping between the shrubs and trailing her fingers lightly along the unfinished pine. Then she bent awkwardly and put her eye to a knothole.

All she could see were branches.

She moved three or four feet to a gap in the planking.

Through it she could see the neighbouring street, across a patch of well-mown grass. In the middle of the patch was a lawnmower — stationary but still running. The council worker who should have been pushing it was nowhere to be seen.

Catherine frowned. Then wondered if he was relieving himself somewhere close by.

That was what she'd seen! The top of a man's head moving towards the neighbours' conifers for a bit of privacy.

And here she was, spying on him.

She straightened up and stifled a giggle.

She was being silly. If someone really planned to kill you, she was pretty sure they didn't call you up first to tip you off. Or leave a note to that effect, for that matter! She assumed they just . . . well . . . *killed you*.

She wasn't going to do this to herself. She'd made her choice and her choice was that the burglar was bluffing. He'd been trying to scare her, but Catherine refused to be scared because that would mean he'd won.

She walked quickly back up the garden to the house — deliberately not looking behind her.

It was probably a cat on the fence. Chips was a lacklustre defender of the realm, and tougher cats often stopped by to taunt him.

She shut the back door firmly behind her and stared out at the garden. There was nobody there.

There never had been.

Catherine leaned her forehead on the glass and stroked her tummy reassuringly. "We chased him out, didn't we, Crimpelene? We chased him out and won a prize."

She smiled at her own silliness.

Now. What was she doing?

Oh yes — mucking up the baking. Maybe there was still time to put the bananas in the cake . . .

Catherine turned towards the oven and gasped.

The oven was open, and the cake tin lay upside down on the tiled floor.

Oozing batter.

DS Reynolds was quite looking forward to seeing Marvel.

He'd done a hell of a job on the capture house, and expected a gruff *Good job, Reynolds* at the very least.

Elizabeth Rice had gone to the police warehouse with him but had turned out to have appalling taste in stolen goods, so her only contributions were a bottle opener for the kitchen, some family photographs, and a PlayStation she'd brought from home.

He, on the other hand, had gone through the Aladdin's cave of stolen goods with his usual flair. There wasn't a great selection of furniture, so apart from the beds, he'd chosen an eclectic mix of mid-century teak, and ironic armchairs in velvet and wool. There were dozens of prints and paintings and lamps to be had, and ornaments of varying quality, so he'd been sparing with those. But when it came to gadgetry, he'd gone for all the high-end burglar-bait he could find — Apple laptops and digital cameras, a Sony TV, and a classic Bang & Olufsen stereo. All the stuff in the police warehouse was eventually auctioned if it was not claimed, and Reynolds made a note to bid for the B&O himself.

He'd got curtains there too. Green velvet and fully lined, although that did make them heavy, and the stool he was standing on to hang them was wobbly at the best of times.

There was a mountain bike and a skateboard for the garden that supposedly belonged to Mattie, the spotty son they were "borrowing" from Rice's sister. There were a couple of photos of Mattie on the bookshelf, along with a photo of Rice at a beach bar in a coral-coloured bikini.

Her stomach was very flat.

Reynolds had been hard-pressed to find anything as carefree. The most informal picture he had showed him wearing baggy grey shorts during a hiking trip he'd taken to the Lake District a few years back. A watery sun bounced off the puddles.

"Nice legs, Glen!" Rice had laughed, and Reynolds had blanched.

He was Glen and she was Michelle. Rice had chosen their undercover names and, in order to maintain cover, they were also under orders from Marvel to dispense with any acknowledgement of rank for the duration of the assignment.

Reynolds thought that was a big mistake.

Still, he had the master bedroom and Rice had a single bed in the room that Mattie wouldn't be sleeping in, so he hoped the "sir" was implied.

They had to share the bathroom, however, and Rice had already joked about what she'd called his "vast array" of toiletries.

She had brought a toothbrush.

Just a toothbrush.

"Did you bring toothpaste?" she asked, and when he confirmed that he had, she said, "Oh good. I thought you would."

He had a good mind to hide it.

Rice had wheedled £200 out of Marvel for extras and they'd made an ascent on HomeFayre, where Reynolds had spent the lot on those little personal touches that made a house a home — candles, vases, picture frames and other assorted knick-knacks. He had brought one of his old watches from home — a defunct Bulova — and even a couple of dozen books; not as bait, but simply as a cultural counter to the bottle opener and PlayStation. He'd made a careful selection to impress Rice, but it was wasted. She had recognized Pushkin, but only because "he makes vodka too!"

Reynolds had sighed like an island.

Despite Rice's ignorance, he was pleased with the results.

Phones, pictures, cameras, games console, food in the fridge, comfortable beds . . . Goldilocks would love it.

If he found it.

And if he found it, they'd certainly find him . . .

Before he and Rice had even pulled up in their Tivi Rentals truck, the police technician had installed cameras and silent alarms — over doors, in corners and on sills.

"Don't fuck with the cameras," the tech had told them. "Not a fucking inch."

Reynolds pursed his lips at the language. There was no need for it.

He almost thought he *would* fuck with one of the cameras, just a little bit. But he wouldn't. He was a rule-maker, not a rule-breaker.

The stool tipped, and he clutched at the wall for support and felt his heart bound into his mouth.

"All right?" said Rice with a brief glance. Then looked back at the TV, where she was playing Grand Theft Auto. Apart from flirting with the postman, it was all she'd done since they'd got back from Exeter.

"I don't even know why you got curtains," she said. "We're only going to leave them open."

"What's for supper?" he said.

"Supper?" Rice frowned at the TV screen, as if she'd never heard the word before.

"Yes. I thought you could make something to eat while I'm doing all the work," he said pointedly.

"Oh, you mean tea," she said. "I thought we'd get a McDonald's."

"I don't eat McDonald's," he said.

"What!" she said incredulously. "Everybody eats McDonald's!"

He corrected her. "I think you'll find that everybody doesn't."

It was like talking to a child. And, like a child, Rice wasn't pulling her weight. He had a good mind to tell her so, but he found it difficult without the evident buffer of rank.

He'd be sure to let Marvel know, though. Reynolds wasn't a brown-nose, but there was nothing wrong with letting your senior officer know who was a valuable member of the team and who was coasting.

"There's Frosties," said Rice, leaning this way and that on the stolen sofa as she mowed down pedestrians. "I only bought breakfast. I thought we'd be eating out a lot, as we're trying to get burgled and — *ah shit!*"

There was a screech and a crash and a flying mailbox and Rice threw down the controller. Then she got up and walked over to Reynolds to watch him hooking up the curtains.

When she picked up the folds of thick green material, he thought she was finally helping, but instead she wrapped the curtain tightly around his legs and her shoulders.

Reynolds froze. They were bound together by velvet, and her arm was warm against his hip.

"What are you —"

Rice giggled and held her camera at arm's length and took a photo of them both.

Reynolds flinched in the flash.

"We need a picture together," she said. "To make it look real."

"Yes," said Reynolds. "Good idea."

Rice unwound herself from the curtain just as the door opened and Marvel walked in, holding up a six-pack of Guinness.

"House-warming gift," he said. "Hope you've got a bottle opener."

Rice disappeared into the kitchen and Marvel sat down and patted the Guinness on his lap like a Pekinese.

"Guinness, Reynolds?"

"No thank you, sir. I'm not a stout man."

"Didn't think so," said Marvel.

Reynolds watched from the corner of his eye while Marvel looked around the room critically — taking note of every little thing.

"I don't know why you got curtains," he said. "We'll only be leaving them open."

Reynolds was stung. But before he could respond, Rice came back into the room. She put two mismatched pint glasses on the table and handed Marvel the bottle opener.

"Just got it today," she said.

"Good work, Rice," he said gruffly.

There were new people at Number 23. Glen and Michelle and their son Mattie.

Shawn hadn't seen the son yet, but he'd seen his mountain bike lying in the front garden. It was a nice bike. Specialized. Expensive. Just thrown down in the grass.

The kid deserved to have it nicked.

Michelle was cute. Cute and chatty. Dark hair, pale skin, with nice freckles on her nose. Shawn didn't have time for a girlfriend, but if he did, she'd be his type.

She'd been grateful when he'd told her about signing for her parcels.

He hadn't seen Glen yet.

They didn't have a dog.

Shawn kept a pocket full of treats for dogs. Big dogs, little dogs, angry dogs, friendly dogs, scary mastiffs and yappy terriers and soppy Labradoodles . . . they were all putty in Shawn's hands once he'd reached into his pocket. Even the cagey-looking German Shepherd with the I BITE sign on his owners' gate would slink out of his kennel looking justifiably embarrassed to be betraying his master's security for a handful of kibble.

Not having a dog wasn't a deal-breaker — it was just they were a convenient way in. People loved talking about their dogs. Their name, their funny little ways.

Whether they might bite the postman . . .

They loved talking about their cats, too. Indoor, outdoor, cat flap, window . . .

It was another hot day and Shawn was in shorts but long sleeves.

The shorts revealed strong, brown, hairy legs. The sleeves hid the needle tracks.

Shawn had started on heroin when he was just sixteen, and in fifteen years had been in rehab fourteen times. Each time he'd relapsed within days of his release, and his family had finally understood what Shawn had known from the very first time a needle had delivered paradise to his veins:

He was *never* going to give it up.

How could he? How could anyone?

So Shawn had become a functioning addict. He had a good job with the Royal Mail, and supplemented his salary with side jobs. A bit of decorating here, a bit of computer wizardry there.

A bit of theft.

In his youth he'd been something of a legend in Tiverton for the offbeat nature of what he called "pranks".

Once he'd stolen a carnival float with a mechanical pig on it.

Another time he'd led the police on a tranquil chase down the towpath, directing operations and shouting encouragement to his pursuers from the deck of a stolen barge.

It wasn't all harmless high jinks. He'd nicked a stack of state-of-the-art hospital beds. As they were unloaded from one lorry, Shawn and his team had loaded them on to a second lorry outside another exit. All it had taken was three easily stolen sets of porters' uniforms and good timing, so that as the real porters wheeled one bed into the hospital, Shawn's men were ready and waiting to take possession of the next one — and make a sharp left down a different corridor. They'd stolen every other bed. Nine, in all. Shawn had had a customer waiting in Poland, and had cleared nearly eight thousand pounds on the heist.

But it had been a hassle. Right from the tip-off, through the planning and execution, it had been a big effort. Far too big for someone whose greatest ambition was to sleep it off, and now Shawn preferred jobs that required as little effort as possible.

And a job that required no effort at all was simply being friendly. Shawn had an open, honest face and a cheerful smile. Being friendly came naturally to him and he was as friendly to the customers on his daily rounds as he was to their dogs and cats.

He collected letters from the elderly to save them the walk to the post box, and when he left a customer a note saying there was a parcel in the wheelie bin, then that was where they always found it. So Shawn was a popular man — and a trusted one, and in brief doorstep instalments the people of Tiverton told him all manner of secret things . . .

Mrs Cobden at Lowman Road revealed that her husband had left her for another man.

Mr Singh up near the cemetery confessed that he'd unintentionally poisoned his neighbour's cat while trying to rid his shed of rats.

And Lisa Trevithick down Cowley Moor told him she'd always found him "interesting". It was seven thirty in the morning but she was already tipsy, and fully made up, so he'd accepted her invitation to come in for a quick cuppa, and they'd enjoyed many a quick cuppa over the next six months until her husband came out of prison.

And Shawn kept those secrets. He never gossiped about gay Mr Cobden, never told Mrs Angel next door that Tigger had died from eating rat poison, and he still bought Ricky Trevithick a pint whenever he saw him in the Soldier's Rest. They'd gone to school together, after all, and Shawn saw no reason to fall out with a mate just because he'd shagged his wife.

The truth was, he found it easy to keep secrets — because he didn't care about them. About *any* of them. The only thing he cared about was heroin and how to get it.

So he made his rounds and nobody ever complained about — or even noticed — a bit of junk mail missing here or there.

But if ever a customer asked him to pop any parcels in the tool shed because they were off to Thailand for a week, or to Sidmouth for their anniversary, or just to have a minor procedure at BUPA overnight . . .

Well, then Shawn Bridge passed that information on to his little brother Louis, who paid him thirty quid a pop.

Jack found his mother.

He was on the hard shoulder and she was in a field full of cows, speaking on the orange emergency phone.

She waved at him, and he waved back.

"Why's the phone in the field?" said Joy.

"That's just where they put them," he said.

They stood in the hot sun and watched their mother hang up and start towards them, but as she did the field began to slope, so that she was walking downhill. At first it was OK. At first she just walked faster and faster, but soon the slope was a mountain and she had to run — out of control — her arms held out as if she were on a tightrope, and still the field continued to tip, from a mountain to a wall, and she couldn't stop.

"Mum!" shouted Jack and started to run towards her — to catch her — but he was too late. Too slow. And she just *lifted* off the field and ran through the air with her white maternity dress flapping and folding around her flailing limbs as she fell down, down down down down —

Jack woke with a grunt. For a moment he lay panting in the darkness, wondering where he was and where *she* was and if there was still time to catch her . . .

132

Then he tensed.

The smallest noise.

There was someone in the house.

He was out of bed in an instant, moving silently and with practised speed across to the window. It opened easily on to the roof of the garage. That's why he'd chosen this room.

He hung from the sill by latex fingertips, and could just feel the tiles beneath his toes. When he let go, he slid, but he let it happen — rolling on to his back, with his bag clutched to his chest, so that he could dig his heels into the guttering.

A new house like this, it would hold.

It did.

He turned. He swung. He hung. He dropped. Softly as a cat, on to the back patio, next to the bike he'd found in the hallway. It was a blue Eddy Merckx. Worth a hundred quid of anybody's money.

Jack hitched his bag on to his shoulders. He stood in the shadow of the house, waiting.

Low voices. Car doors closing gently so as not to wake the neighbours.

They were supposed to be in Cumbria.

Maybe it had rained.

He waited until he heard the front door close and then got on the bike and rode away, past the sleepy Lego houses, down the hill to the old town.

The bike was fast and light and it felt like flying.

A hundred quid. Or he'd bloody keep it!

The sky was turning pink. A light was already on in the Busy Bee and, as he flashed past, Jack could see Mr

Dolan on the phone behind the sloping bank of chocolates.

Jack was fifty yards from home when he saw Joy.

She was in a dirty pink nightdress, barefoot, and with her lank hair hanging in her face. She was bent almost double with the effort of dragging two fat quires of newspapers along the pavement, with a sound like the roar of a waterfall in the silence of dawn.

SCCCCRRRRRRAAAAAAAPE.

SCCCCRRRRRRRAAAAAAAPE.

Jack dropped the bike alongside her. "What are you *doing?*" he hissed.

Joy didn't look at him and didn't stop dragging.

SCCCCRRRRRRRAAAAAAAPE.

"*Shit!*" he said, and grabbed one of the stacks. She shoved him aside and he shoved her back and took it from her, and lifted it off the ground and carried it awkwardly the twenty yards to the front door and slung it inside.

He came back for the second one.

Joy straightened up. Watched him take it.

"Get inside," he said.

She did.

He slammed the door behind them. "What the *fuck* are you doing? What if somebody caught you? What if the police come? They'll take us away!"

Merry came halfway down the stairs in her knickers. "What's happening?" she said, but they didn't look at her.

Instead Joy glared at Jack, panting — her pale eyes barely visible behind her wild hair. She bent to drag a

134

bundle of papers into the front room and Jack stamped on it. The hard plastic tape bit into her fingers as it was wrenched away.

"Ow!" Joy stared into her cupped hand in shock, then lunged at Jack, smearing blood on his face.

He recoiled and slapped her away.

"Yaaaaa!" she shouted, flapping her arms as if he were a crow on the hard shoulder. "Yaaaaa!"

"Don't!" cried Merry. "Don't fight!"

"You're crazy!" Jack yelled at Joy. "Fucking crazy!"

Joy flapped her arms one more time, then turned and ran into the front room. She dropped to her belly and kicked frantically through the tunnel in the newspaper wall, like a mermaid in a dirty pink nightdress.

Jack stood in the silence, shaken by the madness.

There was a knock at the door.

They both turned to look. Through the little glass porthole they could see the top of a grey head.

Jack got awkwardly to his feet and hauled the stacks of papers out of the hallway and into the front room with two loud thuds.

The person knocked again.

They weren't going away. Jack looked at Merry and put his finger to his lips.

She nodded. He opened the door.

"Is everything all right?" said the new nosy neighbour in a dressing gown.

"Yes."

"I heard shouting."

"Yes," said Jack. "That was me. I'm sorry."

The old woman's eyes darted past him, seeking an explanation.

Over her shoulder, Jack saw the bicycle, still lying where he'd dropped it in the street.

"I fell off my bike."

He edged past her to pick it up.

"Oh." She stepped aside to let him wheel it in inside. "Are you all right?"

"Yes thank you," said Jack. "I'm fine. Sorry to have disturbed you."

He half closed the door, but the old woman kept talking.

"Is your father home?"

"Actually he's working."

She put her hands on her hips as if she didn't believe that for a minute.

"I've moved in next door, you know. Mrs Reynolds."

"Yes," said Jack. "Hello."

"Hello," she said, just when he needed her to say *Goodbye*.

There was a long silence.

"Hello, Mrs Reynolds," called Merry from the stairs.

"Hello," she said.

"I'm Jack," said Jack. "And this is Merry."

"We've met," said Mrs Reynolds.

There was more silence.

"Mrs Reynolds' lawnmower is broken," said Merry suddenly. "Maybe you can fix it?"

"Yes," said Jack. "I'll come round and have a look, if you like."

Mrs Reynolds frowned as if this was not good news. But she was left with no response to make other than, "Thank you."

"OK, bye then," said Merry cheerfully.

"Bye then," said Jack.

"Goodbye," said Mrs Reynolds reluctantly, and Jack closed the door and leaned his forehead against it.

Shit.

Later that day he walked back up to the Busy Bee and reinstated the newspaper deliveries, much to the delight of Mr Dolan.

In a box on a low shelf were fake plastic vampire teeth, tipped with blood. Jack picked out a set for Merry.

He reached into his pocket, but Mr Dolan gave a magnanimous flap of his hand.

"The teeth are on the house."

"There's something going on next door," said Mrs Reynolds.

She stood at the back window with a dinner plate in each hand, like the Scales of Justice.

"Hmm?" said Reynolds, noncommittally.

His mother was an inveterate curtain-twitcher. At the last house, she'd been convinced that the neighbours were growing pot and had made him climb over a wall and peer through a shed window, all because the husband had a ponytail.

And sharp hearing.

He'd come outside, and Reynolds had had to pretend his mother's non-existent cat had got lost in their garden, and then didn't know what colour the cat was when Ponytail Man had wanted to help with the search.

He still got flustered thinking about it, and didn't want any repeat.

So he tried not to be drawn into her nosy-parker paranoia by pretending he hadn't heard her.

Instead, he wondered what Rice was doing this weekend.

138

Glen and Michelle had gone to the Reading Festival.

Reynolds had baulked at even the virtual idea, but Rice had been twice before, and said he'd love it if he ever really tried it.

"As much as the Big Mac?" he'd asked sarcastically, and she'd just rolled her eyes as if he was her dad, being square.

In reality, Rice had gone to the movies with Eric, and Reynolds was spending the weekend with his mother. They'd had breaded hake with peas, oven chips and a lemon wedge. She'd been eating the same thing for supper since 1992.

"Did you hear me?" she said sharply. "I'm telling you, there's something going on!"

"Sorry," he said. "What?"

"Something funny," she replied. "There's a boy and a small girl. The girl told me her father works away and her brother and sister look after her, but I've never seen a father or a sister, and she said her brother's twenty but the only boy I've seen looks all of twelve."

He joined her at the window, but it was getting too dark to see the garden next door, let alone the ages of any children that might be in it.

"Well," said Reynolds, "do they seem neglected?"

"They're very thin."

"Well, there are too many fat children now," said Reynolds, taking the plates from her and putting them in the dishwasher.

"I had to go round at six the other morning!" said his mother. "I was woken by the shouting and yelling. The boy said he'd fallen off his bicycle, but it was more than that. And the little one runs wild. Digging in the dirt and mowing the lawn at all hours. And she talks about nothing but vampires and killing old people!"

Reynolds said nothing. Just let that minor bit of melodrama hang in the air — and then blow away on the wind.

Sometimes that was enough.

"What's for pudding?" he asked after a minute.

"Apple tart. Just warming it through."

"Mmmm. Lovely," he said, and let her get on with it, while he wandered into the other room, where the computer was. He'd bought it for her so she could email her sister in Australia, but he noticed the last message sent was the one he'd sent when he'd shown her how it all worked.

"I don't see what's wrong with a letter," she had sniffed. And when he'd told her that email could deliver her message to Australia virtually immediately, she'd frowned and said, "How annoying."

Rice had sent him the photos she'd taken. Her standing in front of the B&O stereo. Him arranging photos on the mantelpiece. That one of them, bound together by green velvet, with her arm around his legs . . .

She was smiling happily, and the flash had brought out her freckles.

At the time Reynolds had been so conscious of her touching him that he'd only blushed and teetered, but in the photo it all looked very natural. As if Elizabeth Rice was happy to have her arm around his legs — and he was happy to have it there.

They looked as if they were just goofing around.

They looked like people in love.

Reynolds hoped Rice hadn't shown it to Eric. She'd said he wouldn't mind about their arrangement in the capture house, but Reynolds had seen Eric and thought he looked like the kind of man who might mind very much indeed. Eric wore grey tracksuit bottoms and a Gold's Gym T-shirt with the sleeves cut off in the middle of winter. As if even short sleeves were too namby-pamby for him. He was no taller than Reynolds, but he was so muscular that his head/neck combo formed a dome on his shoulders — of the kind that might contain a stuffed Victorian pheasant, rather than a brain.

Reynolds didn't want any trouble. Especially over someone like Elizabeth Rice. She didn't hang up the wet bathmat. She left the TV on when she wasn't watching it — wasn't even in the same room! She didn't put a clip on the Frosties to keep them fresh — just crumpled the plastic down into the box and hoped for the best. She dropped a knife in the sink with butter and Marmite on it and considered it "washing up". She left the top off the shampoo. *His* shampoo. *And* his toothpaste — which she used as if it were her own. And Reynolds couldn't even hide it, because there was nobody else in the house, so she'd know it was him — and that would make him look petty.

And she'd complained about hair blocking the shower drain.

Reynolds had stood his ground on that one. It wasn't his. His hair had always been firmly anchored to his head, thank you very much!

Rice had backed down with a tiny little smile that made him want to slap her.

Reynolds had known living together would be difficult. But it had been much harder than that, and he was relieved that the "establishing the house" period was at an end. They'd be back and forth, of course, until they caught Goldilocks or gave up trying, but the week-long relentless twenty-four-seven-living-with-Rice time was over, and Reynolds felt as if he'd weathered such a storm that he was grateful for the safe haven of breaded hake and a lemon wedge with his mother.

"Cream or ice cream?" she called.

"Cream, please," Reynolds called back.

"Oh I forgot to tell you," she went on, "the lawnmower won't start. Could you have a look at it?"

"When I get a minute!" he shouted.

He did ponder showing his mother the photo of Rice with her arm around his legs. She took his celibacy very personally, and it would get her off his back for a good long while if she thought he was actually living with somebody. With shift-work it would be simple for her not to meet his supposed girlfriend for months, and by the time she got insistent, he could easily have broken up with Rice. Reynolds was not a naturally deceitful person, but he was heartily sick of his mother getting all misty over babies on TV ads, and going on and on about his chunky cousin, Judith, who plopped them out like a sea turtle laying eggs.

It wasn't that Reynolds didn't like women — or want a woman — just that he always thought he could do better than any of the women he actually knew. And if he could do better at some point in the future, what was the point of doing anything at all with what was available to him now?

He wasn't an animal!

With a sigh of regret, he decided showing his mother the photo of Rice would only open a can of worms.

But he did save it.

He'd save the others too, of course. Maybe he'd create his own personal record of the progress of the Goldilocks investigation. It might be useful at some point in the future. Some clever reference system he could do for each investigation he was on. Or a feature for the *Tiverton Gazette* once it was all over.

But for now, he'd just save that *one* . . .

His phone rang in his pocket and he flinched guiltily.

It was Marvel.

"Where the hell are you?" he shouted. "There's someone in the house!"

The house belonged to Glen and Michelle Lee, who had gone to Reading Festival and wouldn't be back until Sunday.

Jack knocked on the front door. Nobody answered, of course.

He walked boldly down the side of the house and into the back garden.

The guttering was brilliant, as expected.

Shawn hadn't mentioned a cat, but they'd left the bathroom window open . . .

Stretch, hang, wriggle, and he was in.

There were a lot of toiletries to avoid on the sill.

He went downstairs, his footfall so soft that even he couldn't hear it, and unlocked the back door in case he needed a quick getaway. Louis's voice in his head: *Make sure you can get out before you get into it.*

Then he went into the front room.

The first thing he did was close the ugly green curtains. It was easier said than done because they had been hung so badly. They didn't meet in the middle, but Jack wasn't too bothered. He turned on the light anyway. At the front of a house it was less suspicious than a torch beam in a dark room. Anyone who knew Glen and Michelle were away would assume someone was there to feed the cat or pick up the post, if they cared enough to assume anything at all.

He looked around the room and was disappointed.

The place was sparsely furnished — as if Glen and Michelle had only just moved in. Sure they had the big TV and the B&O stereo, but he wasn't about to carry either of those out of the house in his backpack.

There was a camera on the coffee table, though. A Canon Ixus. Forty quid's worth, and easy to carry. He put it in his bag and moved on.

On the bookshelf were photos of Glen and Michelle. Two separate photos. Glen had pale, knobbly knees, and looked like the kind of man who'd rather stick pins in his eyes than go to a music festival. Michelle was at a beach bar, wearing an orange bikini and drinking a lot of drinks that required the shelter of a small umbrella.

She was out of Glen's league — but Jack thought that was good. Maybe he bought her expensive jewellery to make up for it.

If he did, Jack would find it.

He ran his eye along the spines of the books: Pushkin, Camus, Dawkins.

No vampires.

There was a watch. Jack shook it and held it up to his ear but it wasn't working. He'd take it anyway. Bulova was a good make. He put it on. If he was stopped, a camera in his bag was logical, but a watch should be on his wrist.

He turned to go upstairs, hoping for better. At the very least there would be a bed for him that wasn't covered in papers and musty with mouse shit.

He was almost out of the room when he halted — his gut telling him that something wasn't right. Jack backed carefully into the room again and turned a slow, puzzled circle, seeking the source of his disquiet.

And then he stopped dead, and his heart thudded.

On the mantelpiece was a photo frame. And in the frame was a photo of two children . . .

And a fucking beach ball.

And before his brain even processed why or how, Jack's gut told him to run.

So he did.

Fast.

Marvel was furious.

"What the hell!" he kept muttering and saying and shouting. "What the hell!"

Nobody else said anything very much, although Toby Parrott did murmur "Oh dear" several times as they watched the CCTV footage, which only seemed to make Marvel even angrier.

"How the hell did he know?" he shouted. "What the hell scared him off? You two?" he said, jabbing a demanding finger at Reynolds and Rice. He glared at them in turn, apparently assuming one of them was to blame, then stared back at the TV screen and hit Play for what felt to Reynolds like the zillionth time.

The first fleeting sight of the burglar was as he walked along the landing.

"He came in through the bathroom window," said Marvel grimly, "although you did your level best to barricade it with Brylcreem, Reynolds. God knows why the camera there didn't pick him up. If it had, we'd have caught him red-handed . . ."

This time he acted out the whole crime in time to the CCTV pictures, in a clumsy facsimile of the intruder they were almost one hundred per cent sure was Goldilocks.

"Down the stairs, no problem," he went on, walking on the spot, "and through to the back door" — he unlocked the door in the air — "and then back in here, and pulls the curtains and turns on the light . . ."

In time to the lithe, hooded figure on the TV, Marvel clumped heavily to the curtains and pretended to pull them. "I knew these things were a mistake the minute I saw them," he fumed. "They gave the cocky little sonofabitch privacy. Made it easy for him to search the place without arousing suspicion."

Reynolds' neck burned. Half embarrassment and half anger. He could see which way this was going. Right before his eyes, Marvel was building a case. Not against Goldilocks, but against *him*.

"So he puts on the light," Marvel said from the switch by the door, "and then picks up the camera and puts it in his bag and all's going great guns, and then he finds the watch and shakes it . . ."

He shook his fist at his ear, standing beside the shelf, his eyes darting about to see what the burglar might have seen or heard from that very spot. And he moved towards the door.

"And this is where he stops."

Reynolds' fists tightened by his side. He knew what was wrong. He knew what Goldilocks had seen — had known it the very first time they'd watched the footage.

Now all he could do was sit there and wait for Marvel to see it too.

The DCI turned where Goldilocks had turned, and faced the mantel square on. "Something here . . ." he said. "Look — see him looking . . ."

Reynolds gritted his teeth so hard that they creaked. The photo. The photo! The bloody bloody photo!

The Brylcreem was nonsense. The curtains were an excuse. But the photograph was his fault, and his alone. He had bought the frame in HomeFayre and made a mental note to replace the stock photo. It wasn't a big thing. It was a small thing. But Reynolds prided himself on getting the details right, and so he'd planned to change it. For that one of him and Rice together, perhaps.

Whatever it was, he *was* going to replace it.

But he'd had so much to do! He'd done the whole bloody house on his own! Every bit of decorating and arranging and set-design he'd done alone while Rice had sat on her arse and done nothing, and *still* he would have remembered except that the curtains had taken so long to hang because of the weight of the fabric and the wobbly stool and because he hadn't eaten anything since lunch, and Rice had bought nothing for supper but bloody Frosties!

Reynolds felt like crying. He really did. It wasn't fair! It just wasn't! Any second now Marvel would see the stock picture in the frame and put two and two together and then go ballistic and shit on him from a dizzy height . . .

There was a silence of such length and weight that it was all Reynolds could do not to leap up, dash the frame into the hearth and then commit hara-kiri with the shards, he felt so tense and hard-done-by.

They all flinched as Marvel slapped the mantel with such force that the guilty photo frame toppled on to its face. He righted it and said, "What the fuck did he see?"

"I have no idea, sir," said Rice.

"Neither do I, sir," said Reynolds.

"Beats me," said Parrott.

Marvel sighed and looked around the room one last time, with the air of a man standing in the splinters of his home after a twister. He seemed utterly at a loss, and completely defeated.

Finally he pinched his hairy nose and said, "Back to the bloody drawing board then."

And that was it.

Reynolds couldn't believe his luck.

He saw Marvel to the door. Watched him back angrily out of the drive and squeal out of the cul-de-sac like Starsky and/or Hutch. Then he closed the door and sagged against it.

Marvel really didn't know! He didn't know that the photo frame was the missing link in the chain of disaster. Didn't know that Reynolds had screwed up the whole operation, cost the force several thousand pounds, and was the cause of their continuing failure to catch one skinny little thief who was now making two police forces look like fools.

Reynolds decided not to tell him.

He went back into the front room to find Elizabeth Rice holding the HomeFayre photo frame in one hand and the beach ball picture in the other.

150

"I never liked this picture," she said and, right in front of him, she crumpled it up and threw it in the hearth.

Parrott frowned at her in confusion.

But Reynolds looked her straight in the eyes and said, "Neither did I."

Later that night, as he watched Middlesex surrender to Yorkshire in a disgraceful display of so-called cricket, Marvel took stock.

The capture house had failed.

He didn't know why it had failed, but he felt sure that it must be something that Team Goldilocks had done wrong.

Not him, though. He'd done everything right. No, somebody else had screwed up, and when he found out who, and how, he'd have their guts for garters.

His money was on Reynolds. After all, he'd chosen everything for the house and dressed it all alone. Marvel knew that because Reynolds had made a huge song and dance about it — even taken him aside and told him that Rice had been a lazy cow.

Not that he'd used those words.

Not made a meaningful contribution to the operation, was how he'd put it.

The bloody smarty-pants.

Well, thought Marvel, Reynolds was hoist with his own whatchamacallit — because if all Rice had contributed was a PlayStation, a bottle opener and a photo of herself in a bikini, then he could find no fault with her.

The Middlesex batsman knocked off his own bales with a rash sweep that was more Babe Ruth than W. G. Grace and Marvel groaned. He switched off the TV and poured himself another angry whiskey.

Regardless of who was at fault, the capture house had failed. Which meant *he* had failed. And the worst thing about it was he had failed just when he needed to make a stunningly good first impression.

Marvel knew only too well that one lousy case — one dumb move — could make a cop a laughing stock, and put the kibosh on any hopes he'd had of promotion.

As he stared moodily into his Jameson's, Marvel felt his back against the wall, only weeks since his back had been against another wall, on another force.

Then he downed his drink and thought, *Fuck it.*

Back-to-the-wall, seat-of-his-pants, skin-of-his-teeth — that was how he had always worked best. In the Met, he'd had a solve-rate that rivalled the best in the force. The best in *any* metropolitan force. And that was for murder — not this B&E bullshit! He wasn't about to admit defeat to a perp called Goldilocks. And he certainly wasn't about to admit defeat three weeks into his tenure in Taunton. Or Tiverton. Or whatever the hell hick place he was in. With all the sheep and the sky, he found it hard to keep track.

Six weeks, he thought. If the capture house was to fail, six weeks was at least a reasonable length of time. A face-saving length of time. After six weeks, he would feel OK about telling Detective Superintendent Cullymore that they'd given it a fair crack, but that to go on might be an expensive experiment in diminishing returns.

Marvel totted up the broad figures in his head. The capture house had been operational for three weeks and was costing the Avon and Somerset force about four thousand pounds a week in running costs, what with rent, bills and overtime. Six weeks instead of three would mean spending twenty-four thousand pounds instead of twelve.

What the hell, thought Marvel. That's what taxpayers are for.

So he told Reynolds and Rice to give it another week or so to see if they could lure Goldilocks back to the capture house.

And when he next reported to Superintendent Cullymore, he told him everything was going just fine.

Catherine While was shopping and thinking about sex.

Not in a dirty way. In a scientific way.

She had come to the conclusion that pregnancy freed one from the shackles of sexuality in all social situations.

Catherine knew she was young and reasonably pretty, and yet men no longer seemed to find her attractive. They had stopped flirting with her and started being helpful instead. At first she had missed the occasional frisson of an innocent flirtation, but she'd quickly embraced the altruism of the opened door, and the surrendered seat in the doctor's waiting room.

Women, too, were sweeter. Quicker to smile, and more considerate of her back, her feet, her bladder. As if her distended tummy were a tethered blimp, advertising the fact that she had had all of the sex she was going to need for a good while yet and so was a sister to be protected, rather than the Competition.

Sex had evaporated and Catherine enjoyed the kinder world that was its residue.

She picked up a wheel of Stilton and wondered idly whether her thought was new, or only new to her.

154

Either way, it made her feel better about everything. It helped her to let go of the fright and the fear. To remember that most people were kind, most places were safe — and most lies remained forever undiscovered . . .

Catherine put the Stilton back and scolded the baby: "You can't have blue cheese, silly!"

She put a piece of good, firm Cheddar in her trolley instead and rolled around to the meat aisle, where a tall man in a thick burgundy jumper was sniffing the bacon, so she veered away and into the bakery aisle, which was a minefield of jam and icing.

"What do you fancy?" she said.

The middle-aged woman next to her said, "Excuse me?"

Catherine blushed. "Sorry, I was talking to the baby."

The woman looked down at Catherine's tummy and laughed. Then she bent over and addressed Catherine's navel directly. "I bet you fancy a nice bit of coal, don't you? Mine were all devils for coal. My mouth was black as the ace of spades!"

Catherine cocked a thumb at her belly. "This one ordered cold butter beans for a week, breakfast, lunch and dinner!"

"Mad, innit?"

"Mad," agreed Catherine cheerfully, and rolled on towards the Mr Kiplings. Baby wanted Bakewell tarts.

"Baby's not getting Bakewell tarts," she told it sternly. "You can have a nice apple when you get home. Yum!"

Then she shed her smile and sighed. Who was she kidding? Shopping was no fun since it had become an obstacle course of denial. Her trolley contained so much foliage that it was like pushing a mini-greenhouse around the supermarket.

Maybe she would go to the café and treat herself to tea and cake. If it was carrot cake, it would be almost like having one of her five-a-day, wouldn't it?

Maybe she should get a fish pie.

Enough!

Catherine felt suddenly as hungry as hell and a little tearful. She steered rapidly to the tills and paid for half a load of shopping she didn't want. She'd come back another time for the rest, when she had more willpower.

It had rained briefly, but the sun was out again with a vengeance, and the tarmac was already starting to steam around the glittering cars.

Catherine opened the back of the pea-green Volvo and lifted the first bag from the trolley. It split, and all her shopping went rolling about the car park. Peppers and onions and cabbages and leeks.

She almost cried.

Oh stuff it, she thought, I'm just backing over that healthy shit and going home for a nap.

But a boy appeared from nowhere, nimbly dodging about, stretching under cars, picking everything up and handing it all back to her, filling her arms with groceries.

"Oh!" she said. "Thank you."

He nodded and — without offering or being asked — quickly transferred the rest of her shopping from the trolley into the car.

Catherine started to feel better as she watched pregnancy-related altruism in action.

"That's so kind of you," she said when he'd finished. "Do you work here?"

"No," he shrugged, "just passing."

"Lucky for me," she said, and wondered if she should tip him. Her grandmother would have tipped him. Made him stand there for an age while she rummaged in her purse for an inadequate coin.

"My grandmother would tip you," she smiled.

"I don't want a tip," he said, and she thought he would leave, but he didn't leave. He just stood there, pale and skinny, in scruffy jeans, Adidas trainers and a blue hoodie. She had thought he was about twelve, but now she realized he must be older, because he had the start of mild fuzz on his chin and cheeks. He had narrow, pale grey eyes and looked hungry.

"Can I buy you a piece of cake?" she said suddenly. "I was just going to treat myself."

She *was* going to treat herself. Why the hell not? And why not treat him too? Repay his small kindness with one of her own. Make a human connection.

Her huge belly made it OK to offer.

But she was still surprised when he said yes.

By the time they had stood in the queue with a tray for five minutes, Catherine was regretting her invitation.

The boy was not chatty. Barely made eye contact. They shuffled to the till in silence, sat down in silence.

How were they going to eat cake together?

"Counts as one of your five-a-day," Catherine joked as she cut the nose off her slice of carrot cake.

The boy didn't laugh. "I eat five a day," he said. "I try to stay healthy."

He didn't look healthy. He was so thin that it verged on undernourished. But he wasn't eating his cake.

Probably on drugs, Catherine thought, and immediately chided herself for having an uncharitable thought about someone who'd done her a favour.

She babbled through the guilt.

"I try to stay healthy too," she said. "Because of the baby, of course. But even when I'm not ... y'know ..."

The boy nodded at her cappuccino. "My mother said you shouldn't drink coffee," he said. "When you're expecting."

Catherine was amused by his use of the word "expecting". It sounded very old-fashioned coming out of his young mouth.

"This is decaf," she smiled.

"Or smoke," he added.

"I don't," she nodded, "luckily. But my mother smoked with me. I weighed less than six pounds."

"Is that bad?" he said.

"Yes, quite," she said. "Of course, she claims it was normal. People weren't as educated back then, were they?"

As if he would know, she thought. He was a child. His idea of back then was probably last Christmas.

For the first time in her life, Catherine felt old. A fat old lady waddling about, mothering strangers, made confident by her lack of sexuality.

The boy stared into his tea but didn't drink it. The silence stretched. Catherine put a piece of cake in her mouth, and then quickly another. She wanted to finish it fast so she could go.

I have to dash, but you enjoy the rest of your cake.

"I don't know how much I weighed," the boy finally said. "I think I used to know, but I've forgotten."

"Your mum will know," said Catherine. "To the ounce!"

"She's dead," he said.

"Oh," she said, "I'm sorry." And she really was. Sorry his mother was dead — but more sorry she'd mentioned her. How awkward!

There was a gaping silence, and then the boy said, "She was murdered."

"Oh no!"

It was all Catherine could say. What else was there? The only logical thing to say after that bombshell was to ask when and how and did they ever catch him and are you all right . . . And none of those were questions you asked of some stranger you'd only just met — or anyone in a coffee shop.

But the boy looked at her properly for the first time, as if he wanted her to ask questions — as if *daring* her to ask.

159

Catherine bit her lip. She didn't want to ask. She didn't want to know.

She had to get this back on a more normal, formal footing. She spoke stiffly. "I'm sorry for your loss."

The boy gave no acknowledgement of her words — just continued to stare straight into her face. She avoided his eyes and looked at the counter, as if it were the most natural thing in the world, when told someone's mother has been murdered, to check for muffins.

"A stranger killed her with a knife."

Catherine gasped.

She felt sick. Tossed about and queasy. A little boat on a high sea. Holding on to the sides of the table to ride out the storm she'd called down upon herself.

"Stop it," she whispered. "Stop it, please."

But the boy didn't stop it. Instead he leaned forward to close the space between them and said softly, "She was pregnant too."

The blood drained from Catherine's head. She gripped the edge of the table so hard that her fingers went white.

"What?" she said, cocking her ear towards him like a deaf person. "What did you say?"

"You heard me," he said.

Catherine *had* heard him. That was why her mouth was open, her breathing shallow. Unconsciously, she splayed a guardian hand over her unborn baby.

"She was killed with *that knife*."

"The knife . . ." Her voice cracked. She tried again. "The knife you left in my house?"

"No!" The boy looked surprised.

160

"No," he said again. "The knife I *found* in your house."

Jack Bright withdrew the knife from the mud-crusted hiking boot, then slowly frowned at it — confused by recognition.

The shell handle shimmered like oil on water. The blade was serrated on one edge, curved on the other to a cruel point . . .

He felt Pam's grip on his wrist; heard the inhuman howl of their lives falling apart, and he knew — somehow he knew — that the knife — this knife! — had murdered his mother.

He dropped it with a panicky clatter and backed away from it on his knees, dazed by fear and uncertain memory.

Then his head snapped up at the exorcist cry:
"WHOEVER'S THERE HAD BETTER GET THE HELL OUT OF THIS HOUSE!"

Catherine got up too fast. She winced as her tummy bumped the table side. People looked at them. She wanted to slap the boy, but instead she bent over him, trying to keep this private.

Civil.

English.

Her trembling betrayed her. "If you ever come near me again," she said quietly, "I'll call the police."

The boy looked at her with eyes that were as cold and as grey as the ice on a dirty lake.

"No you won't."

161

Jack was electric with fury.

He had broken into Catherine While's home and left a knife by her bed and a note threatening to kill her.

She would see them. She would call the police. The police would investigate. Connections would be made. Knots would unravel. The man who'd killed his mother would finally be caught.

None of this had been in any doubt for Jack . . .

Until it hadn't happened.

Now he had nothing. Not the knife, and not the killer.

He should never have left the knife behind! He should have taken it with him. Gone straight to the cops and told them where he'd found it and what it meant . . . But he couldn't do that because he didn't *know* what it meant. Was Adam While the *muffled voice*? The *unidentified male*? He didn't know, and didn't know how to find out. Only the police could do that and he wasn't about to ask them because, like Louis said, they always got you for *something*. And if he was nicked for burglary, then Joy and Merry would be in care before the day was out.

162

Jack couldn't let that happen.

That's why *she* was supposed to call the police. Tell them about the knife. The note. The cake on the kitchen floor. The late-night phone call.

Why wouldn't she call the police?

"Shit!" he shouted. "Shit!"

Near the little police station was a phone box.

"Police, fire or ambulance?"

He couldn't speak.

The orange phone dangling on the twisted wire.

"Hello. Police, fire or ambulance?"

He took a deep breath. "Hello."

"Do you want police, fire or ambulance, sir?"

Jack looked at the police station. "I want to report . . ." he said. "I want to report . . ."

What *did* he want to report? Jack didn't know. A murder? He wasn't reporting a murder because they already knew about the murder. It was a murderer he wanted to report, but he had no proof. He knew where the proof *was*, and his gut felt it, and it all made sense in the darkness inside his head, but once he brought it out into the light so he could see it, the proof turned to dust, like one of Merry's vampires.

He couldn't risk losing what was left of his family for dust.

"Sir? Can you tell me the nature of your emergency, please?"

Jack hung up.

Then he beat the phone to death against the wall.

Catherine couldn't remember driving home from the supermarket, but she must have, because here she was, in the driveway, and shaking so hard that her teeth chattered and her fingers fumbled on the seatbelt catch, making the panic rise inside her.

Screw utmost serenity! She had to tell Adam! She had to tell the police! She got a jagged pang of regret for burning the card in the sink. She saw again the paper turned to soft ash, washing down the plug hole.

Idiot!

But she still had the knife. The knife would be enough. They could get DNA off the knife. They could get DNA off anything. Fast, too! She'd seen it on TV. Let them nail the little bastard. The lying, thieving, stalking little *shit*. If he'd left her alone, she would have left *him* alone, but now she didn't care if they gunned him down in the *fucking street*!

The seatbelt finally popped open and she hauled herself out of the car.

It took her three goes to get the quivering key into the lock.

She went upstairs as fast as the baby allowed, her chest heaving from fear as much as exertion.

Chips slunk off the bed but she ignored him. She opened her bra drawer and slid her hand to the back.

She couldn't find the knife.

She checked again, slower this time.

It wasn't there.

She pulled the drawer out completely and tipped it on to the bed.

164

A jumble of silken wire and ribbon and lace.

The knife was not there.

She yanked open her knicker drawer. Her sock drawer. Her jumpers and T-shirts and jeans.

Not there.

But it must be! It must be there! She had pushed it to the back. It had fallen down inside. It must have . . .

She pulled all the drawers out, piling them haphazardly on the bed in a noisy wood-and-cotton Jenga, then sank awkwardly on to her knees, holding the bed for support, to check inside the dark shell of the wooden chest.

It was empty.

The knife was gone.

The little shit had broken back in and taken it. When? Why? To get his so-called proof? Or just to mess with her head? To show her he could come and go as he pleased? Just to scare her?

It had worked before and it was working again.

She wasn't safe.

Her baby wasn't safe.

None of them were safe!

The skin on the back of Catherine's neck crawled with unspeakable dread.

"Are you looking for this?"

She screamed.

Catherine pressed a hand over her heart to stop it bounding clear out of her chest.

"Oh my God, Adam! What are you doing here?"

"Are you looking for this?" he repeated.

She looked down at the knife in his hand. The brutal blade. The handle of shell.

There was no lie Catherine could think of fast enough. "Yes."

"What's it doing in your underwear drawer?"

"What were *you* doing in my underwear drawer?"

"Don't fuck about, Cath!"

Catherine was surprised. Adam had never spoken to her so rudely. He rarely swore.

She rose awkwardly from her knees, using the corner of the chest to haul herself upright, then sat on the edge of the bed and pushed her hair out of her eyes.

He looked at her intently.

She took a deep breath. "Somebody left it by the bed."

"Who?"

"I didn't tell you only because I didn't want to worry you."

166

"Who?"

"Someone broke in, Adam. While you were in Chesterfield."

"A burglar?"

"Yes."

"A burglar broke in and left this knife by your bed?"

"Yes."

"And you didn't call me?"

"I didn't want to worry you."

"Did you call the police?"

She hesitated, and Adam gave a short, incredulous laugh.

Because it sounded so stupid. Catherine knew that and felt her face grow warm with shame.

"What could they have done? I chased him out of the house with that horrible vase that Valerie gave us. I never even *saw* him. He didn't *take* anything!"

"So a burglar broke in just to leave this knife next to your bed?"

His sarcasm stung.

"And a note," she said defiantly.

"What did it say?"

"Adam —"

"WHAT THE FUCK DID IT SAY?"

"'*I could have killed you.*'"

The words were shocked out of her.

There was a stunned silence and Catherine worked hard not to cry. This was all so unexpectedly horrible. Adam was being so mean to her. She looked up at him, willing him to reach out and touch her, to hold her, to tell her he loved her and she'd done the right thing and that it was all going to be OK . . .

But he didn't. He just stood there, flushed with anger.

"Where is it?" he demanded coldly. "Let me see it."

For a moment Catherine was so confused that she didn't know what he was talking about.

"What?"

"The note."

"I . . . I burned it."

"You *burned* it?"

"I burned it. In the kitchen sink."

"I don't believe you."

She blinked up at him. "What?"

"You're lying to me."

"I'm *not!*"

"You *are!*" he cried. "It makes no sense! A burglar breaks in and you don't call me? Or the police? He doesn't steal anything but he leaves this knife? By your *bed*? You say there was a note but you burned it? I'm not a fucking idiot, Catherine!"

"Adam —" She reached for his hand but he shook her off.

"Are you having an affair?"

"*What?*" Catherine was blindsided.

"Someone was here in our bedroom and you're lying about it. Are you having an affair?"

"An *affair?*" She grappled with this new twist.

"Is that why you've stopped having sex with me? You're getting it somewhere else?"

"I'm nearly eight months pregnant, Adam!"

"Tell me the truth, Cath."

"I *am* telling you the truth!"

"Who is it?"

"Nobody!"

"Just tell me who it is. I won't be angry. I just have to know."

"It's *nobody*. Adam, you're being ridiculous."

"Don't tell me I'm ridiculous!" he shouted. "I'm trying to protect you! You and the baby! And all this time you've been lying to me. I *know* it! That phone call! The wrong number. You lied to my face! So don't tell me I'm ridiculous, Catherine, just tell me the fucking truth."

His lip trembled, and in a blinding flash Catherine realized that Adam was more than just angry . . .

He was *scared*.

She *had* lied to him, and because of that he'd jumped to the wrong conclusion, but it wasn't an illogical one, wasn't ridiculous.

Catherine's heart ached for the man she loved.

"This *is* the truth, Adam. Please believe me. I didn't tell anyone about the burglary because I didn't think they could do anything, and I just couldn't face the drama. The hoo-hah. But *I* was being ridiculous, not you. I see that now. Believe me, I wish I'd called you. I wish I'd called the police. But I didn't. And the longer it went on, the harder it got to tell anyone!"

She took his hand and this time he let her hold it.

"I feel terrible about lying to you. But I just wanted to forget all about it and stay calm. For the baby . . ."

She placed his hand gently on her tummy under her own. "For *our* baby . . ."

He stood for a moment, head bowed. "Who is he?"

"God, Adam! He's just a boy!"

Adam took his hand from hers.

"You said you never saw him!" The accusation was back in his voice.

"*That night*," she said. "I never saw him the night he broke in."

"But you've seen him since?"

Catherine sighed deeply and nodded. "Today," she said. "Just now, at the supermarket. And he's just a boy, Adam. A skinny, scruffy little kid."

"Why did you meet him at the supermarket?"

"I didn't meet him! He just came up to me in the car park."

Catherine paused.

Mentally edited.

She didn't want to say that she'd bought the boy tea and cake when Adam was apparently so alert to betrayal.

"He admitted he'd broken in."

"What else?"

"Just . . ." she hesitated.

"What else?"

"He told me some crazy story about his mother being murdered with that knife . . ."

She looked down at the knife, loose in Adam's hand now — its vicious tip pointing at the floor.

"This knife?" He looked confused. He held it up to show her, as if there might be another one.

170

She sniffed back tears. "Yes. That's why I came straight home to find it."

"What were you going to do with it?"

"I don't know. Take it to the police. Let them sort it out. Just . . . get it out of the house."

Adam said nothing, just stared down at the knife in his hand.

"He said he found it here," she said tentatively.

He nodded, focusing on the knife. "Of course," he said. "Because it's mine. But I haven't seen it for so long I thought I'd lost it, to be honest."

He sat down beside her with a sigh, and took her hand in his. "I'm sorry I shouted at you, Cath. You gave me a fright."

Relief washed over her like a balm.

"*I'm* sorry, Ad. And I'm sorry I didn't call you that night."

"I can see now how it happened," he said. "You were alone and frightened, and worried about protecting the baby . . . It was all too much to deal with at one time."

She nodded vehemently. That's exactly how it had felt. Too much to deal with at one time.

"You made one bad choice, that's all."

"Yes," she nodded.

One bad choice. And so many consequences.

"It *was* him on the phone that night . . ."

"I thought so," he said grimly.

"And I think he flattened Rhod's tyre. Jan found a note on our car. It said *Call the police.*"

"He sounds psychotic," said Adam seriously.

171

"Maybe," she nodded wearily. "Or maybe he's just getting his own back because I chased him out of the house. Either way, if he wanted to scare me, then he's doing a bloody good job."

She felt her chin tremble and then Adam took her in his arms. Finally Catherine allowed herself to be comforted by him, and it felt so good and warm and safe that she wished she had let it happen weeks ago.

"Why are you here?" she snuffled into his chest.

"Huh?"

"Why aren't you in Cornwall?"

"Oh. The place in Hayle cancelled. I thought I'd turn round and surprise you."

"Well, you certainly did *that!*"

They both smiled small, tremulous smiles and Adam stroked her hair.

"*Should* we call the police?" she whispered.

There was a long silence.

"Not if you don't want to. But I think I should talk to him."

She sat up in surprise. "Talk to the boy?"

He nodded firmly. "We need to know whether he's actually dangerous or just a nasty little bully who can be scared off by someone his own size."

"*Twice* his size!" said Catherine. "You could squash him flat!"

Adam raised a droll eyebrow, as if that might have to be an option.

"Seriously, Adam. I don't want you doing anything . . ." She'd been going to say *silly* but she switched to "heroic".

172

"Heroic?" he laughed. "Me?"

"Don't make me worry about *him* calling the police on *you*."

He held two fingers to his temple. "Scout's honour."

"When were you ever a scout?"

"In my head, I've got all my badges."

Catherine smiled and Adam kissed her.

"Don't worry," he said. "I only want to talk to him. Just to make sure he won't come back."

"You think he'll come back?" said Rice.

Reynolds looked at Rice over the breakfast table. She was crunching through a bowl of her infernal Frosties. He'd had to go out himself and buy yoghurt and berries and good rough oatmeal.

"No."

"Then why are we still here?"

Reynolds shrugged.

"I don't really mind how long we stay," said Rice, and looked around the kitchen. "It's bigger than my place. I like it."

Reynolds put more salt on his porridge. "Don't you miss Eric?"

"No," said Rice.

Reynolds waited for her to say something more, but she didn't seem to think that it needed further explanation.

Which it obviously did, so he asked why.

"Dunno," she said, like an annoying teenager.

He wasn't going to *beg*. But he thought it was interesting.

"Going anywhere nice tonight?" he said, carefully neutral. They were both going out almost every night now in the remote hope that Goldilocks would come back.

"Movies," said Rice.

"Anything good?"

"Who cares?" she said with an impish smile.

Reynolds got up and brusquely scraped the rest of his porridge into the bin. He would be dining with his mother tonight.

Again.

It was her birthday and he was taking her out to a restaurant that served breaded hake. Still, it was better than staying in and having to listen to her paranoia about the devil-child next door or her whine about the lawnmower.

His phone rang. It was Mr Passmore to say that the insurance company was querying his claim.

"But I gave you a crime reference number," said Reynolds.

"And I gave it to the insurance chap who came out," said Mr Passmore. "And I told him you thought it was Goldilocks and all, but now they're giving me the runaround."

"On what basis?"

"On the basis they don't want to pay up, by the sound of it."

"Well," said Reynolds, "I'm afraid that is between you and your insurer, Mr Passmore. It's nothing to do with me."

"But now they're saying it wasn't a burglary. And *you're* the one who said it *was*. So how can that be nothing to do with you?"

"Once we have issued a reference number, it becomes a matter for the householder and insurer. We do not get involved with insurance claims unless there has been some wrongdoing on the part of the householder."

"Are you saying I'm trying to diddle the insurance company?" said Mr Passmore snippily.

"Not at all."

"Well then, what about the investigation?"

Reynolds paused. It wouldn't do to tell Mr Passmore the truth about burglaries. So he spoke carefully. "I can't disclose procedural details, sir, but the investigation into Goldilocks is ongoing."

"And that will involve my case?"

"If your case is found to be linked to Goldilocks, then of course."

"I thought you said it *was* linked!"

"That is yet to be determined, sir."

"And how do you determine it?" said Mr Passmore.

"Well," said Reynolds, "when we catch him, we ask him."

There was a long silence on the line.

"You *ask* him?"

"Yes, sir."

"And you just *believe* him?"

"Well, sir," said Reynolds, "usually any criminal who's arrested, and faced with evidence he feels will stand up in court, will ask for other offences to be taken into consideration for the purpose of sentencing. At that point there's really no mileage in the offender saying he *didn't* carry out a particular burglary, because that means he could be tried for it at a later date and sentenced for it separately and possibly do another spell in jail."

"Well," said Mr Passmore, "I'm still very surprised that you'd take the word of a criminal."

"It's called confession," said Reynolds. "We're all for it."

If Mr Passmore noticed the sarcasm, he ignored it. "So how close are you to catching this Goldilocks character?"

"As I said, sir, I can't —"

"All right. All right!" said Mr Passmore impatiently. "So while we all wait for a thief to be caught and to tell the truth, I have to put up with my insurance company calling *me* a liar, do I? Calling *you* a liar, in effect, Sergeant Reynolds."

"I've been called worse," said Reynolds, which was true.

"*Fine!*" said Mr Passmore, and hung up.

Reynolds cleared his throat. Then he put a clip on the Frosties and picked up his car keys.

Rice winked at him. "Hot date, *Glen*?"

"Don't forget to leave the window open, *Michelle*."

Jack couldn't remember a time when he wasn't angry.

It was always there, like an itch. Sometimes mild and ignored, sometimes so big and sore that his slight frame could not contain it, and it burst like a boil, spewing violence and bitter hatred that left him hollow.

For a short while.

He always filled up again. Easily, and to the brim.

He wished it would stop. He wished *he* could stop. Every time he woke up, still tired, in a stranger's clean, comfortable bed, he wished for a childish miracle that would turn back the clock to before the hard shoulder.

Sometimes he felt as if he'd never left that road. Or that day. As if he'd been stuck there ever since his mother had disappeared, and everything that had happened since was a dream, a mirage, a fake life that he couldn't discover how to escape.

Sometimes his need to be free of it all was so strong that he packed a bag and planned a route to somewhere — anywhere — where he could forget his past, get a job, go back to school, start at the beginning again.

He wouldn't miss anything.

Not the house or the town.

Not Joy, rotting away in a dungeon of useless news.

He certainly wouldn't miss himself — this dirty, angry, sneaky little *thief* that he'd become, waking each day from a nightmare into exhaustion and grief, then lurching from there to anger and hate and destruction.

And back to exhaustion.

Sometimes he wondered what his mother would say if she knew what he was doing . . .

Shit! He should leave this place. He should have left it already.

Only Merry kept him coming home.

Only in-the-way, book-to-read, mouth-to-feed Merry.

Who would bring Merry books if he didn't? *Good* books, not stupid kids' books about Spot the dog and the Cat in the Hat. Who else would understand that she needed vampires in her life, and Donald in her arms, and a worm hotel and a lawn to mow?

Nobody.

Nobody in foster care, anyway.

He couldn't just abandon her, because she'd already been abandoned. Twice.

And that made him angriest of all . . .

"I fucking hate my mother."

Baz was at a playdate, so it was OK to swear.

Louis shook his head. "Nah, you don't."

"She didn't love us."

"She loved you," Louis said firmly. "You know that."

"Bollocks. If she loved us, why did she leave us?"

"Mate," said Louis carefully, "she didn't mean to leave you. She was murdered."

"Serves her fucking right. I don't even care any more. I don't even care who killed her."

In the defiant silence, Louis stroked his own leg with a slow, seeking thumb.

Two Blundell's boys went past in their posh blue-and-maroon uniforms — shiny leather satchels on their backs. They stopped to feed their sandwiches to the ducks, then moved on.

"I hated my mother for a while."

Jack didn't look at him.

"I used to be so angry with her. Always getting nicked and going inside and leaving me to pick up the pieces. Having to keep all the balls in the air. The job and the yard and all the heat and hassle of it, and nobody helping me. I mean, you know what Tammy and Victor are like, and Shawn . . . shit! I mean, I love them all, but they're right useless bastards."

Jack nodded in agreement.

"Everybody thinks it's a bed of roses, getting left with a business to run and money coming in and shit, but it's not. It's a pain in the arse. I didn't ask for it and I didn't want it and I was like, what the fuck, bitch!"

He laughed. Then he went on, "But now I've got Baz and I know —"

He stopped and shrugged.

"What?"

Louis went on more slowly. "I know you only want your kids to be safe and happy, you know? And I know you do your best, but you don't always get it right. Not even *half* the time! So, anyway, now when I go to visit my mother, or even just get a letter, I get, like, reminded how hard it is and that she's trying, even if she keeps screwing up. And I know she's trying because she loves me. And then all that angry shit just fades away . . ."

Jack glared at the canal. "What's your point?"

"Jeez, I don't know!" laughed Louis. "I don't even know if there is a point. All I'm saying is, when you have a kid, then suddenly you understand how easy it is to make mistakes, see? And you forgive your parents a bit, you know?"

Jack said nothing.

"But you can't go and visit your mother or get a letter from her. So you *never* get reminded that she loves you because . . . you know," he shrugged, "she's dead."

Jack picked at the end of the wooden bench.

"And that's not her fault," Louis went on. "Or your fault. It's only the fault of the bastard that killed her."

Jack nodded.

"You gonna hate anyone," said Louis, "make it *him*."

"She's mowing the lawn," called Mrs Reynolds. "Come and see."

Reynolds sighed and stared at the kitchen ceiling, then he got up and trudged upstairs and joined his mother at the back-bedroom window, because he knew he would have to in the end, so he might as well get it over with.

Next door there was indeed a small child mowing the lawn with a large petrol lawnmower. The handle was as high as her head, and she had locked her elbows and was leaning into it at a frightening angle in order to get the machine to move. Often it got stuck and she'd shove and yank until it got going again, and then walked it backwards in the other direction to avoid having to turn it round at either end of the mercifully small garden. Now and then she stopped and left it running to remove a large brown rock from her trajectory. After the second time, Reynolds realized it wasn't a rock, but a tortoise.

"You see?" said Mrs Reynolds accusingly.

"I don't see what you're worried about," he said.

But his mother was determined to find fault with her new neighbours, and if she couldn't criticize the

182

mowing, she had other ammunition. "She's a terrible little liar, too, and hangs off my fence like a chimp. She'll break it one day and then who'll pay for it? Not the scruffy brother, *that's* for sure!"

"Why don't you wait to cross that bridge if you ever come to it?" he said soothingly.

It didn't soothe his mother one little bit. She made a *hmff* noise that meant *This isn't over*, and stomped downstairs to finish making the supper.

Reynolds stood at the window for another moment.

He watched the little girl stop to wipe her sweaty face on the bottom of her T-shirt, exposing pale ribs.

Skinny as a pin!

Then she pushed her straggly nothing-coloured hair behind her ears, puffed out her cheeks and leaned into the mower once again.

"I tell you what," he mused to nobody but himself, "she's making a bloody good job of that lawn."

There was a knock at the door.

Adam.

He'd only left for Ludlow five minutes ago. And he had a key, of course. Even so, that's who Catherine expected to see when she opened the door.

Instead it was the burglar.

A shock ran through her and she gasped so loudly that Mr Kent across the road looked up from washing his car.

"What do you want?"

"The knife," said the boy bluntly.

He looked just the same as he had in the supermarket car park. The same unwashed jeans, the same blue hoodie. The same home-cut hair and dirty grey eyes.

Catherine shook her head. "I don't have it."

"Where is it?"

"I don't have it."

"*Shit!*" The boy shifted his weight and looked around, as if somebody nearby might have an answer that suited him better.

"It's my husband's knife," she said. "And he's very angry about this whole thing, so I wouldn't hang around here if I were you."

"But I need it."

"Well, he found it and now I don't know where it is," she said, "so you're out of luck."

And she made to close the door.

The boy put out a quick hand to stop it shutting. It bounced back at Catherine and gave her a fright.

"I can find it," he said. "Can I come in?"

"No, you cannot!" she said incredulously. "And if you don't leave right now, I'll call the police."

"Go on then," he said, stepping away from the door. "Call them."

"I *will*."

"Go *on* then!"

Catherine hesitated. She hadn't expected the conversation to take this turn. She wasn't sure what she *had* expected. Maybe a threat? Or an apology? Both seemed unlikely — but both seemed more likely than *this* — a burglar demanding that she call the police!

"This is *stupid*," she said. "Just go away!"

"Are you all right, Catherine?" Mr Kent called out. He'd stopped washing his car and now stood holding the big yellow sponge in both hands against his chest, like a parade rifle.

"I think so," she called, with what she hoped was just the right amount of weight to keep him alert without inviting him to come over and get involved. "Thank you, Mr Kent."

It worked. He continued washing his car, but glanced over often, and with comforting suspicion.

When Catherine looked back at the boy, he carried on as if they'd never been interrupted.

"It's not stupid," he said. "My mother was murdered. And the knife that killed her is in *your house*."

Something in the boy's eyes and determined tone was so completely *honest* that it took the wind out of Catherine's angry sails and, suddenly, the only emotion she felt was pity. Whatever had happened to the boy's mother — whether she'd been murdered or died of cancer or had just left her family for a new life — he'd clearly been traumatized by it.

"What was your mother's name?" she said gently.

The boy looked wary, but said, "Eileen Bright."

"And yours?"

He hesitated. He looked around the estate again, for an alternative line of questioning. For a lie, perhaps.

He didn't find either.

"Jack," he said finally.

"Jack," said Catherine more kindly, "the knife belongs to my husband. He'd actually lost it and was quite pleased to have it back! But there must be a million knives out there just like it."

"No." Jack shook his head forcefully. "That's the one."

"How do you know?"

"I don't know how I know," he frowned. Then suddenly he wobbled. He bit his lip and looked away across the gardens, tears sheening his eyes. "I just *know*."

Catherine felt a pang. He was a thief, but he was still only a child.

"But it's not logical, is it?" she told him gently.

186

"*You're* not logical!" he shot back. "If you were logical you would have called the police!"

"That may be true," Catherine smiled. "But I'm pregnant, in case you hadn't noticed. And sometimes logic takes a back seat."

The boy looked at her sharply — as if she'd said something of real import.

"What do you mean?"

She shrugged. "Pregnant women do crazy shit."

Then she half smiled, but he didn't. He just stood there, frowning, as if he were thinking of something else. Someone else.

"Jack," she said firmly, "you have to understand that your break-in was terribly upsetting for me. It's very lucky for you that neither of us want to extend that upset by going to the police, because of the baby coming so soon. Really we just want to forget it, and so we were prepared to let it go. But now you're making that very difficult for us!"

There, thought Catherine. *That's telling him!*

But the boy didn't look as if he were even listening to her.

"You said your husband found the knife?"

"Yes."

"Then he must have been looking for it."

She stared at him blankly.

"*That's* logical," he said slowly, as if he were just working it out himself. "*If he found* it, then he must have been *looking* for it."

"I don't see —"

"And *that* means he must have known it was missing. So it *can't* have been lost!"

Catherine opened her mouth to contradict him. Then she closed it again.

She *did* see . . .

"He lied to you," said the boy, and Catherine flushed at the truth.

What were you doing in my underwear drawer?

Adam had never answered her question — just demanded answers from *her*.

Butterflies battered the walls of her tummy and chest, fluttered in her throat.

Mere seconds before, she had had a firm grip on the situation. Now she felt . . . *lost*.

And suddenly it was the burglar who was looking at *her* with pity!

"Can I come in?" he said.

She hesitated.

I could have killed you.

He could have killed her.

"*Please?*" he said.

And Catherine While held open the door and let him in.

Jack couldn't remember the last time he'd entered a stranger's home through the front door.

Everything looked different in daylight. The house was full of light and air and space and calm.

So *clean*.

The living room where he'd picked up the phone was decorated in plum. There was a rug in the shape of a big plummy heart. In the study, the laptop he'd once put on the kitchen table was back on the desk. There were two wire in-trays overflowing with paperwork, and a roll of Christmas wrapping paper was propped, unfurling, in a corner.

In the bright kitchen there was a silly sign over the sink that said, *The Great Unwashed*. A fluffy white cat brushed against his leg and then hurried to its bowl and mewed plaintively.

Catherine While stood in the centre of the room. She looked pale and confused. *She* looked like the stranger in the house.

"Do you want to sit down?" he asked cautiously.

She sat down.

Jack didn't want to stay any longer than he had to. He'd watched and waited patiently for Adam to drive away in the white van with the red rosette on the back, but he was used to getting into and out of a house *fast*, and he already felt twitchy just standing still in this one.

He glanced back towards the front door, and the stairs.

"I'll find the knife."

"No!"

"But that's why I'm here."

"*Wait*," she said. "Let me think."

Jack was frustrated. What was the point of letting him in if she wasn't going to let him find the knife? He should have just broken in again and taken what he wanted. For a moment he almost did that anyway — run upstairs and start to hunt down the murder weapon.

What could she do?

Call the police?

But if *him* taking the knife to the police had ever been the best solution, he would have done it the last time he was here. There was still a chance to try to convince *her* to do it.

Without threatening to kill her.

He wished Louis were here, with his gift of the gab. Louis could talk anybody into anything.

He *had* to get the knife. He *had* to make her believe him!

"He lied about the knife. And he slashed that man's tyre too."

"Who, Adam?" she frowned. "Don't be silly."

190

"I saw him do it. He came out and stuck a knife in it twice and went back inside."

Catherine While looked pale. She clasped her tummy as if clinging to a rock in a fast-flowing river.

"You *have* to call the police," he said urgently.

"I . . ." she started.

Then the cat flinched in sudden warning and Adam While walked into the house.

Jack froze — wide-eyed — then dived for the back door.

Locked!

Shit!

He turned the key and yanked it open —

And something hit him so hard on the back of the head that it knocked him clear out of the house.

"Adam! No!"

Jack staggered, dropped to one knee on the painful patio, got up, nearly pitched over with momentum.

Kept going.

Someone grabbed the back of his hoodie and held on. Jack tried to pull away. The man hit him again. Hard, in the ear.

"Adam, *no!*" Muffled now. "Adam! *Stop!*"

Adam didn't stop. He hung on. He shouted, *"You little shit! You little fucker!"*

Jack swung round, twisted to face him, ducked and pulled backwards, stripping himself out of his hoodie and tee — leaving them dangling from the man's hand as he ran bare-chested across the lawn and through the flower bed and on to the fence, and launched off the top into the soft green arms of the fir trees beyond.

A big fist gripped his foot in mid air, interrupting his arc. He tipped and covered his face and fell awkwardly, skimming the tree and hitting the fence.

He bounced into the dirt, stunned and staring up at the cloudless blue sky.

And then Adam While came over the fence like an angry bear, and Jack rolled to his feet and ran again, through the neighbours' garden, down the side of that house, across the little patch of front lawn where a woman pruned a rose —

"*Oh!*"

— and out into the street, legs blurring and lungs sucking in air, and arms pumping so hard that he thought he might take off and fly the rest of the way home.

Or die.

"You little *shit*! I'll fucking *kill you*!"

Jack risked a glance over his shoulder. While was still coming. Bigger and older, but fury kept him in the race.

Jack kept running.

Kept sucking.

Kept looking behind him.

Until — finally — nobody was there.

Only then did he slow. Only then did he stop to take stock of the grazes and scratches and soon-to-be-bruises on his arms and chest and back, and the blood that ran from his ringing ear.

He went the long way home, along the canal, where he washed the blood from his face and chest. He winced at the pain in his ear. His knee hurt from the patio. He felt a little sick, and the back of his head throbbed.

But Adam While had killed his mother.

Now Jack *knew* it was true. He'd seen it in the man's eyes, felt it in his fists. The same brutal hands that had murdered his mother and his unborn sister had punched him, grabbed him, ripped the shirt off his back.

I'll kill him, he thought, and was shocked by the surge of hot pleasure that came with the words.

Jack was used to anger, but he had never before felt murderous.

He did now.

His blood fizzed, and his fingers twitched in anticipation. Adam While on his knees. He'd beat him to death as he pleaded for mercy. Bring his hammer down, claw first, lever slabs of skull from the top of his head, spatter his brain, break his teeth, puncture his eyes, wrench off his balls in bloody handfuls. Leave him in the road for the crows to pick over, the way Adam While had left his mother for nine days.

Nine long hot summer days . . .

In the scrub in a lay-by. Like waste. Like *rubbish*.

He sprinted through the town, pale blood still running in wet rivulets down his chest and ribs, his ear shouting in pain with every step.

The homeless man looked up as he passed.

"You're bleeding!" he said, and started to rise, but Jack left him behind and kept running all the way home.

The sun was leaving the sky, but he could hear the lawnmower out back, and was grateful that Merry wasn't there to ask questions.

He ran upstairs and took his other hoodie off the hook on the back of the door where he kept his clothes so the mice couldn't piss on them.

He grabbed his backpack. His hammer. He'd go in through the bathroom window. They wouldn't be expecting it. Not tonight. He'd kill Adam While while his stupid wife screamed and screamed and wished she'd *called the fucking police*!

All his weariness was forgotten; his fear was forgotten.

Only anger remained.

He slung the backpack over his shoulders and turned to go.

"I'm hungry."

Shit!

The sudden silence was the absence of the lawnmower.

"There's no cereal," said Merry. She held Donald to her chest like a shield, his scaly toes resting on her collarbones, his face looking trustingly up into hers.

"Then eat something else."

"There is nothing else. And I'm *hungry*. We all are."

"What the *shit*, Merry," he snapped. "You never fucking *stop*!"

194

She flinched. He didn't care. She stared up at him with big scared eyes to make him feel guilty.

"It's not my fault," he snapped. "For *fuck's sake*, stop *nagging*!"

"I only —"

"I'll bring you something for breakfast, OK?"

Her lower lip wobbled. "But I'm hungry *now*."

"There'll be food in the morning, Merry! Jesus!"

"OK." Merry nodded miserably. She hitched Donald up, and turned her head and wiped her nose on her own skinny shoulder.

She could wait for breakfast.

"And a book?" she hoped.

"Don't push it," he said, and stormed down the stairs.

Catherine While waited for Adam to come home — scared in a way she'd never been before.

Not scared that she might fail an exam or crash the car or get mugged on the way home from the shops — but scared for her entire future, and that of her child.

She waited, her ears alert to every sound, her eyes searching the garden, then the road, then the garden, then the road, for any sign of Adam *or* the boy. She called Adam's phone. It rang in the van that was parked haphazardly in the driveway.

The events kept replaying themselves in her head like a horrible movie she couldn't un-see. She'd never seen Adam so angry. Never seen *anyone* so angry. What if Adam had caught the boy? What if he'd beaten him to a pulp? Or had chased him on to the railway line where he'd been chopped into pieces, or knocked him into the canal where he'd sunk like a stone? What if bystanders had made a citizen's arrest? What if the handcuffs were being snapped around Adam's wrists, even while she sat here and dithered?

Even worse, what if Jack had killed Adam? Turned on him with a knife or a stick or a chunk of concrete? What

196

if Adam were only so long coming home because he was *dead*?

Tears boiled over in Catherine's eyes as her panicky mind darted from one dreadful conclusion to the other.

If Adam were dead, what would become of her?

Or arrested for murder, what would become of her?

Either way. *What would become of her?*

She almost laughed — it sounded so melodramatic. And yet it was all she could think of, as the minutes ticked slowly away until they became parts of an hour — and then an hour itself, and then two hours — and still Adam did not come back.

She nearly called the police.

She really nearly did.

But if the worst had happened, she wasn't in a hurry to hear it. And if it hadn't, she didn't want to alert the police to the fact that her muscular six-foot-two-inch husband had assaulted, and was now hunting down, a skinny boy.

A police siren whooped and she froze, but it passed.

Not for her.

And please, not for her Adam.

Her Adam, who'd vowed to love and honour her, who had bought their microscopic dot of a baby banana pudding and a train that blew bubbles. *Her Adam*, who worked so hard to pay the bills and who had given up his sporty car for a Side Impact Protection System, and who sent her postcards from Derby and Warwick and Falmouth with wry notes and funny doodles that made her giggle and feel safe and adored.

Her Adam — who'd ignored her cries and pleas to stop, while he'd punched a boy bloody, then torn the shirt clean off his back and chased him over the fence and down the road . . .

Like a madman.

It got dark, and Catherine prayed. She felt stupid but she did it anyway, for the first time since childhood. Begging a snubbed deity to do her this one favour: to let Adam come home safe, and without having done anything — ever — that they'd all live to regret.

When he left home, Jack was angry with Merry. But by the time he broke into the house on Brooksia Close, he was only angry with himself.

It was his fault that she was hungry. He'd been distracted. Since finding the knife, he'd been distracted. Hadn't worked so much. Hadn't brought food. Hadn't brought books. He'd taken his eye off the ball.

He gritted his teeth. Being in charge was *relentless*.

No wonder his father had given up.

There were slim pickings in the kitchen of the Williams family, who had gone to Disneyland Paris and whose cupboards were filled with junk food.

Finally Jack chucked a net of oranges and a pint of milk into his backpack. He emptied the rest of the rubbish out of their fridge and into the washing machine and considered it a personal favour.

There was a bookshelf at the top of the stairs and Jack went through it, sweeping out rejected titles in angry armfuls and tumbling them to the floor, then trampling them while he looked at others, careless of torn covers and ripped pages.

There were only two vampire books and Merry had read them both, but he found Stephen King's *It*. It was good and thick, and Merry might as well get started on clowns . . .

He had never read the book himself, but when he was about eight he'd watched the TV film with his father and it had scared the shit out of both of them. The horror that lurked around every normal corner . . . Afterwards his mother had yelled that he was too young to watch it, but afterwards was too late, and Jack was glad. The film had become something they'd shared — he and his dad.

He'd thought that had meant something, but he'd left them anyway.

Suddenly the fact hit Jack like a physical blow. He stumbled sideways on the slippery book covers and clutched the bannister for balance, bent over and breathless with loss.

He missed his father.

He missed the kind and the funny and the strong parts of him that he'd almost forgotten existed before the weakness and the fear and the crying. He missed how, when they were little, he and Joy would climb him like monkeys up a tree; the way he'd wrapped Loopy the gerbil very gently in tissue paper, and put a little scatter of sunflower seeds in the shoebox they'd buried him in; the time Jack had burned a hole in the living-room carpet with a magnifying glass, and his father had covered it up with the couch so Mum wouldn't see . . . And the day Jack had learned to ride a bike in the park — his father's hand *there* and then *not*

200

there, but still close enough in case he needed catching . . .

Jack panicked.

One minute he was standing on a stranger's landing, feeling as dizzy as a small boy on a runaway bicycle, and the next he was skidding off the books and half falling down the stairs in his haste to get out of the house.

It was past midnight and the only sound in the whole of Tiverton was his own rubber footsteps echoing through the Pannier Market, and past the crescent of the Half Moon pub and down Gold Street, where a barn owl swooped over him, so low that he could have reached up and brushed its pale feathers with his fingers, before tipping a wing in salute to the statue of Edward VII and disappearing over the canal.

He ran on, still not knowing why, except that Merry was hungry *now*, wasn't she? She was hungry *now*! And it was his job to take care of her. His job to catch her so she wouldn't wobble and fall . . .

He cut across the supermarket car park, where a single escaped trolley under a security light was the star of the show. Past the garage that sold cars nobody could afford, and finally — panting — on to his street.

At the freshly painted front door, Jack stopped. He dropped the book and the backpack. Couldn't feel his legs.

The little glass porthole was broken.

And through it he could see that the house was on fire.

It was nearly one in the morning before Adam finally came through the front door, and when he did, Catherine attacked him.

"Don't you *EVER!*" she shouted, flailing at him. "Don't you *EVER* do that again! I've been *frantic*. What would have happened if you hadn't come back? If he'd stabbed you? Or you'd killed him? What would have happened to me and the baby? What would have — *happened* — *to* — *us*?" She slapped him on every word, on the arms and the shoulders, furious with relief, until she finally ran out of energy and fell into his arms and cried and cried and cried.

"You scared the *shit* out of me!" she sobbed. "You macho dickhead!"

"I'm so sorry, Cath," he said, gently stroking her hair, her back, her tummy. "I just snapped. I *was* a macho dickhead. I'm so, *so* sorry I scared you."

He soothed her and murmured to her until she finally stopped crying, then he made them both tea, which they drank at the kitchen table, perched awkwardly on wooden chairs instead of relaxing in the living room, because that would have seemed too forgiving.

"Where have you *been*?"

"I couldn't catch the little bastard —"

"Thank God!"

"So I went to the pub."

She was surprised. Adam wasn't a big drinker, and she couldn't smell it on his breath. But then, her nose had been filled with tears all evening.

"Which pub?"

"The Half Moon."

He'd run all the way into the centre of town, then. He must have tried very hard to catch the boy. Been very angry . . .

Catherine shivered at what might have been.

"Why are you even here?" she said, only just thinking about it. "And not in Ludlow?"

Adam sighed and rubbed his face wearily with his hands. "I knew something was up, Cath. I was watching the house."

Her eyes widened. "You were *spying* on me?"

"Of course not," he said, surprised. "You're my wife! I wanted to be sure you were OK. I was worried about you — and obviously for good reason. This kid threatened to *kill* you, Catherine! And he was in our house! What would have happened if I hadn't been here?"

Catherine bit her lip. "I don't know."

"Well, I wasn't going to sit around and find out."

"But what about work?" she said.

"Let *me* worry about work," he said. "I've done so much overtime they owe me a month."

Catherine hesitated. Adam was only a salesman. Not irreplaceable . . .

Then she let it go and nodded dully. She *would* let him worry about work. She had to; she had no spare capacity to worry about anything new.

Adam covered her hand with his, and she didn't move it.

He gave a huge, cleansing sigh. "Anyway, he's had a good smack on the head and a big fright. I don't think he'll be back again. And if he ever *does* come back, we'll call the police and have the little sod arrested. Deal?"

He smiled reassuringly and Catherine looked into his eyes. They were so kind that it was hard to reconcile them with the way he'd attacked Jack . . .

"Deal," she whispered.

"Good," he said, and they went upstairs together.

While Adam showered, Catherine got ready for bed. She took out her nightdress — so big it was like a sheet — and laid it on the bed and stood over it — unseeing.

Then she picked up the phone and called Jan. She apologized for the hour. It was fine; Jan was up.

"Oh good," said Catherine, and stopped and didn't know what to say next.

"Is everything OK, Cath?"

"Yes," she said. "I just . . . How's Rhod?"

"Great!" said Jan enthusiastically. "I really think he might be the one, you know."

"I'm so happy for you," Catherine heard herself saying. "That's super news."

"Thanks!" said Jan, and wittered on for a little bit about how well Rhod treated her, and how much he earned doing whatever it was that he did, because she *still* wasn't sure, *hahaha* . . .

"What happened with his tyre?"

There was a confused pause where Jan stopped talking about her golden future with Rhod and readjusted to Catherine asking about a flat tyre.

"Oh," she said, sounding a little put out. "It wasn't faulty at all. It had been slashed."

Catherine turned slowly and stared into the mirror on the wall next to the bed. "Really?"

"Yes! Can you believe it? In that quiet little road, right outside your house! They said something very sharp had gone right through the wall in two places! So of course he didn't get a refund."

"Of course," said Catherine.

Another silence.

She wasn't sure how the conversation with Jan ended, but she knew she'd hung up.

Slowly, she removed her clothes.

In the bathroom, the shower was switched off and she could hear the small sounds of Adam drying himself, humming snatches of song — something by The Beatles — and then doing his teeth.

By the half-light of the hallway Catherine stood, naked, and stared down at her huge tummy — shiny and stretched to accommodate the baby they were looking forward to with such pleasure. It was a view she'd enjoyed many, many times over the past months

— marvelling at her tightening swell and disappearing feet.

She always felt joy and wonder.

But tonight the joy didn't come. And neither did the wonder.

Instead Jack Bright's words spiralled and twisted inside her head. The words that had made her invite him into their house like a vampire . . .

If he found it, then he must have been looking for it.

Adam said the knife had been lost. But he knew it was gone. And had searched for it hard enough to find it in her underwear drawer.

And then he'd lied to her about it.

So tonight Catherine looked down at her tight tummy not with joy, but with a strange queasiness.

Because for the first time, alongside their precious child grew a tiny seed of doubt.

And she *hated* Jack Bright for planting it there.

Jack yanked his key over his head — sucking in a sharp breath as the string snagged on his sore ear, and then coughing out smoke.

He shoved open the door, and flames bounded at him like happy dogs, before the door hit something solid and bounced back at him, engulfing him in a single genie-like puff of grey smoke.

Joy and her *fucking papers!*

"*Joy!*" he shouted. "*Merry!*"

He covered his face with his crooked arm, ran through the fire and dropped to all fours and, on the floor, found air and eyesight again.

The fire was only behind the door — the flames licking the walls almost to the ceiling, and crawling along the carpet — but the smoke was thick and choking, and heading for the stairs . . .

Jack doubled over with coughing. He groped for the handle to the door of the living room and pulled it shut to stop the advance. If the fire got in there, nothing would save the house.

He scurried up the stairs on all fours, to stay low, coughing all the way.

"Merry!" he croaked at the top. "The house is on fire!"

Her room was already blurred with smoke. She was there, almost buried in her paper bedding.

He shook her roughly, terrified that he was too late, that she wouldn't wake up.

"What's wrong?" she said crossly.

"The house is on fire!"

Jack pulled her out of her nest, then dragged her by her wrist into the bathroom and slammed the door behind them.

"It smells," she yawned, and then coughed.

"That's the smoke," said Jack, grabbing a towel and running water over it in the basin. Then he threw open the window and lifted Merry on to the sill.

"You go out the window and slide off the kitchen roof into the garden and then stay far away from the house. Do you understand?"

"Why can't I just stay in here?" said Merry. "If the fire's out *there*?"

"Because the fire will come and get you."

"Fire can't *move*!" she said, looking sceptical.

"Yes, it can," he said. "Faster than you can run."

Merry's eyes grew wide with fear. "But what about Donald?"

"He'll be fine."

She started to cry. "But he can't run fast and the fire will come and get him!"

Jack hesitated. Then he shouted, "Shit!" and took a deep breath and went back out on to the landing.

The smoke up here was thicker now. He took two paces and fell over something, which turned out to be Donald, making a slow run for it.

Merry's face lit up as Jack pressed the hard dome of pet into her chest. Then he stood on the edge of the bath, picked her up under her arms and lowered her and Donald from the window to the gently sloping lean-to roof.

"Sit down," he said. "Be careful."

Merry turned and looked up at him, one hand on the sill, the other around Donald. "Where are *you* going?" she said.

"To get Joy."

"But the *fire!*"

"Just go!" he said. "And don't come back!"

He slammed the window so she couldn't get back in, then hesitated for a brief moment, taking stock, making choices.

The bag of money was stashed on top of the wardrobe in his bedroom. Was there time to get it and throw it out of the window after Merry?

No.

Shit.

Jack covered his head with the dripping towel and ran downstairs.

The flames had made an arch around the front door but were taking their time spreading up the hallway. However, the smoke billowed eagerly behind him as he entered the front room — crowding in, creeping along the paper passages and sliding over the canyon walls like a thick grey search party. Jack slammed the door

209

closed on it but enough had come in with him to make him cough, and he could see more sneaking under the door and between the hinges.

"Joy!" he shouted at the wall, but he choked so badly on the word that she may not have heard him.

He hoped that was why she wasn't answering.

Jack shoved at the wall of newspapers. They didn't budge. Not even an inch.

"Joy!"

He dropped to his hands and knees.

As he started through the tunnel, he realized just how tight it was. He had to lie flat on his stomach and pull himself along with his elbows like a soldier under wire, although the sides of the tunnel were so close that even that much movement was difficult. The papers pressed his shoulders, his hips and his head at all times. He had thought the tunnel would be flimsy and easily collapsed, but now that he was inside it, it felt absolutely solid. The front of the living room was only a few feet away through the wall, and yet he felt that at any moment he might get stuck and be unable to move forwards or backwards. That he would suffocate here, and then burn, and firemen would have to pull his charred body out by the ankles.

He hoped to God that Merry was safe at the bottom of the garden.

The wet towel helped with his breathing but not with his vision. He wiped his eyes but they only welled with tears again as smoke and evil ash filled the air.

"Joy!" he tried again.

Nothing. He kept going.

It can't have taken more than twenty seconds to get through the paper wall, but it seemed to last a lifetime.

Finally his shoulders were free and he dragged his legs after him and stood up. He lifted the towel to peer around him. The streetlight shone through the window that Joy had stolen from the rest of the house, illuminating her half of the room.

She wasn't there. There was a narrow bed made of neat stacks of papers. It had Joy's duvet on it. Bambi and Thumper. He hadn't seen it for years but recognized it immediately. Beside the bed was the crib that had been bought for their new baby sister, although all it held now was Joy's old doll, Martha.

Smoke rolled lazily over the paper wall like storm clouds, and Jack doubled over with coughing.

"Joy!" he yelled — angry now, and suddenly scared too.

He couldn't go back through the tunnel. He'd have to go out through the window. Then round the back to get the hose. He'd have to run to the end of the row of houses to get over the back garden wall from the riverbank. Vital minutes lost. But it was the only thing to do now.

The window was locked.

Desperately he jerked the handle.

Still locked. Where was the key! Was there a key? Blinded by acrid smoke, he felt along the windowsill. Nothing but papers that fell to the floor.

Stupid with panic, he bent to pick them up. He coughed and dragged in smoke and coughed again. He sank to his knees, and then to his hands and knees, and then realized that he wasn't picking up the papers any more, but suffocating — right here under the window where he'd crouched with Joy and Merry on the day they'd first met Louis Bridge.

Now that he knew he was dying, Jack decided to get up.

In his mind that's what he was doing, but in reality he sank even lower, on to his elbows and knees, then slumped sideways against the wall, feeling nothing on the outside of his body, but inside there was a huge dull pain deep in the middle of his chest, where his lungs were no longer breathing air, but smoke and ash and carpet chemicals . . .

How stupid, he thought as he slid gently down the wall on to his nose, his lips, his cheek, his ear . . . *How stupid to leave me in charge.*

Cold, hard water hit Jack in the face, making him splutter and roll over and cough and cough and cough.

"I *told* you he wasn't dead," said Merry.

The spray blasted ice into his ear and ran in waterfalls down his neck and back and chest, soaking him, choking him.

He covered his head with his arms and shouted, "Turn it *off*! Turn it *off*!"

"Turn it *off*!" squeaked Merry, and it finally stopped soaking him, although he could still hear it falling nearby.

Jack gasped for air and wiped his eyes. Joy stood in the middle of her paper room, lit by the streetlight, with the garden hose in her hand — the silvery water blossoming into the air and down again like a liquid umbrella that rained around her. Her face was white, her lips blue, and she wore the same pink nightdress Jack had seen her in last, but so dirty now that it was grey, and so wet that water ran off it and on to her bare feet in sheets.

Her pale eyes bored into his face — they were the only part of her that looked alive.

Jack shivered in the freezing water that pooled under him and croaked up at Merry, "I told you to stay out of the house."

"Joy and me put out the fire with the hose," Merry shrugged. "And I cut my foot."

She lifted it to show him. The gash under the ball of her foot was still bleeding. He sat up, slow and dripping. "How did you do that?"

"There was glass in the hall." Merry held up a chunk of glass, but it was not glass from the porthole — this was thick and dark brown. The bottom of a bottle. Most of the label had been burned off, but Jack could still read the *ness* of *Guinness*.

Even before he put it to his nose, he could smell the petrol.

Adam While.

The coincidence was too great. Jack had thought he'd outrun him. He'd thought he'd won. But at some point While must have stopped trying to catch, and started to hide and to follow.

Followed him all the way home. Tried to kill him. Could have killed them all.

Jack felt a sudden uneasy concern for Catherine While. Did she know what her husband had done? What he was capable of doing?

"I hate you," said Joy.

"I hate you too," said Jack wearily. He leaned forward in the sodden mush and got awkwardly to his knees.

"Shit," he said. "What a bloody m —"

Joy hit him. Not with a hand, or an arm, but with her whole body, bowling him over, scratching, biting, pulling his hair, and all with the hose in one hand, still spraying. It was like being hit by a wave and tumbled over rocks: so wet, so cold, so disorientating that he thought he might drown right here in the front room.

"Yaaa!" she screamed. "YAAAA!"

Jack fell on to his back and tried to push her off him, but she straddled his chest with sharp knees, punching his head with the sprayer so that every blow was both hot and cold. Jack covered his face and tried to turn away from the blows while Joy continued to spit at him.

"You shouldn't be in charge! You said we'd find her and we didn't! And you promised everything would be OK and it's *not*, and I *hate* you! *I hate you!* I HATE YOU!"

"Stop!" shouted Merry from a long way away. "Joy! Stop!"

And finally Joy did stop.

Jack spluttered as she hung over him — the water dripping off her face on to his protective hands.

"I don't *want* to be in charge," he said. "But *somebody* had to be."

"*Daddy* was in charge."

"But he was *shit* at it. He was just a cry-baby."

"Because he was *sad!*" Joy shouted.

"I was sad too!" Jack shouted back. "But I didn't get pissed every night! I didn't lose my job! I didn't fuck off to get milk and never come back! I stayed here and I did my *best*."

"But . . ." Joy started, and then her mouth struggled to keep a shape. She was going to cry; Jack remembered when she used to do that all the time and get her own way. None of them cried now. It never got them anywhere.

She sat up on his stomach. She wiped her wet face with her wet arm, and looked around the paper room slowly melting into itself as the hose ran and ran and ran.

"But," she said again, "I don't *like* your best."

"I don't like it too," sniffed Merry. "And neither does Donald."

Jack didn't know what to say. He didn't know what to do. He only knew that he'd failed, and it felt like shit.

Joy climbed off him slowly. Then she crawled away through the tunnel with the hose.

"Will we have to move now?" said Merry, looking around miserably. "Because I only just mowed the lawn."

"No," he said. "Everything will be OK." The words sounded hollow to Jack's ears — a promise he'd already failed to keep.

He sighed and sat up in a squelchy puddle of dirty water. The smoke was clearing and by the streetlight he now saw that the walls of Joy's little room were festooned with hundreds of newspaper cuttings. Maybe thousands — hanging from the stacks like fish scales.

This must be where all those holes had ended up. Jack imagined Joy bent over the papers by night, muttering and cuttering like Rumpelstiltskin . . .

Crazy.

But as he stared at them, he realized the cuttings weren't about crazy things.

They were all about their mother.

Headlines and articles and tiny little snippets.

Mum-to-be, Mum-to-be, Mum-to-be . . .

And photos. The one of their father crying. *Abandoned Joy.* The small and blurry photo of his mother, repeated around the walls.

There were other pictures he'd never seen. Images that sparked memories in him that he'd have sworn were lost for ever. Photos of *Call-Me-Ralph* and his big moustache. Of Merry in the crook of their father's arm in front of their blue and peeling front door. Of his mother's coffin, covered in daisies. Jack remembered how they had picked the daisies from the verge near the roundabout. He hadn't wanted to. Hadn't wanted to pretend the world was anything but vicious and ugly.

His eyes roamed the walls, eagerly seeking the photo of them all together, with their hair in their eyes, but it wasn't there.

So this was how Joy spent her life — remembering the last days of the life she'd had *before* . . .

For the first time, Jack felt sorry for her.

For the first time, he realized that she was not crazy — only heartbroken.

And for the first time, he wondered if they were the same thing . . .

Somebody knocked at the door.

Jack and Merry looked at each other, wide-eyed. He moved towards the tunnel, but before he could start through it, they heard Joy open the door.

"Shit," he hissed. He and Merry sat cross-legged, facing each other. Listening.

"Hello, dear. Is everything all right?"

"*Mrs Reynolds!*" said Merry in a stage whisper.

"Sssh!" said Jack with a finger at her lips. She batted him away and said loudly, "I'm *whispering!*"

"Yes," said Joy. "Everything's all right."

There was a long pause and Jack could only imagine the woman looking Joy up and down, wondering if this was really what "all right" looked like.

"Has there been a *fire?*"

"Yes," said Joy. "But Daddy put it out, thank you."

Merry giggled and, instead of being cross with her, Jack giggled too.

"Oh good," said Mrs Reynolds doubtfully. "As long as everything's all right . . ."

"Yes," said Joy. "But thanks for coming."

They heard Mrs Reynolds pass the window, then heard her door open and close behind her.

"You said you'd fix her mower," Merry reminded him.

"*You* said I'd fix her mower!" he said, wringing water out of the bottom of his T-shirt.

"That's Mummy," said Merry, touching one of the small and blurry pictures beside his head. "I remember her." Then, before Jack could contradict her, she glared at him and insisted, "I *do.*"

But he only nodded. He was in no mood to argue with Merry. Let her imagine that she remembered their mother. Where was the harm in it, he thought. Let her imagine whatever she needed to.

"She waved goodbye and I didn't want her to go," said Merry.

"When?" said Jack.

"That day when we were walking and it was so hot, and you carried me, remember?"

Jack nodded vaguely. Merry was only recounting what she'd overheard, what she'd read, what she'd *imagined* down the years. He wondered suddenly if that's how everybody constructed their own past — with the experiences of others, and photos and headlines and snatches of reality, all mashed together into memories they claimed as their own. For the first time, he thought that the photo of them all, happy and with the wind in their hair, might never have existed either. Maybe it was all in his head and he'd only imagined it on the fridge, and the little frame he'd stolen from HomeFayre would be empty for ever . . .

He shivered. He should get up and put on some dry clothes.

But Merry was rambling on, her finger on the little picture: ". . . and the fox with its guts hanging out and Joy chased the birds and Mummy was in that car —"

"What car?"

"You remember," Merry encouraged him. "The car that slowed down. Going the other way."

It was like a slap in the face.

He had forgotten the slowing car. He'd *forgotten* it. Had never talked of it! Had never even *thought* of it, from that moment to this, but *instantly* he was back there — on the hard shoulder, where he'd been a thousand times before, and could feel once more the heat through his shoes, and the sun on his face, and the leaden weight of his sister on his shoulder, grizzling and wriggling . . .

"What was she doing?" he whispered.

"Waving goodbye," said Merry, and raised her own little fingers in sad memory. "And I said, 'Mama! Mama!'"

Jack's heart beat so hard that it hurt.

He remembered it now. He *remembered it all*. The car slowing down . . . The driver had looked at him and he'd looked away. Shaking with fear.

But *Merry* hadn't looked away. Hanging over his shoulder, looking back down the road, watching the car speed up again, Merry had cried and reached out for something.

Or someone . . .

Mama! Mama!

Someone small and blurry . . .

Jack felt dizzy. He rocked forward on to his knees, fighting for air. Then he put his forehead on the soggy paper floor, as if praying.

"What's wrong?" said Merry.

"I feel sick," he choked. "I feel sick."

Merry patted his back gently. "There, there," she said, just like his mother used to do to him.

To *them*.

Merry was only two when she'd gone.

But she *did* remember.

They *all* did.

Baz was on a rusty little tricycle, riding slow circles around a precarious pile of timber. He saw Jack before Louis did, and waved.

"Ja'!" he said. "Ja'!"

Jack had never been to Bridge Fencing. Louis didn't like the boys there, mixing straight with crooked. He was in the middle of the yard, talking to a tall fat man and a short thin one, when Jack skidded to a halt beside them.

"I know who killed my mother."

Silence fell like lead.

Then, "You go on," said the tall fat man. "We're not in a hurry."

"Cheers, mate," said Louis, and took Jack's elbow and half led, half marched him to the wooden shed that he used as an office.

He turned angrily, but Jack didn't even let him start. "I found the knife that killed my mum."

"You what?" said Louis. "Where?"

"In a house up on the estates."

"Whose house?"

"A man called Adam While."

"Let's see it."

"I don't have it," said Jack. "I left it there."

"*Why?*"

"I didn't know what to do. He wasn't there, so I left it next to his wife's bed with a note. I thought she'd call the police, but she *didn't*."

"Why not?"

"*I don't know!*" cried Jack. "And now Adam While's trying to kill me."

"Yeah?"

"Last night. He set my house on fire."

"On fire? Is everything OK?"

"It's a mess, but it's all right. Joy and Merry are fine."

Louis nodded. Then he said, "How do you know it's the same knife?"

"I just know," said Jack. "I don't know how. But I know, all right?"

Louis frowned. "Hold on," he said. "You saying someone was in that house when you broke in?"

"Yeah. His wife."

"Bloody Shawn!" said Louis angrily. "I'll have his *guts*. That's aggravated burglary! That's serious shi —!" He caught himself and they both looked at the doorway where Baz was sitting on his trike, looking up at them with interest.

"Shenanigans," finished Louis, and waggled his fingers at Baz. Baz giggled and waggled his back.

"Ja', I'm riding a bike!"

"That's . . . Baztastic," Jack told him.

Baz laughed. "Watch me!"

"I'm watching."

They both watched Baz rumble away until he was out of earshot.

"It doesn't matter about Shawn," said Jack. "What matters is, what do I do now?"

"Well, you *don't* go to the cops," said Louis sharply.

Jack was silent.

"You haven't told them already, have you?"

Jack chewed his lip. "No, but he's *dangerous*, Louis. I could see it in his eyes. He hit me and chased me right through town and then followed me home like a nut and set fire to the house while Joy and Merry were in there. They could have died!"

Louis frowned. He looked across the yard at Baz.

Then he said, "Listen, mate. We can take care of this bastard. Just don't go to the cops. You think you're going in there about one thing, but they'll get this Goldilocks shit out of you too, and then you're fucked. And if you're fucked, *I'm* fucked and all the boys are fucked too!"

"What about his wife?"

"His wife can take care of herself."

"No she can't."

"Why not?"

"She's pregnant . . ."

"Shit!" said Louis. "She's not your mum, Jack."

"I *know* that!" said Jack angrily. "But still . . ."

"Listen," Louis lowered his voice threateningly. "You do whatever you want. But if you drop me in this, we're *over*, you understand?"

"But I have to find out who killed her, Louis. I don't know how. I only know that's the only way it's going to stop. All this thieving and lying and hiding. I just want it all to be over! You know what you said about Baz? You were right. I just want Joy and Merry to be happy and safe. I want them to have beds and a bath and to go to school — even if it means going to prison! And I just want to sleep without dreaming of her *every fucking night*."

"Awwww, *shit!*" Louis punched the wall so hard that Jack flinched and Baz stopped dead and looked back towards the shed, squinting in the sunshine.

Louis came closer to Jack now. Close enough to hit him if he wanted to.

"This here is my fucking *life*," he said. "Don't come here again."

Then he strode away across the yard. He plucked Baz off his tricycle as he passed, and carried the squirming toddler with him towards the two patient customers waiting in the timber shed.

Jack watched his only friend disappear into the darkness.

Detective Sergeant Reynolds had a quiet night in.

He opened a bottle of white Burgundy and made himself chicken gujons and wilted spinach, with tarte au citron for dessert.

He laid a place and ate at the table — *like a human being*, his mother always said — and then watched *University Challenge*. This week was St Hilda's College, Oxford, against Hull. It was a contest as uneven as it sounded. Reynolds scored more alone than Hull did as a team, and by the end of the show the northerners were sent packing like pregnant housemaids.

Reynolds topped up his glass and opened his book. It was a wonderful book on Churchill. He'd not read a better one.

He wondered what Elizabeth Rice was doing.

Probably something quite lowbrow with Eric, he imagined. Paintball. Or the pub.

He wondered which pub.

He closed his book and went to bed early.

DS Reynolds woke at four, thinking about Mr Passmore and his insurance claim. Poor chap. The trauma of a burglary and then the bloody company trying to disclaim! Reynolds' finely tuned sense of justice was pricked.

Later, on his way to the capture house, he called DCI Marvel and sought his advice.

"Sounds like the company's being difficult, sir. I just wondered if there was anything we could do to help him."

"Steady on with the *we!*" Marvel grumped. "Insurance companies disclaim for good reason. Don't get involved."

Don't get involved. What a lovely sentiment for an officer of the law to hold, thought Reynolds.

"But if it's a Goldilocks case —"

"Which it's not," said Marvel.

Reynolds frowned. If it *wasn't* a Goldilocks case, then he'd made a horrible mistake. *Two* horrible mistakes, in fact. First in treating it like one, and second — much worse — in telling Mr Passmore that it was one. Two horrible mistakes, when he wasn't used to making *any* mistakes at all. So he still thought it highly unlikely that he'd made one now.

"I hate to labour the point, sir —"

"Look," interrupted Marvel. "You said the local paper has been all over this story for a year, right?"

"Right," said Reynolds.

"So a lot of the details would have been in the paper, right?"

"Right," said Reynolds again, although he wished Marvel would stop saying "right" at the end of every sentence, which required him to answer by repeating the word like some dreadful cockney.

"So anyone could have copied Goldilocks, right?"

Reynolds baulked at another *right*, but finally had to say it anyway, because Marvel *was* right.

"Right."

"Anyone including Passmore," Marvel went on. "See, he knows food is taken, but not that Goldilocks steals healthy food. He doesn't know Goldilocks targets detached houses, when he lives in a terrace. He knows Goldilocks sleeps in the beds, but didn't know he sleeps in the *kids'* beds — you see where I'm going?"

Reynolds did.

"But the clincher is what the kid with the thing on her lip said."

The little girl on the sofa with the sun-blistered lips.

"What did she say?" asked Reynolds.

"She said, 'But *that* TV's broken.' As if it was *already* broken."

Reynolds hardly remembered it. But it was a child getting mixed up. Not something on which to take a policing decision!

"I wouldn't even have noticed it," said Marvel. "Except that her father jumped all over her, like he was trying to cover up a slip."

Reynolds nodded slowly. He *did* remember that. Mr Passmore butting in, drowning out his daughter with angry rhetoric about the thieves. He hadn't appreciated before the ambiguity of the child's comment — or her father's rush to respond in a way that made her words fit with his own version of events.

"But the TV *was* broken," said Reynolds.

"I'm not saying it wasn't," said Marvel. "I'm just saying it wasn't broken by a *burglar*. My guess is that the new TV got broken and Passmore did all the rest to make it look like a Goldilocks burglary, expecting a windfall, but the loss adjustor smelled a rat. Now he's shitting himself because he smashed up his own house and he's not getting paid for any of it!"

Marvel laughed heartily, then hung up.

Reynolds pulled into the driveway of the capture house behind Rice's battered little Toyota, and sat for a moment, worrying. He'd expected some bullshit from Marvel about hunches and instincts, but the DCI's logic was annoyingly logical, and his memory sharp. What was worse, Marvel's suspicions had first been raised by a question of *semantics* — something Reynolds considered his own personal territory.

It was humiliating.

Reynolds could hardly bear to countenance the possibility, but maybe he *had* made a mistake. He liked to do everything *right*. The thought of having done something *wrong* was disconcerting. And the thought of anyone else *knowing* he'd done something wrong was unbearable.

He ran a worried hand through his hair and frowned. It felt thinner than usual. And he would know; he often checked.

Rice had claimed his hair was falling out in the shower.

Suddenly Reynolds needed to see a mirror.

Right now.

He threw open the door of the car.

"Hello, Glen," said the woman who lived next door.

"What?" said Reynolds.

"Hello," she said, her smile faltering.

"Hello," he snapped, and slammed the door, rushed inside and ran upstairs. The bathroom mirror was on the windowsill where he'd propped it. He picked it up and realized that behind it was a camera he was supposed to not fuck with.

Oops. No wonder they hadn't seen Goldilocks come in until the cameras in the living room had picked him up.

Too late to worry about that now! Reynolds tried to get a good angle to see the back of his head but it needed two mirrors.

"Hi," called Rice from downstairs. "Is that you?"

Stupid question. He didn't bother answering.

Rice had a mirror in her room.

Reynolds went into Rice's room and crossed to the mirror on the wardrobe. He turned and angled both mirrors, and frowned.

His hair *did* look a little —

Reynolds froze — staring into the glass.

Behind him, in the bed, somebody stirred. And then was still again.

Eric!

Oh God, Rice had brought *Eric* back to the house with her! When they were supposed to be out, getting burgled! She'd known it would be empty and had brought her dome-headed boyfriend there and shagged him in her little single bed. At least, Reynolds *hoped* that's where they'd shagged! And now Eric was asleep in the room they'd created for their imaginary son.

Reynolds was stung.

It was silly, but he was stung.

He was Glen and she was Michelle, and now she'd brought another man into their fake house and it felt like she'd betrayed their fake marriage. He knew he had no right to feel slighted, but he did anyway.

He stood for a moment, still holding the mirror, not knowing what he should do.

Ignore him?

Go downstairs and confront Rice?

Or shake Eric awake right now and demand that he leave?

But what if Eric punched him? Reynolds thought that was a distinct possibility — especially if he'd seen the photos of Glen and Michelle wrapped together in cosy green velvet . . .

Maybe he should just creep out of the room and pretend it had never happened?

Then his backbone stiffened.

On *this* he *knew* he was right: Elizabeth Rice had overstepped the bounds of professional conduct one too many times. This was a place of *work*, and Reynolds knew he had both the professional right and the moral high ground to wake up the no-necked gym-bunny and kick him out of the capture house.

In fact, it would give him enormous satisfaction to do *just that*.

He strode to the bed, put a firm hand on the man's shoulder and shook it hard.

"Rise and shine," he said.

The moment he touched him, Reynolds knew it wasn't Eric. It wasn't even a grown-up. The shoulder was too small, the body too easy to shake.

And the head on the pillow too . . .

. . . golden.

The interview room at Tiverton police station was tiny but it served many purposes. There was a table — small and Formica — up against one wall. Metal shelving ran down the opposite wall, and was stacked with copy paper and notebooks and toilet rolls, almost up to the high, narrow strip of window just under the ceiling. An old coffee machine and three mugs stood on the draining board of a grimy little sink. A broom and mop and bucket stood guard behind the door, while a photocopier hummed gently against the back wall.

It was the Swiss Army Knife of rooms.

"Let me just move these," said DC Parrott, shifting several boxes of Bic pens off the little table. Then he opened three wooden folding chairs with a hospitable flourish.

"Is that all the chairs?" said Marvel.

"Lucky to have *them*!" said Parrott defensively. "Mostly we only got one or two men on shift, and there's no call to be sitting down!"

Marvel let it go and sat down. The chair was little better than a stool. It was small and hard and uneven and tipped back and forth every time he moved, which made him feel like an elephant on a tightrope. Reynolds sat next to him, the boy opposite. There was a recorder on the table between them, but Marvel didn't touch it.

Marvel jerked a thumb at the coffee machine.

"Fire that up, Rice."

"Yes, sir."

Parrott had taken up a position at the door, but his folded hands almost touched the back of the boy's head, and the mop leaned into his shoulder like a dreadlocked girlfriend.

"Wait outside, Parrott. There's no room in here."

Parrott looked disappointed, but said, "Yes, sir," and left.

Marvel tipped awkwardly forward and put his elbows on the table. "We can't formally interview you without a parent or guardian present," he started.

"That's OK," said the boy. "I *want* to talk."

"Until a parent or legal representative is present, I don't want to hear it."

The boy shrugged. "But I'm going to say it anyway."

"But unless you're properly represented and safeguarded and the interview is recorded, it's not admissible as evidence."

"Fine by me," shrugged the boy, and gave the smallest of smiles.

Marvel glared at him.

The whole Goldilocks thing was most unsatisfactory. For a start, it was no fun to discover that they'd all been outwitted by a child. Fourteen going on twelve, skinny as hell, with dirty blond hair and a peach-fuzzy face. And it was pure luck that they'd caught him at all! He'd broken back into the capture house — although God knows how the fancy bloody cameras kept missing it — and fallen asleep there! He could have cleaned the place out and they'd have been none the wiser.

The kid hadn't even tried to escape when Reynolds had found him. The DS kept trying to make it sound like a great bit of policing on his part, but Marvel could tell that all he'd done was shake him awake, as if for school!

And so the Goldilocks myth had become an embarrassing damp squib. He wasn't some Raffles-type cat burglar; he was just a lazy little thief who'd finally overslept in the wrong bed.

Marvel was sorry he'd ever got involved.

"Can we ask him about the Passmore house, sir?" said Reynolds.

"Ask him anything you want," snorted Marvel. "None of it's admissible."

Reynolds pursed his lips.

"What's your name?" said Marvel.

He didn't expect an answer, but he got one.

"Jack Bright."

"That your real name?"

"Yes."

"So what went wrong this morning, Jack?" said Marvel. "Alarm clock not go off?"

"Nothing went wrong," said the boy.

"Ohhhh," said Reynolds sarcastically, "so you *wanted* me to catch you!"

"Yes."

"Rubbish!" said Reynolds. "Nobody *wants* to be caught."

The boy shrugged. "Well, I did."

"If you wanted to be caught," said Marvel, "why not just hand yourself in?"

"Because I want to make a deal. And if you think I'm Goldilocks, then I have some . . ." The boy hesitated, searching for the word.

"Leverage?" said Marvel.

"That's right," he nodded. "Leverage."

"But you *are* Goldilocks," said Reynolds anxiously. "Aren't you?"

The boy shrugged.

"Just tell me, did you burgle a house down on St Peter Street? Steal a camera and smash a big new Sony TV? Take pizzas from the freezer?"

The boy shook his head. "I don't eat pizza."

Marvel laughed at Reynolds. "He's Goldilocks, all right!"

Then he turned back to Jack Bright.

"What kind of deal? What's so important that you're prepared to risk getting nicked for all those burglaries?"

The boy suddenly went quiet. A shadow passed across his face, and Marvel was surprised to see his bottom lip tremble, as if he might cry. It was fleeting, but it looked real.

Finally, he took a deep, shaky breath and said, "Murder."

The hairs on Marvel's neck sprang to attention.

Murder.

"Rubbish!" said Reynolds. "I caught you red-handed. You can't wriggle off the hook now by trying to distract us with some stupid lie."

But Marvel only leaned back in his chair and re-appraised the boy.

"Please," he said with an elaborate twirl of his hand. "Distract us."

So Jack Bright told them about the murder of his mother.

To his amazement, they remembered it. Even Marvel, who had apparently been in London at the time. Jack was so used to being invisible that seeing the sombre nods and murmurs of recognition was a strangely encouraging experience.

It made things easier. He grew more confident.

He told them what he thought they needed to know. Not everything. He told them about the home schooling, his father leaving, his sisters. The way they'd all slowly disappeared.

He left out Smooth Louis Bridge. The newspapers. The vandalism.

Strangely, the memory of photos torn and toys smashed and posters ripped off walls made him feel worse than the theft of thousands of pounds' worth of jewels and phones. He didn't want to hear those memories out loud.

But he told them about the burglary.

As he talked, he watched their faces. Marvel was intent, Reynolds sceptical, Rice sympathetic.

When he described finding the murder weapon in Adam While's hiking boot, Marvel shifted in his seat as if he couldn't wait to bound out of it.

He interrupted Jack. "Where's the knife now?"

Jack hesitated. "I left it there."

"In the house? Why?"

"Because . . . if I took the knife out of the house, how could I prove it was ever there? And even if you *had* believed me, I'd have been in the shit for B&E."

"True," said Marvel. "But you're in the shit now."

"I had no choice," Jack shrugged ruefully. "I left the knife next to Mrs While's bed. And a note threatening to kill her. I wasn't *going* to, you know? I just thought she'd call the police, but she never did."

The three officers swapped surprised glances.

"And it made me think, maybe they're *both* in on it! And *then* I started to think, maybe they'll get rid of the knife and then I'll *never* find it and then he'll get away with killing my mum!"

He stopped for a moment, his heart marking the urgency.

He calmed down.

Carried on.

"And so I went back to try to get it, but he'd already found it and his wife didn't have it and then he showed up even though he should have been at work, and he hit me and chased me . . ." Unconsciously, he touched his ear. "And after that he tried to burn down my house, so —"

"He tried to burn down your house?" said Marvel.

"Two nights ago. He put a petrol bomb through the front door."

"Was anyone hurt?"

"No," said Jack. "We put it out."

"You have any proof it was Adam While?"

"No," said Jack, "I can't prove *anything*. That's why *you* have to get involved."

He looked at Marvel intently, but the man only shrugged and folded his arms.

"Maybe I don't want to get involved. Maybe I don't have time to get involved with one old murder case while we've got a hundred new burglaries to clear off the books."

He raised a meaningful eyebrow at Jack, who only pursed his lips. Marvel might outweigh him by a fat margin, but he wasn't about to be provoked into giving up his leverage.

Marvel gave a short laugh.

"All right then," he said. "But at least tell me why you left the capture house so quickly the first time you broke in."

"Capture house," said Jack, tasting the words in his mouth. "Is that what it is?" Then he nodded his cautious approval. "It's not bad."

Marvel shrugged. "Then why weren't you captured?"

Reynolds interrupted: "Sir, shouldn't we be cautious about leading questions in the Goldilocks case? Particularly with a juvenile . . . ?"

"Fuck Goldilocks," said Marvel, and Jack smiled.

"The photo on the mantelpiece wasn't real," he said. "It was just the picture they sell with the frame. Those two kids with a beach ball, you know?"

Marvel glanced at Reynolds, who reddened furiously.

"Well," said Marvel, "I know *now* . . ." He leaned forward. "So, what makes you think the knife you found in Adam While's boot is the murder weapon?"

238

Jack stuck out his chin defensively. "I just know."

"That's not helpful, is it?"

"I knew the minute I saw it. It was like I *felt* it too! It's got a white handle, made of some kind of shell, I think, all blue and white like clouds, and the blade is curved on one side and the other is sort of jagged."

"Serrated?"

"Yes, serrated."

Marvel shrugged. "It sounds like a lot of knives."

"It's *not* like a lot of knives," Jack said angrily. "It's the knife that killed my mother!"

There was a moment of silence.

"Say that's true," said Marvel, pinching his nose. "Why would Adam While keep it if it ties him to a murder? The murder weapon's the *first* thing a killer gets rid of. Keeping it doesn't make any sense."

Jack *knew* it didn't make any sense. He battled to keep a lid on his frustration. "I *know*," he said, "but he *hid* it. Like it was important. Like it was *secret*. And he lied to his wife about it. Said he'd lost it, but he *knew* it was missing from his boot, and he went looking for it! I feel like —"

"Feelings aren't facts," Reynolds interrupted.

"But sometimes they *feel* like facts!" Jack shot back.

Marvel snorted and nearly laughed, and Jack wiped his sweaty palms on his jeans.

"I want to make a deal."

Marvel looked at him sharply. "What kind of deal?"

"If I'm wrong about the knife, then I'll plead guilty to the Goldilocks stuff."

"And if you're right?" said Marvel.

"You arrest Adam While," said Jack. "Instead of me."

Marvel was interested, Jack could see.

"*Instead* of?" said Reynolds, and turned to Marvel. "But then what about the Goldilocks case?"

Marvel spoke carefully. "I think I need to speak to the senior investigating officer in the Eileen Bright case."

"Sir?" said Reynolds warily, but Marvel just got to his feet.

"You wait here, all right?" he told Jack. Then to Rice: "Get him some breakfast."

"What about the deal?" said Jack.

"We'll talk about that when I get back."

"Sir?" said Reynolds again, but Marvel ignored him again.

"You promise?" said Jack.

Marvel snorted again. "This isn't nursery school."

"*You promise?*"

"I promise," said Marvel. "Happy now?"

DCI John Marvel left the little room with a scowl on his face, but with a light step and a belly that buzzed with anticipation. It wouldn't have mattered to him what deal Jack Bright had demanded, he would have said yes.

The boy had had him at *murder*.

"Call me Ralph," said DCI Stourbridge, and shook Marvel's hand with expansive good cheer.

Marvel scowled. He disliked familiarity, and first names in particular. They made him uncomfortable and he didn't use them. He also disliked facial hair, and Stourbridge had a ridiculously bushy joke-shop moustache.

So they were off on the wrong foot, but that was the only foot Marvel knew how to put forward.

"Marvel," he said bluntly. "I'm looking at the Eileen Bright case."

Immediately Stourbridge's big, open face clouded over and his moustache drooped. "Ahh," he sighed. "Very sad case."

"Any unsolved murder case is very sad," said Marvel, and the moustache looked surprised — then a little offended.

"Strictly speaking," Stourbridge said stiffly, "the case was only half ours. Devon and Cornwall had the missing person, and we found the body. It was never established where the murder actually took place."

Now that Stourbridge looked less cheerful, Marvel felt better about everything.

"You ever heard the name Adam While?"

"Adam While?" Stourbridge looked surprised. "Yes. But not for a very long time. He was picked up near the scene a week or so after the body was found."

It was Marvel's turn to look surprised.

"How near the scene?"

"In the same lay-by. Said he'd stopped for a pee, but we brought him in for questioning. We didn't have any reason to keep him or charge him, so we let him go. He was only in custody for a few hours."

Marvel grunted. It was a coincidence, but he was not a man who scoffed at coincidence. He'd never worked a case where coincidence hadn't played a part, either in the commission of the crime or the solving of it.

"Was While's name ever released to the public?"

"God, no," said Stourbridge. "Feelings were running very high on this one. No reason to start a witch hunt! We pulled him in, eliminated him and let him go."

"Was he ever mentioned to Eileen Bright's family?"

Stourbridge shook his head. "It's a long time ago, but I don't think so. There just wasn't any reason."

Stourbridge shifted in his seat and frowned. "What's your interest, John?"

Marvel shot him a warning look about first names, but the man misinterpreted it and softened his tone sympathetically.

"You seem troubled —"

"I'm not *troubled*," said Marvel. "I'm just doing my job."

There was an awkward silence, then Stourbridge said, "I have the Bright file right here, if you want to see it."

Without waiting for Marvel to say whether he did or not, Stourbridge opened the bottom right-hand drawer of his desk and pulled out a well-stuffed grey folder. "I keep it here," he said. "So that . . . you know . . ."

He didn't finish the sentence, but Marvel *did* know. The bottom right-hand drawer of his own desk at Lewisham nick was where he'd kept those very few case files that remained open and unsolved. Every week — sometimes more often than that — he would remove one and pore over it obsessively during his lunch hour, or when everybody else was heading home. Picking at the scabs of his own failure.

The photo taped to the wall inside his front door — of the little girl on the BMX bike — had been taken from a folder just like the one Ralph Stourbridge was holding out to him now. Her name was Edie Evans and Marvel still thought about her every day.

"Thanks," he said, and took the file from Stourbridge. He didn't ask whether he could take it away — he wouldn't have allowed anyone to take *his* files away with them.

"Can I get you a cuppa?" said Stourbridge, pointing at the door.

"Thanks," said Marvel. "Two sugars, whatever it is."

Marvel sat down in Stourbridge's chair and started to go through the file. It was well organized and he could tell immediately that Stourbridge had done a thorough job. There were even photos of Arthur Bright and each of his children. Bright looked cheerful and ignorant of impending disaster. Marvel barely recognized the smiling schoolboy that was Jack. His hair properly cut; his brow unfurrowed.

He easily found the record of the brief detention of Adam While. There was a photo of him, looking tired and a little cross, with his hair sticking up on one side of his forehead, as if he'd been clutching at it in frustration. He was clean-shaven, and wore wire-rimmed glasses and a shirt and tie. He looked like a businessman late for a train.

There was a brief, typed note.

Mr Adam While, a 35-year-old male of Leaburn Road, Tiverton, was detained voluntarily at 11:20 on September 6, 1998 in the lay-by where the body of Mrs Eileen Bright was found on August 29, 1998. Nothing of relevance was found during a search of Mr While's person and car (see Appendix C). Mr While was questioned on September 6 (see Appendix D) and released at 19:25 the same day without formal arrest, charge or bail. NFA.

NFA.

No Further Action.

And there hadn't been.

Before Marvel could look at the Appendices, Stourbridge came back in and put a cup of tea beside him.

"Thanks," said Marvel. "Was the victim sexually assaulted?"

"No."

"And she died from a single stab wound?"

"To the stomach," said Stourbridge. "She bled to death."

There was another silence, but this time it wasn't awkward at all. This time Marvel knew they were just two coppers thinking about the same thing: the horror of stabbing a pregnant woman in the stomach.

At least, that's what *he* was thinking about.

"This While been in trouble before or since?"

"Nothing. Not even as a kid. Nice house, good job, married man. We had no hook to hang him on. And believe me, if we could have, we would have."

Marvel grimaced. It sounded like While was just in the wrong place at the wrong time. But there was that coincidence. Jack Bright and Adam While. Connected across the years.

Somehow . . .

So John Marvel did something he rarely did.

He shared.

"Eileen Bright's son says he broke into Adam While's house and found the murder weapon there."

Stourbridge's moustache fairly bristled.

"Her son? He can't be more than . . ."

"Fourteen," supplied Marvel.

"Fourteen?" said Stourbridge. "Time flies."

"Says he found the knife in the toe of a boot in While's wardrobe."

"Impossible," said Stourbridge.

"Why?"

"Because it's downstairs in the evidence room."

Marvel felt sucker-punched. He'd almost believed the boy. Almost bought the story. Now he felt stupid and cheated.

"Shit," he said, and glared at Stourbridge as if it were all his fault.

"We found it within hours of finding the body," said Stourbridge apologetically. "It'll be in the file." He held out his hand. "May I?"

Marvel handed the file over, and Stourbridge found the information quickly. "Seventeen forty-five on the twenty-ninth. It was only twenty yards away from the body."

"And While was picked up on September sixth."

"That's right."

"How did you know he was there?"

"We had cameras and surveillance on the lay-by for the duration of the search and for a month after we reopened it."

"Nothing before that?"

"If we'd had cameras on it before that, we wouldn't be having this conversation," said Stourbridge flatly. "Afterwards, a few cars stopped, a couple of people got out and threw away litter or walked the dog. Lorry drivers slept there overnight. A few of them peed. While was the only one who went over the barrier and stayed there for any length of time."

"What's the terrain like?"

"Long grass, scrubby trees. It slopes down away from the road. Those motorway lay-bys are longer than you think. All in all, we're talking an area about the size of a football pitch."

"You *were* lucky with the knife!"

"It was our only break, to be honest. The killer could have thrown it anywhere between here and John o'Groats."

Marvel pursed his lips, then asked, "Who found the body?"

"A lorry driver named Royston Ash. Another one who stopped for a pee."

"Was he eliminated as a suspect?"

Stourbridge nodded. "He said he only went down to check it out because he'd picked up loads of stuff in lay-bys over the years. I remember he even came clean about a couple of bags of cannabis leaf he'd found up near Cambridge. Admitted he'd filled a shopping bag and sold it to his mates. Anyway, he only went a few yards before the smell tipped him off. He was traumatized by finding the body, and wanted to help. He seemed straight to me."

Marvel nodded. He liked a good hunch himself, and was open to the instincts of others.

"How long had she been there?"

"A while."

"So she was probably killed shortly after being taken?"

"We assume. There was no sign that she was kept anywhere else."

"So an impulsive act," said Marvel.

Stourbridge nodded. "Poor woman was just in the wrong place at the wrong time."

"Did you show the knife to While?"

"Yes. No response. I don't think he'd ever seen it before. But you know how it is — we were clutching at straws."

Stourbridge sighed, and Marvel felt his pain. He could see that the murder of Eileen Bright had been a tough case. Two police forces, two crime scenes more than a week apart, no witnesses. No wonder they'd picked up While and given him a hard time.

No wonder they'd had no reason to hold him.

Chumming the river.

"When did you reopen the lay-by?"

Stourbridge consulted the file briefly. "The evening of the fifth."

Marvel tingled. Not a big tingle, just a little one, but a tingle nonetheless. "So While was detained in the lay-by on the first possible day he could legally be there?"

"That's right."

"Had you released the description of the knife to the press by then?"

"No. We held it back."

"So the killer wouldn't have known it had been found."

"That's right. In fact, we've never released it to the public. It's all we've got to tie the killer to the crime."

"Then how the *hell* would Jack Bright know what it looks like?"

Stourbridge shook his head. "I have no idea."

Marvel frowned. "Can I see the knife?"

The evidence room at Taunton was a bright and airy place — completely unlike the dingy cavern in the basement at the old Lewisham station.

DCI Stourbridge chatted as he led Marvel through the neatly marked shelves.

"You say the boy broke into While's house?"

"Yeah," said Marvel. "Seems he's been supporting the family through burglary for over a year."

"Jesus," frowned Stourbridge, "I remember him. Poor kid. What happened to the father?"

"He left."

Stourbridge sucked air through his teeth. "What a shit."

Marvel made no comment about a father leaving his children, but he liked Stourbridge better now that he'd said "shit".

Stourbridge knew exactly where he was going. Marvel could tell he came here often. They stopped in front of a rack of boxes and Stourbridge opened one without hesitation and handed an evidence bag to Marvel.

For the second time today, the hairs on the back of his neck stood up.

Even through clear plastic, the knife exuded menace. It was open, so its jewel-like handle couldn't hide its true purpose, which was the swift and merciless imposition of death. Curved on one side, serrated on the other, just as the boy had said. But more than that — Marvel noticed that the thumb stud was inlaid with a small but brilliant diamond.

And between the blade and the handle was a black crust of old blood . . .

"Was it found open like this?"

"Yes."

"Wiped?"

"Yup," said Stourbridge. "And yet thrown away."

Marvel understood what he meant. Wiping the knife clean of prints spoke of control; throwing it away close to the body spoke of panic.

"Odd," he said.

"No odder than stabbing a pregnant woman in the stomach."

"You're right," said Marvel.

It made him uneasy. The crime was so . . . *personal*.

"You sure it wasn't the husband?"

"Sure as we could be," Stourbridge sighed. "Although I'm never sure of anything until the jury foreman says *guilty*."

Marvel snorted his appreciation of *that* legal nicety.

"Arthur Bright was in pieces from day one. Missing wife; three traumatized kids. I don't think he even understood that he might *be* a suspect, you know? I think he honestly believed that it was all a mistake and his wife might come home any time. When we found her body it broke him and — from what you say about him leaving the kids — he probably didn't recover —"

Stourbridge stopped with his mouth open, staring at the knife in the bag.

Then he said "Shit" for a second time.

"What's up?" said Marvel.

"I just remembered something." Stourbridge shifted uncomfortably and smoothed the ends of his moustache. "I took the knife with me when I went to tell Arthur Bright that his wife's body had been found. See his reaction. Shock tactics, you know? But I was clutching at straws."

He glanced at Marvel sheepishly but Marvel only shrugged. Sometimes you had to break somebody apart, just to look inside them to see if they were guilty. If they were, you'd done your job. If they weren't — well, you'd done your job then too.

Either way, the person got broken.

It was collateral damage.

Stourbridge continued, "I had the knife with me just in the bag. I should have put it in a box or something but I didn't. And the kid was right there . . ."

"You think he saw it?" said Marvel.

"I think so. The WPC who came with me said he got very agitated. She had to restrain him from following me."

"So that's how he knows what it looks like."

Stourbridge rubbed his jaw as if he had toothache. "Not my finest hour."

Marvel shrugged again. He'd had many hours that were not his finest. He was a murder detective. The interests of the corpse came first. He changed the subject with uncharacteristic tact. "What was the motive?"

Stourbridge glanced at him gratefully. "The only motive we could come up with was robbery. Eileen had a purse with her when she left home. She was taking the kids to buy school shoes in Exeter, and she stopped for petrol at the M5 junction. We carried out fingertip searches around each scene — the abduction, the car, and the body dump. That's how we found the knife, but we never found the purse."

"Robbery seems logical."

"Yeah," said Stourbridge, "but her card was never used, so . . ."

He shrugged and Marvel nodded. Sometimes things didn't fit. Or they *did* fit, but you never discovered exactly *how*. It was the nature of the murder beast.

"Can I have a copy of the file?"

"Sure," said Stourbridge. "I'll have it sent to you."

"Great. And can I borrow this?" said Marvel, holding up the knife in the bag.

Stourbridge hesitated. Marvel could see that he didn't want to let the murder weapon go.

It wasn't doing anybody any good where it was, but he still understood. When a case was unsolved, every clue — no matter how small — might turn out to be vital. The compulsion to keep hold of every single thing was extreme.

Especially when that thing was the murder weapon.

So he was sympathetic, but he wasn't about to show that to Stourbridge, or he wouldn't get what he wanted.

Finally the big man sighed and said, "For Christ's sake, don't lose it."

Stourbridge walked Marvel to his car and they shook hands there.

"Thanks," said Marvel.

"Any time you want to compare notes, just call me," said Stourbridge. "I think about it all the time anyway — might as well bore somebody new."

"I will," Marvel said and got into his car. He checked his watch. It would take him thirty minutes to get back to Tiverton — well within the few hours he'd promised, even if it wasn't with the news the boy wanted.

"Oh, and remember me to Jack," said Stourbridge. "I'm sorry he's gone wrong, but there's always time to go right."

"I will," said Marvel again, although, in his experience, once a kid had gone wrong, the road back to right was a hard one to find.

Jack found his mother.

He was on the hard shoulder and she was alongside him in a car — looking out of the passenger window, smiling, and with one bare arm dangling down, her hand patting the metallic door now and then, as if to encourage him to keep up.

Everything was so clear! Even the tiny golden hairs on her arm that trembled in the breeze created by slow motion.

Her wedding ring made the tiniest *tink* against the door panel.

He couldn't see who was driving the car, but he knew it wasn't his father.

Slow down, he said.

Hurry up, she told him.

As if in response, the driver dipped the throttle and the car went a little bit faster.

Jack broke into a jog.

Wait! he said.

You're too slow, she said, and the car accelerated again so that now Jack was running along the hard shoulder, and it was raining, but only from his knees down, so that his trainers slapped and splashed while the rest of him baked in the August sun.

The car pulled away and his mother looked back and patted the door.

Tink. Tink. Tink.

Jack sprinted after the car, hot air burning holes in his lungs.

Mum! Wait! Call the police!

His mother shrugged her bare arm and gave a sad little smile.

It's too late, she said, and the car got smaller and smaller and its engine faded into the distance . . .

Jack woke with a start, with his face on the cool surface of the Formica table, next to an uneaten Big Mac and a cup of Pepsi sitting in a puddle of its own sweat.

He straightened up, disorientated, and breathing hard. The nightmares scooped him out, and it always took him a moment to leave the dream and return to reality.

"All right?" said DC Rice.

But before he could properly gather himself, the door opened and Marvel walked in.

He sat down and moved the burger box and the wet Pepsi out of the way, then placed a clear plastic bag on the Formica table between them.

Jack looked up at Marvel in happy wonder.

"You *found* it!"

Marvel cleared his throat. "This is the murder weapon —"

"I know! I —"

But Marvel held up his hand and went on: "It's been in the Taunton police evidence room for the past three years."

Jack frowned and shook his head. That couldn't be right! It would make everything else . . . *wrong*.

"But . . ." he said haltingly, "it's Adam While's knife."

"No it's not," said Marvel. "DCI Stourbridge — you remember him?"

Jack paused and then said uncertainly, "Call-Me-Ralph?"

Marvel nodded. "He tells me that on the day it was found, he brought this knife to your home to show it to your father. He thinks you might have seen it then. Do you remember that?"

Jack stared at the knife. "I . . . I don't know," he said. "I don't remember."

"Adam While's knife might look the same. It's probably one of thousands just like it," said Marvel. "But his knife didn't kill your mother."

Jack felt hot and cold. If the knife in Adam While's house was one of thousands, then everything he'd done, everything he'd risked, was all for nothing.

"But — but it's the same knife!" he stammered. "Even if they're different, they're the same! They *must* be connected. Because . . . because why would he hide it in his boot? If it wasn't the one, why would he hide it? And he lied about it to his boot! Why would he lie about it if it didn't *mean* anything? *Why?*"

"I don't know why," said Marvel. "But I do know it's not because it was the murder weapon."

Vaguely Jack felt Rice's sympathetic hand on his shoulder. It made him want to cry or to scream, but he didn't even have the energy to shake it off.

"What about our deal?" he said softly.

Marvel sighed and shook his head, and Jack felt as if he were falling through space — light years from anything to grab on to.

He'd blown it. He had no leverage. Nothing to trade. He'd gambled his family's future on making a deal with the police . . . and he'd lost. Louis was right. They'd get him for *some* fucking thing. And Joy was right too. He was *shit* at being in charge. Even worse than their father.

Now the remaining fragments of his shattered family would be lost to him, and probably to each other, for ever.

A sudden harsh pain made him grimace and he clutched at his chest — right in the middle, between the sharp sweep of his ribs.

This is how Mum felt.

Jack knew that suddenly. Knew it like breathing.

She had been in charge, that sunny August afternoon a lifetime ago. She, too, had risked her family's future, without even realizing it and never dreaming she'd lose. Never dreaming that a stranger in a car would stop to help her, and instead drive her away and put a knife — *THIS KNIFE!* — through her and her unborn child.

Because who would ever dream that such a thing could happen?

Nobody.

She'd made a mistake. And who could blame her?

257

Nobody. *Nobody!*

Not even him.

And Jack also knew that when his mother had finally understood what was happening to her — what was happening to *all* of them — she had felt this same horror. The same fear. The same searing guilt. The same unbearable sadness.

"Mum!"

The word was ripped from a place so deep and dark inside Jack Bright that it tore his throat, and rang hoarsely around the little room where the photocopier hummed.

Then he put his head on his arms and wept.

They locked him up.

The police station was so small that the holding cell was little more than the twin of the interview room, but with a peephole and a flap in the door, and without the photocopier.

Someone at the little station had taken pride in it though, and had made it more comfortable than was the norm. There was a single mattress on the bench-slash-bed. There was a box of old wax crayons with which the prisoners could draw or write on the walls — which they apparently did with unequal parts talent and filth — and on the sill of the long, high window was a posy of fake flowers in a plastic pot, which the prisoners couldn't reach, but which they could enjoy, if their eyesight was good enough.

"Well, this isn't so bad, is it?" said Rice encouragingly. "There's crayons."

Jack walked into the middle of the room, silent and dazed.

From the doorway Reynolds said, "That bed'll be *just right* for you, Goldilocks."

"Bit mean, isn't it?" said Rice sharply.

"Bit mean, isn't it, *sir*," he snapped back.

"Jack?" said Marvel. Then again, "Jack?"

When Jack turned to look at him, he went on, "When the duty solicitor gets in we can take a proper statement, all right? Until then, have a kip. You look like shit."

"But I have to go home," said Jack. "They've only got oranges."

Rice touched his arm gently. "I'll call Social Services, all right? They'll sort things out."

Angrily he shook her hand off his arm. "They'll put them in care!" he shouted. "I have to go home! I'm in *charge*!"

"Sorry, Jack," said Rice.

Parrott closed the door and locked it.

As they stood outside the cell, Marvel turned to Reynolds. "You and Parrott go back to the capture house and start dismantling it."

"Yes, sir."

"Parrott, is there a safe here?"

"Yes, sir. Behind the front desk."

Marvel handed him the knife. "Be sure to put that in it before you go."

"Yes, sir."

Parrott disappeared down the dingy corridor.

"Rice, get someone to pick up the kids."

Rice pulled a face. "But sir —"

Marvel's phone rang and he answered it.

"Hello, John," said Ralph Stourbridge irritatingly. "Am I right in thinking you mentioned Adam While's wife?"

"Yes," said Marvel. "What about it?"

"Well, I was boring a colleague about the case just now and it turns out this colleague knows Mrs While's cousin. She tells me Mrs While left her husband the day we picked him up."

There was a crackling silence.

"The *same* day?" said Marvel incredulously.

"The same day," said Stourbridge. "And I have to tell you, John . . . that bothers me."

"Yeah," said Marvel. "It bothers me too."

Adam While's wife opened the door looking like a whale.

She was hugely pregnant.

"Mrs While?" said Marvel.

"Yes?"

"Detective Chief Inspector Marvel. Can I come in?"

Mrs While looked worried. "Why?" she said. "What's wrong?"

"Nothing," said Marvel. "Nothing's wrong."

Reluctantly, she opened the door.

Marvel was always amazed how just *saying* that nothing was wrong could reassure people to the point of compliance. Even when there was *loads* wrong. Marvel wasn't above a little white lie — or a big black one — in this regard. The job was all about getting inside and sitting down with people. Get them to make you a cup of tea, and you were halfway to a confession.

Marvel prided himself on his skill as an interviewer. On his way over in the car, he'd decided only to address the period immediately after the Eileen Bright murder. Unless it came up in the course of the conversation, he didn't plan to touch on the burglary at all, now that it was clear that the knife Jack Bright had found was a red herring. A red herring that had set wheels in motion, but a red herring nonetheless.

Mrs While was a pretty girl, but had an anxious air about her that made Marvel suspicious. He liked that. *Suspicious* was his default setting, and he liked to know that he might actually have a valid reason to believe the worst about people.

He followed her through to the kitchen, hoping she'd put the kettle on.

Catherine didn't put the kettle on. Her mind bubbled instead.

The policeman had said there was nothing wrong. But when was the last time somebody sent the police round to deliver good news? So although he'd *said* nothing was wrong, there plainly *was* something wrong.

Adam and the boy. It must be.

What had one of them done?

But if something *had* happened, surely the detective would have been legally obliged to use some other form of words, even if it was ambiguous? Maybe *Nothing serious* or *There's been an incident* . . . Something like that?

So she walked him through to the kitchen — really only because she didn't know what else to do, and because it gave her a moment to process these thoughts in her anxious head.

"Do you mind if I sit?" she asked. She patted the top of her tummy and gave him a meaningful smile, but he didn't smile back. Only inclined his head briefly to show that he had no objection.

Rude!

Catherine had got so used to people accommodating her pregnancy that she felt a spark of resentment at the man's lack of interest.

She didn't offer him a seat.

He didn't seem to care. Just stood in the middle of the floor, got out his notebook and flipped through it.

"I wanted to ask you about your husband."

Catherine's heart skipped an anxious beat. "Why? she said. "What's wrong? Is he OK? You said nothing had happened! But something's happened, hasn't it? So what's happened?"

The detective held up his hand as if she were a collie and he a shepherd. It made her hackles rise.

"Don't panic," he told her firmly.

"I wasn't panicking," she snapped. Although she had been, a little bit.

"As far as I know, Mr While is fine. I'm just filling in some gaps in an old case."

"What old case?"

"It's a simple thing," he said. "I understand that when Mr While was questioned about the incident on the M5 a few years back, you left the family home."

"The incident?"

"Yes," said the policeman. "Detective Chief Inspector Stourbridge tells me you left the family home the same day your husband was questioned. I wonder if you could tell me why?"

Catherine frowned. "I'm sorry," she said, "but I haven't got the faintest idea what you're talking about. And you just saying it again in a different order doesn't help!"

She smiled briefly at him, but the detective sighed as if she were being very stupid indeed, when *he* was the one who'd got things wrong!

She didn't like him.

At all.

"Look, I don't know what's going on here," she said briskly, "but I'm eight months pregnant, in case you hadn't noticed, and I don't need the stress, Mr Marble —"

"Marvel," said Marvel.

"Whatever!" said Catherine. "I don't know what you're *talking* about!"

"Look, Mrs While, it's not a big deal. I'd just like to know why you left your husband that day, and why you came back."

"I've never *left* my husband!" said Catherine. "On *any* day! I never left, and so I never came back! And who's Detective Chief Inspector Starbridge when he's at home? I've never heard of the man!"

"DCI Stourbridge was the detective in charge of the Eileen Bright murder investigation."

The baby turned to cold lead in Catherine's tummy.

There was a huge rushing sound in her head, as if her thoughts were a giant wave crashing on to the beach of her brain.

Eileen Bright. The boy's mother. The boy's pregnant mother. The woman he said had been murdered with the knife that had been left next to her bed!

The knife she'd hidden and Adam had found.

Or was it the other way around . . . ?

Jack Bright had fixated on it, and now the fat ugly policeman had too. It was a mistake. A misunderstanding. She knew that, but she couldn't work out whether what the man was saying was *all* wrong, or just bits of it.

Catherine's head buzzed like a bad radio.

"I don't know what you're talking about." She stood up dizzily, and clutched the corner of the table for support. "I think you should come back when Adam's home."

"It's not Adam I want to speak to," said Marvel. "It's you."

"No," said Catherine, shaking her head slowly. "You need to talk to *Adam* about this! You need to come back!"

"No, *you* need to answer my questions, Mrs While. We can do it here or you can come down to the police station and do it there. Anything else will be considered obstructing the course of justice."

"I'm not going *anywhere!*" said Catherine, feeling the tide of panic rise inside her. "I don't know what you're talking about and I'm not going *anywhere!*"

She tried to barge past him, but he held her arm.

"Go away!" she cried. "Leave me alone!" She flailed to free herself, slapping his face with the back of her hand, grazing his brow with her engagement ring. He grabbed her arm in an iron grip and twisted her back down into her chair.

She shrieked.

"How dare you?" she cried. "Let me *go*! I'll report you! I'm *pregnant*! For God's sake, you moron! Can't you see I'm fucking *pregnant*?"

"So what?" he said. "Congratulations on being a mammal."

Catherine burst into tears of humiliation and fury. She twisted her head and bit his arm, but he saw her coming and she only tore a hole in his shirtsleeve.

Then, as if in a parallel dimension, Catherine felt him putting her in *handcuffs*. As if she were a criminal! Or someone in a soap! Bending her hard over her own giant belly, pulling her hands together behind her back . . .

"Please don't," she whimpered. "You're hurting my baby!"

He relented. He let her up and stood over her, panting and red-faced. Her ring had caught him above the eye and he was bleeding. He spoke in breathless snatches.

"Angela While," he said. "I'm arresting you. For . . . obstructing the course of justice. And . . . resisting —"

"I'm not Angela While," sobbed Catherine.

"What?"

"I'm *Catherine* While."

She and Marvel looked at each other, fleetingly united by mutual confusion.

Then he said, "Shit," and Catherine felt all the blood drain from her face. Her voice shook.

"Who the *bloody hell* is Angela While?"

It took Marvel half an hour to get hold of Ralph Stourbridge.

"Wrong Mrs While," he announced when he finally did.

"I didn't know there was more than one."

"Well, there's at least two," said Marvel. "And this one's fucking *furious*."

Jack found his mother.

She was under the apple tree on the hard shoulder, sitting with her back against the barrier, examining the small bright red fruits as if for worms.

He stopped his bike at the edge of the shadow it cast across the tarmac.

A line he could not cross.

Hi, he said. *How are you?*

Wormy, she said, and tossed the apples across the road, where they rolled and bounced like cheeses.

Don't get in the car, he said.

What car? she said, and Merry — who was suddenly next to Jack — said, *That car*, and a blue car pulled up.

Merry ran towards it.

Don't get in the car! cried Jack, but his mother got up and brushed her hands against the front of her white summer dress, and followed Merry and together they got into the car.

NO!

Sound of car driving off.

Jack pedalled after it, but he had forgotten how to ride a bicycle and kept wobbling and having to put his foot down, and get the pedal back up to the top, like a small child without a parent to steady him.

At last he just stopped on the dusty tarmac and watched the blue car disappear around the bend.

In the back window, Merry held up a single sad hand in goodbye.

Mama!

The word on his own lips woke him in the tiny police cell — curled and shivering with sweat. He sat up slowly on the narrow bench and waited for the nightmare to fragment around him. But it took a very long time to fade, and even when he knew he was fully awake, the miserable feeling of failure remained.

Jack looked up at the little pot of fake flowers on the high sill.

He needed catching now.

Marvel knocked on Mrs *Angela* While's front door in Taunton. She turned out to be a slightly older version of the new Mrs While. Same blonde, shoulder-length hair, same blue eyes, same rounded face.

Different girth.

"Mrs *Angela* While?" said Marvel cautiously.

And when she nodded he said, "Detective Chief Inspector Marvel. Can I come in?"

The house was a mess created by, and divided equally between, a small boy and a large dog.

"This is Robbie," said Angela While, as if Marvel gave a shit. "And this is Brutus."

She was apparently so smitten with both that she gave no indication of noticing his lack of interest in either. She smiled brightly at him and asked how she could help.

"I've come about Adam While," he said. Then he added, "Your husband?" just to be on the safe side.

"Ex-husband," said Angela.

Marvel felt a tiny bit of equilibrium return to his world.

"Ex-husband," he repeated. "I just have a few questions about an old case."

Her smile switched off. "Eileen Bright?"

A thrill ran through Marvel. A chance remark from him, Ralph Stourbridge musing to a colleague, and suddenly new light might shine on murder.

It was like magic.

He struck immediately while Angela While was still off-kilter. "I believe that you left your husband the day he was questioned about it. Why was that?"

She opened her mouth, but didn't answer immediately.

Instead she sat down and drew her son to her, and hugged him until he grizzled. The dog came over, concerned, and Angela While put a hand on its head. Marvel thought she looked like an old Victorian painting — one of those that told a story and had an apt title. *Waiting for Bad News* or *The Telegram*. Except with Lego bricks strewn about the floor and a TV showing cartoons in the background.

Then Robbie fought his way out of her arms and went back to his toys, and the dog left her side too, and instead sniffed Marvel's trouser leg as if he might make it his own.

"Sss," said Marvel sharply, and Brutus ambled out of the room. A minute later, Marvel could hear him gulping water in big slow laps.

Angela While looked up at him with a blank, slow-motion face.

"You left Adam," Marvel reminded her. "Why?"

"He . . ." she said, and then stopped.

"I . . ." she started, and then stopped again.

Third time lucky, thought Marvel impatiently.

"I have no proof," she finally got out. "Of *anything*. I want you to understand that right up front. If I'd had proof I'd have told police at the time, but I didn't. And I still don't."

So much for the magic, thought Marvel.

"Just tell me what you want to tell me," he said. "I'm only here to listen."

Of course, that wasn't true at all. Marvel would happily arrest her, *and* the kid — and the dog too — if he thought it would help his case. But over the years he had found that in these situations there was rarely any call to be honest with people. It was better to tell them exactly what they wanted to hear if he were to stand any chance of hearing what *he* wanted to hear.

"On the day Eileen Bright disappeared," Angela said, "we had a fight."

"What about?" he said, and lowered himself into a chair without being invited. It seemed the natural thing to do. Angela barely registered the move. Mostly she spoke with her eyes on her son, who was building something unrecognizable, forcing bricks into place with gritted teeth and ham fists instead of fitting them easily together like the smiling children on the box. Marvel wondered if there was something wrong with the Lego, or something wrong with the kid.

Angela While lowered her voice, looked meaningfully at her son and said, "I was pregnant."

Marvel shivered the way he always did when things that had seemed unconnected suddenly matched.

Angela While had been pregnant; Eileen Bright had been pregnant; the new Mrs While was pregnant. It *must* be important. He needed to know *how* . . .

"And Adam got it into his head that I'd cheated on him. I mean, it was ridiculous. There was no chance the baby wasn't his. *No* chance. He *knew* that! But he went crazy. I mean, like, *bonkers*." She half laughed at how bonkers he'd gone, but it was a nervous, mirthless sound.

"Did he ever hit you?"

"Only once." She touched her cheek, remembering the exact spot, however many years later. "He always had a temper. He didn't snap often, but when he did, you knew about it."

"What happened?" said Marvel.

"We'd had lunch with some friends in the Feathers, and someone had made a joke — just a stupid joke about the baby looking like the milkman. You know that thing people say. Just silliness. But Adam wouldn't let it go. When we got home he went on and on about it and got more and more angry, and then *I* got angry too and then he slapped me, and I slapped him back and told him to get out, and he did . . ."

"How long was he gone?"

"I don't know," she said. "Hours? And when he came back it was with flowers and chocolates and a ridiculous gift for the baby — some light-up sword thing from *Star Wars* or *Star Trek*. And he wasn't even born yet!"

"Was Adam behaving strangely at all when he came home?"

274

"Nope," she sighed. "Just full of sorrys and I-love-yous."

She paused, then shrugged.

"We made up and carried on, and when I heard on the news a while later that Eileen Bright's body had been found, I didn't make any connection. I only really paid any attention because she'd been pregnant too, you know? Horrible."

She shivered and rubbed her arms.

"So why *did* you leave?"

Angela screwed up her face as if trying to settle on one thing. Finally she said, "Well, he had a knife . . ."

Marvel got prickles up the back of his neck. "What kind of knife?"

"Like a fancy penknife. But bigger. It cost a lot of money, apparently."

"Was it like this one?" Marvel showed her the photo of the murder weapon.

"Yeah, like that. I couldn't say if it was exactly like that because I don't give a shit about knives, but it was very similar with that pearly handle. He was always fiddling with it and sharpening it and cleaning it. You know what men are like about their things — no offence. It drove me nuts! But anyway, in the time before I left him, I noticed: suddenly he doesn't have the knife any more."

"You mean after Eileen Bright was murdered?"

"Around that time. I can't be sure — that's why I say I don't have any proof of anything, you see? I can't remember the exact timings and I never paid enough attention to the knife to know for sure . . . I just started

275

to notice he's not pampering the knife like a bloody baby, and when I asked if he'd lost it, he said no, it was upstairs, but — trust me — if that knife was in the house, it was in his pocket. So I thought he must have lost it and just didn't want to tell me because apparently it had cost so much. Not that I cared. Adam had a good job, and we never went short, and it's not my money, is it?"

"No," agreed Marvel.

She went on: "So anyway, that was that, and I didn't think any more about it until he called me a few days later and told me he was being questioned by the police, and I was like, *What the hell?* I had no idea what could be wrong. Literally. He told me all he'd done was stop on the motorway for a pee and I thought, is that even a *crime*? I mean, everyone's had a pee by the side of the road, haven't they? But then he said it was near where Eileen Bright's body had been found . . . and . . . it all sort of . . . came together for me. You know — him hitting me that time, the jealousy and the fight over the baby, the missing knife, him being picked up in the same place her body was found . . ."

Her voice became sing-song as she went through the list. Then she sighed and fixed Marvel with a steady gaze. "I didn't even wait for him to come home. I packed a few things and went to my mum's. He kept calling, kept begging, but I wouldn't see him. Then a few weeks later he comes to her house waving that bloody knife, saying he's found it — like that made any difference! Because it wasn't really about the knife. It was over, because in my heart I felt —"

She stopped again.

"That he'd killed her?" said Marvel.

"Oh no!" Angela frowned at him, then lowered her voice to a bare whisper. "But I felt that he was *capable* of killing." She stroked her son's hair and shrugged. "And that was enough."

Marvel nodded. He closed his notebook and got up.

But Angela While didn't look up. Just carried on touching the boy. Raining love down on him through every fleeting fingertip, the way only a parent can.

And as only a child can, Robbie ignored her, and carried on jamming mismatched Lego bricks on to each other.

"Look!" he said, holding up a chunk of coloured rubble.

"That's wonderful, sweetheart," she said with a dazzling smile.

Marvel didn't know how mothers did it.

"Does Adam see his son?"

Angela shook her head and lowered her voice. "No. And I don't want him to. I called him when Robbie was born. I mean, he's got rights, hasn't he? But he said he wasn't interested —" She gave a bitter laugh and blew her nose into a tissue she took from the sleeve of her jumper. "Said he was going to start over again and do it *better* next time."

"Do what better?" said Marvel.

"Who knows?" she sighed. "I'm just glad he's not doing it with us."

Marvel didn't get back to Tiverton until the sun had fallen behind the hills of Exmoor.

After seeing Angela While, he had called Ralph Stourbridge and briefed him on the day's events. He didn't tell him everything, of course. For one thing, he left out the bit about restraining and cuffing the wrong woman — the wrong *pregnant* woman.

Also calling her a mammal. It wasn't an official sexist insult, obviously. Not like *bitch* or *cow*. But Marvel would nonetheless have been very reluctant to hear it repeated in front of a disciplinary tribunal — which is absolutely where it could have ended up if Catherine While hadn't caught his brow with her engagement ring, in a back-handed stroke of good fortune.

He'd made sure she understood that she was *very lucky* that he was prepared to overlook her assault on a police officer while resisting arrest. But she hadn't seemed to be interested in pursuing a complaint about their little tussle. Apparently she'd been so distraught at discovering that her husband wasn't a virgin in a glass box before he'd met her that she'd just wanted Marvel out of the house so that she could weep and plot.

Or whatever it was that a woman did who felt herself scorned.

Either way, Marvel had to admit that he'd had a very close shave. Not his closest, obviously — a man like him, who took risks and lived by his instincts, was sure to have a few near misses throughout his career, and this was just one more — but it would certainly be something to regale his mates with down the pub. If he ever found a decent pub in this sheep-laden shithole.

Or some mates.

What the hell. He didn't care! A close shave always made him feel alive in a way usually only achieved by a near-death experience. Nothing made his heart pound like a precipice sidestepped, a bullet dodged, or the end of an affair.

He shook a cigarette out of the packet and stuck it between his lips, loving the dirty chemical taste of the filter. He didn't have a match, but for now that was enough.

His car bumped over the kerb outside the police station and came to a halt on the pavement. There was no car park at the station, and he really didn't have time to park at the supermarket and walk past the benches like everybody else.

He looked at his watch. It was still light, thanks to summer, and the air was still warm, the sky still blue. Marvel flinched as a sheep baaed somewhere worryingly close. He turned off the engine and just sat — his brain bulging with a million permutations.

Investigating a murder was like doing a jigsaw puzzle in the dark. The constant fingertip-feeling and testing and turning. The picking up and the putting down and the picking up again.

The trying to make things *fit*.

Marvel felt closer right now to seeing the picture on the box than Ralph Stourbridge had ever been.

And further away too, because that picture had been drawn for him by a liar. A serial thief who'd assumed he'd found the knife that had killed his mother in a house he was burgling.

Marvel snorted. That might be the biggest and best coincidence he'd encountered in his twenty-two years in homicide. Or it could be the twisted imaginings of a disturbed delinquent.

If he hadn't wanted a murder case so badly, he would have written it off as the latter.

But he *did* want a murder case.

Very badly.

So he was prepared to consider the former, dig deeper, risk more.

Marvel had a unique technique when it came to solving crime. He liked to consider all the smoke to be fire, just to see where it took him.

So . . .

Adam While *had* assaulted Jack Bright, and set his house ablaze.

A woman who'd once loved While had believed he did have the capacity to kill, and While had hidden that past from the woman who loved him now.

While had been jealous and angry with his *pregnant* wife on the day that *pregnant* Eileen Bright had been killed by a knife.

He had been picked up in the lay-by where the knife had been found close to the body. And had a very similar knife . . .

He *still* had that knife.

It just wasn't the *right* knife.

"Shit!" Marvel yelled at the steering wheel. "Bollocks and *shit!*"

The window was down and a woman wheeling a supermarket trolley said, "No need for that sort of language!"

"How would *you* know?" Marvel shot back at her. Then he put his head out of the window and shouted after her, "Hey! Are you *stealing* that trolley?"

The woman hurried away, looking daggers over her shoulder.

Marvel withdrew, and resumed glaring at the steering wheel. Whichever way he looked at it, the boy was the key.

There was little doubt he was Goldilocks, and with his cooperation it would be an open-and-shut case. In fact, over one hundred open-and-shut cases! Scores of burglaries that could be cleared off the books and boost the force's solve-rate stats in an instant. It would mean that Marvel's first case with a new force would be a wild success. It would go a long way to winning him the status he craved, without the need for years of hard work.

There was only one problem . . .

Marvel couldn't arrest Adam While for the murder of Eileen Bright. Without any connection to the murder weapon, all he had on While was the same non-evidence that Stourbridge had had three years ago.

Plus an ex-wife with a feeling in her water.

Marvel got out of the car and slammed the door hard. He almost bumped into Reynolds inside the glass front door of the little police station.

"Any luck, sir?"

"Some."

"Enough to arrest Adam While?"

"No," snapped Marvel. "Did you finish up at the house?"

"Almost, sir. Got everything in the van that needs to go back to Exeter. Just some personal items and clothing for Rice and me to pick up tomorrow."

"Good," said Marvel. "I told you the capture house would work."

"You did," said Reynolds. "And it did."

"Where's Parrott?"

"He left at the end of our shift, sir."

Marvel ignored the fact that Reynolds was still there past the end of his shift.

"Duty solicitor here?"

"Car trouble, sir," said Reynolds. "I'm a bit wary of keeping the boy this long without legal representation . . ."

"We've put in the call," said Marvel testily. "Not our fault if the solicitor's dragging his heels."

Elizabeth Rice walked in with a bag of apples and a sandwich. "For Jack," she said. "He doesn't eat McDonald's."

"I told you so," said Reynolds.

Rice ignored him and took the key to the holding cell from the WPC with the cider nose who was on the desk. She disappeared down the corridor.

"It's some life he's been leading," mused Reynolds. "Kid his age, supporting the family through crime. It's Dickensian, isn't it?"

Marvel grunted.

Rice shouted something.

Marvel and Reynolds frowned at each other. "What did she say?" said Marvel.

"I didn't catch it," said Reynolds.

They both started down the corridor. "Rice?" called Reynolds, and broke into a half-jog. "Rice?"

Rice was standing in the holding cell with her apples and sandwich.

"He's gone!"

"Spare change? . . . Spare change?"

Feet passed. Somebody dropped something into the ice-cream tub.

"Thank you," said the homeless man.

More feet.

They stopped.

"Spare change?"

But there was no corresponding rattle of money in the box.

The homeless man looked up, and flinched, snatching up the tub as he did, cradling his cash, even as one hunched shoulder protected his ear.

But the boy didn't hit him.

Instead he tossed something at him.

A snake!

The man cried out in fear as it dropped into his lap in poisonous stripes.

But it wasn't a snake. It was a necktie. Red silk with sharp white stripes.

"We need a grown-up in the house," said Jack. "If you still want to come home."

"How the *hell*?" said Marvel.

The mattress was leaned drunkenly against the wall under the window, but the window was still locked. There were crayons and fake flowers on the floor.

"How the *hell*?" Marvel said again — but they worked it out eventually.

Jack Bright had propped the mattress against the wall under the window and had stood on, or bounced off, its precarious edge to grab the flowers from the windowsill. He'd bent the wire stem of a single fake flower into a lock pick and opened the cell door, then somehow sneaked past the reception desk and out of the front door.

"Let's go and get the little bastard," said Marvel.

As his car was parked conveniently outside, they piled into that, with Rice still holding the sandwich and apples.

Marvel started the engine. "Where are we going, Reynolds?"

"Sir?"

"What's the address?"

"Uhhh . . . I don't know, sir."

Marvel looked sharply at him. "You don't know his address?"

"No, sir."

"But you're the arresting officer."

Now Marvel *and* Rice both looked at Reynolds, who started to sweat.

"You didn't get his address?"

"No, sir."

There was a thick silence, and then Marvel said, "Please tell me you read him his rights . . ."

"Sir —" Reynolds started, and Marvel banged the dashboard with his fist so hard that it cracked.

"You bloody *idiot*, Reynolds!"

"Sir, it's just . . . it was a weird situation. It wasn't a normal arrest, you see, as I'm sure you appreciate. I mean, he was there in the bed and . . . so it was all very odd and I admit I was a bit thrown."

"Then what's all that bollocks in your notebook about capturing Goldilocks single-handed! '*Silently I bloody pounced*'! And now it turns out that not only didn't you pounce, but you didn't even read the little shit his rights! Which means he hasn't escaped from legal custody because he was never legally *in* custody! Jesus Christ! We're back to square fucking *one*. No! Square *minus* one, because now he knows we'll be after him!"

"I apologize, sir," said Reynolds stiffly — and in a tone that implied that Marvel should really be getting over it by now.

"Well, bollocks to your apology!" shouted Marvel. "Just *bollocks* to it! I'm not calling Stourbridge. *You* can call him and ask him for the address and explain to him how the Goldilocks prime suspect walked out of a police cell and now we don't know where to find him because you screwed up the arrest."

"Sir?" said Rice from the back seat.

"What?" snapped Marvel.

"Wouldn't Toby know the address?"

"Who the fuck is Toby?"

"DC Parrott, sir," said Rice. "I mean, he's been here donkey's years, and even if he wasn't involved, he's sure to know where the Bright family live, isn't he?"

There was a brief silence, then Marvel said, "Good thinking, Rice. Where's Parrott?"

"I imagine he went home, sir," said Reynolds.

"Well, imagine calling him," said Marvel. "And imagine telling him you need him to cover your arse."

"Who are *you*?" said Merry suspiciously from the living-room doorway. And then, before he could tell her, her eyes lighted on the tub in the man's hand. "Have you got ice cream?"

"No," he said. "Sorry." He glanced at Jack. "I should have brought ice cream," he said. "I should have brought *something*."

"Doesn't matter," said Jack. "We didn't expect anything from you."

"Who *are* you?" said Merry again.

"It's Dad," said Jack bluntly.

She frowned at the man. Took out her vampire teeth and looked him up and down.

The beard. The dirty clothes. The red silk tie looped around his neck.

"You got so tall, Merry!" He stepped towards her, but she slid backwards around the doorframe to keep her distance.

He stopped and touched his cheek and glanced at Jack. "It's the beard. I'll shave it off."

He smiled tentatively. They didn't.

He stared slowly around the scorched hallway, at the granulated carpet, the blistered front door. Then back at Merry.

"What are you reading?"

She looked at the book in her hand — her finger a bookmark — and read the cover to him. "*It* by Stephen King."

He frowned. "Aren't you a bit young for that?"

"It's about clowns in the drains," she shrugged. "It's not *real*."

He gave a shaky laugh. "I've missed you," he said. "I've missed you all so much." His voice was filled with emotion, but his words went un-echoed.

"Where have you *been*?" said Merry.

"Well . . . I went away for a little bit."

"For a *long* bit," she corrected him.

"You're right. For far too long. I'm so sorry."

"Were you sad? Joy said you were sad."

"Yes I was," he nodded. "Very very sad. I felt . . . well, it doesn't matter what I felt. I should never have gone. But every day I was gone I thought about you all and missed you all, and wanted to see you again.

"I would have come home sooner but . . ." He shrugged, then looked at Jack. "But I understand. I do understand."

Then he straightened up and smoothed down the tie as if preparing for a job interview. "But I'm home now. I'll be better this time round. I promise."

He smiled at Merry, but she only stared back at him in blank solemnity.

Jack opened his backpack. "I got you a suit," he said. "So you can get a job."

He hung it over the door to the front room. It was nice. Pale grey.

"Thank you."

"You'll have to get your own shoes."

"Daddy?"

They all looked up.

Joy stood in the living-room doorway, filthy and shining.

She fell into her father's arms, and he caught her.

Toby Parrott didn't pick up his phone for fifteen long minutes. Marvel knew exactly, because he made the increasingly sweaty Reynolds keep trying the number while they all waited for directions in the car.

While they waited, Marvel planned his strategy.

He didn't know who'd answer the door at the Bright home, but he did know he didn't have a warrant. Any other time he could have demanded entry to search for a prisoner escaped from custody. But this time — thanks to Reynolds — the prisoner had never officially been *in* custody and therefore could not be said to have escaped it. In fact, if he took a fancy, Jack Bright could probably sue the shit out of two police forces for keeping him in a cell without arrest or charge or even legal representation. And him a juvenile, too . . .

So, although it wasn't in his nature, Marvel knew he would have to proceed exceedingly carefully. Keep it cordial. Seek consent.

It was irritating, but there it was.

When Parrott finally did answer his phone, Reynolds spoke in low, clipped sentences, and hung up within the minute.

291

"It's on Blundell's Road," he said. "He doesn't have the number, but he says he'll know it when he sees it, so he's meeting us at the car showroom there."

Marvel started the engine and bumped off the kerb and swung the car in a squealing arc. He glanced at his sergeant's anxiously jiggling knee.

"Excited, Reynolds?" he said. "Now you can catch Goldilocks *twice*."

In the warm summer twilight, they carried armfuls of newspapers from the house to the garden.

At first it was a slow process: take a thick slice of newsprint from the canyon wall and carry it outside, where Arthur Bright was building them into a careful pyramid in the centre of the lawn. But the lower the canyon wall got, the more excited Joy became, and her excitement was infectious, so that within minutes all three of them were running in and out of the back door, giggling and bumping into each other in the doorway, shrieking at scuttling spiders, and slipping and sliding on fallen issues of The Times and the Daily Mail and the Tiverton Gazette.

Slowly but surely, one canyon wall completely disappeared from the kitchen, leaving a broad strip of pale floor in its place.

While Joy and Merry carried newspapers past him, Jack stood and stared at the floor — amazed that it had been there all along, and how easy it had been to find it. Then he hoisted another armful of papers off the counter and headed outside.

Finally Arthur held up a hand. "I think that's enough for now," he smiled.

Jack, Joy and Merry watched him, bright-eyed and breathless, as he reached into his pocket and pulled out a box of matches.

"Stand clear now," he said.

It was getting dark when Toby Parrott waved them down in the light that spilled from the showroom filled with luxury cars. Marvel had never seen a luxury car on the streets of Tiverton, and made a mental note to be very suspicious of the dealership when he next had the time.

Parrott jogged over to them wearing a very old tracksuit — bobbly and too short in the ankle. He got in the back with Rice, and Marvel drove slowly out on Blundell's Road.

"I think that's the one," said Toby Parrott, pointing.

"Are you sure?" said Reynolds.

"As I can be."

"If it's not that one, we can just knock on the neighbours' doors," said Rice. "Someone will know them."

"It's getting a bit late for that, isn't it?" said Reynolds.

Marvel frowned at him in the rear-view mirror. "What's wrong with you, man? We're the *police*!" He parked badly and they all got out.

Marvel looked at the neat little terraced house. It was not what he'd expected. Then again, nothing about Goldilocks had been what he'd expected.

The windows were clean and there was a four-foot strip of trimmed lawn behind a low retaining wall.

Spick and span, he thought.

Then he sniffed the air. "Is that smoke?"

The glass porthole in the front door was smashed, and through it they could hear the sound of a child sobbing as if its heart would break.

Marvel stepped up to the door. He hesitated for a second, then leaned forward and looked through the porthole. Inside was very dark, but he could just about make out a small girl sitting on the floor of the hallway, holding a football to her chest and crying her eyes out.

Marvel knocked on the door. The crying didn't stop.

He knocked again, more loudly.

He wrinkled his nose and looked at Rice and Reynolds, who'd been joined by Parrott.

Rice crossed the road to get a better view of the house. "Something's on fire round the back, sir!"

Marvel hammered on the door. "Oi!" he said to the child. "Are you all right in there?"

The child turned her face towards him and slowly shook her head. "No!" she wailed, and went on crying.

"Shit," said Marvel irritably. "Stand clear!" He backed up a few paces and ran at the door. He hit it hard and bounced off, staggering backwards with his arms flailing.

Reynolds grabbed him and stopped him from toppling over the little wall, just as a gaunt, unshaven man in a khaki T-shirt and a red silk tie opened the door.

"Hello."

Marvel fumbled for his ID. "Mr Bright?"

"Yes."

"We're looking for Jack."

"Hold on," said Bright, and looked behind him, distracted by the kid still bawling on the floor. He turned and picked her up and came back to the door with her sitting in the crook of his elbow, still crying, and with her head on his shoulder. Now that she was closer, Marvel could see that what she was holding was not a football but a large tortoise with a patient look on its face, as if it had seen it all before.

"She's upset about the lawn," said Bright cryptically.

"I just *mowed* it!" wept the tear-stained child. "And now it's on *fire*!"

"It'll grow back, Merry. I promise." He patted her back and explained to Marvel, "We're having a bit of a clear-out."

He smiled and Marvel tried to do the same, even though he was itching at the delay. *Keep it cordial*, he reminded himself. *Or they'll sue . . .*

Bright held his daughter a little away from him so he could look at her face. "You're getting salt in Donald's eyes."

The child stopped crying and sniffed down at the tortoise. He put her down and she disappeared into the house.

Marvel opened his mouth to ask after Jack again, but before he could speak, Reynolds said, "That's my tie!"

"Reynolds . . ." he said sharply.

But Reynolds leaned to look around Mr Bright and said, "And that's my suit!" And before Marvel could stop him, Reynolds shouldered his way past the surprised Mr Bright, and took a pale grey suit from where it hung on the living-room door.

"Hey, you can't just come in here!" said Arthur Bright. "Aren't you supposed to have a warrant or something?"

Shit. The W-word! Marvel gave Reynolds a furious look, but he opened the jacket defiantly to show a name label sewn into the lining.

REYNOLDS.

"See?" he said.

And, very slowly, DCI Marvel smiled.

"Mr Bright," he said, "we're coming into your home to search the premises under the Theft Act of nineteen sixty-eight due to stolen goods being in plain view in the house, and in the reasonable expectation of finding further stolen goods therein, and/or the perpetrator of the crime of burglary, during the commission of which said goods may have been stolen. Do you understand?"

"No," said Bright, with a confused look. "Does anybody?"

Jack sat on the grass and watched Joy dance around the fire. Now and then she threw another stack of papers on the pyre, or poked it with an old rake, laughing at the sparks that exploded into the pale evening sky.

Soft grey petals of ash fell all around them like gentle snow.

Merry came out of the house and put Donald in his run, well away from the flames.

"Why are the police looking for you?"

"What?" he said. "Where?"

Merry pointed. "They're at the front door."

Jack scrambled to his feet. Through the flames he saw dark shapes moving in the house, and his throat pulsed with fear.

Those bar stewards always get you for something . . .

For a single, heart-tingling moment he stood there, blank with panic.

Then he hugged Merry hard. "Don't say anything," he said.

And he vaulted over the fence into Mrs Reynolds' garden.

Jack ran to the door and knocked hard.

Mrs Reynolds didn't answer.

He knocked again, looking desperately at the fence, and up at his own bedroom window, where the little photo frame still stood empty on the sill. If anybody looked out of that window now, they would see him cringing here by the door, and there was nothing he could do about it.

He knocked again. *Come on!* he screamed in his head. *Come on!*

And then Mrs Reynolds *was* coming. He could see her through the glass. She didn't look pleased to see him, and for a dreadful moment Jack thought she was going to wave him away and refuse to open the door.

He tried not to look worried. Tried not to look like he was on the run from the police. He calmed his breathing. Straightened up. Mustered a smile.

With a frown, the old lady unlocked the door and opened it.

"What do *you* want?" she said.

"Hi," said Jack. "I've come to fix your lawnmower."

★ ★ ★

298

Jack Bright wasn't in the house.

It wasn't an easy house to search and it had taken them longer than expected. Every room was a maze of newspaper walls and tunnels and dead ends. Just when they thought they'd exhausted the search, they'd realize a pile was a bed they had to look under, or that a wall hid a wardrobe they couldn't open.

Parrott had seen a mouse and the whole house stunk of mould — and something Marvel didn't want to put his finger on. No wonder Jack Bright kept the lawn mown and the windows washed to stay under the radar of the authorities — inside, the house wasn't fit for dogs, let alone children.

In the back bedroom Marvel found an empty photo frame and — on the floor — the crumpled picture of two children and a beach ball.

Despite everything, he'd given a short, bitter laugh.

Now he stood in the twilight with ash falling around him and glared angrily into the crackling fire.

The little shit had given them the slip. He had no doubt that Jack had been here recently. *So* recently that Arthur Bright's stalling at the door had probably made all the difference.

The two sisters stood and watched him silently.

"Where's your brother?" he demanded.

"I don't know," said the older girl.

"I don't know either," said the kid with the tortoise. Marvel pursed his lips.

"You want ten pounds?" he said. "Each?"

"No," said the older girl, just as the little one said, "Yes please!" so Marvel looked only at the little one. He bent down with his hands on his knees to get closer to her level.

"You tell me where your brother is, and I'll give you ten quid."

"Mmmmm . . ." The child screwed up her face as if she were thinking.

"I'll tell you about vampires for *five* quid," she said, holding up five little fingers in case Marvel couldn't count. "Or worms for *three*."

Marvel straightened up. He brushed ashes off his shoulders and headed back indoors, shouting, "Search the house again!"

Like many things in life, there wasn't much wrong with Mrs Reynolds' lawnmower that couldn't be fixed by a good clean and some WD40.

Jack sat on an old can of paint and used a chisel he found in a toolbox to scrape many seasons' worth of stiff, dry grass from inside the skirt of the mower.

He'd shut the shed door. He'd told Mrs Reynolds it was to stop the ashes floating in. At first when he did, he'd just stood there, with his ear pressed against the wood, trying to hear what was going on next door.

But he couldn't hear anything much with the door shut, so he turned on the light and tipped the mower on to its good side to avoid the oil fouling the air filter, and got to work.

Once he'd cleared the underside of the skirt, he could see that more long pieces of grass had wrapped themselves around the shaft of the blade, slowing it up and making it stick. He sliced through them and peeled each one carefully away.

He realized he was enjoying himself. More than that, he felt *like* himself for the first time in ages. Like a boy helping a neighbour. It felt good . . .

He jumped as Mrs Reynolds opened the door. She didn't say anything. Just stood and watched him spray the cleared shaft so that the blade would turn easily.

"How's your sister?"

"Which one?" said Jack.

"The vampire hunter."

Jack smiled. "She's into scary clowns now. She does that. Gets a new *thing* and wants to know all about it. She reads everything. I have to bring her books all the time because she reads them so fast."

He cleaned the plug and topped up the oil.

"Been asking my son to do this for weeks," she said. "He never does."

Jack stood up, primed the mower and pulled the starter. It roared easily into life, but only for a moment because he cut the engine so the shed didn't fill with fumes.

"It's a good mower," said Jack. "It should last for years. But you need to keep it clean underneath or the dead grass will clog it up."

"*Hello!*"

Jack froze and looked at the door. *Marvel!*

Mrs Reynolds went outside, leaving the shed door halfway open, and Jack caught a fleeting glimpse of Marvel peering over the fence. He quickly ducked out of his line of sight. But it was almost dark outside now, and the light was on in the shed. If Marvel came much closer, or the door swung open any further, there would be nowhere to hide . . .

He could see the detective through the crack in the door, leaning heavily on the fence with one hand, holding up his ID with the other. He must be standing on the cold frame. Jack pursed his lips. He'd better not break it!

"We're looking for your neighbour," said Marvel. "Jack Bright. You know him?"

Jack held his breath.

"Oh yes," said Mrs Reynolds, peering at the ID. Then she said, "My son's in the police as well, you know."

Marvel ignored her. "Have you seen Jack tonight?"

"Why?" she said suspiciously. "What's he done?"

"He's wanted for burglary."

"Burglary!" she said, sounding shocked, and looked at the shed.

Jack flinched and willed her to look away — mentally *begged* her — but instead the old woman walked straight towards him. Through the crack, Jack watched her getting closer and closer, his teeth gritted so hard that his jaw ached, hope draining from him like bathwater.

Mrs Reynolds reached for the shed door.

And shut it.

Jack blinked in shock. He heard the key squeak in the lock, then the little scrape of a flowerpot being moved.

"I think you must be mistaken," he heard her say. "Nobody steals stuff around here."

Jack waited for Mrs Reynolds to come back.

He put the paint can close to the wall of the shed so he could lean back and close his eyes. The petrol fumes had dissipated and he could smell the wood. As he drifted, he thought of the timber yard.

Don't come here again.

Jack grimaced at the memory, then relaxed again. His head nodded on to his chest. He was so tired. He could sleep for England.

He was almost asleep — almost on that wonderful cusp between two cruel worlds — when there was a metal scrape and Mrs Reynolds opened the door.

Jack scrambled to his feet and they stared at each other.

"Come with me," she finally said.

He followed her across the patio to the back door.

"Take your shoes off, please."

He did, and they went through the sparkling kitchen to a lounge so light and flowery that it was like summer indoors.

Mrs Reynolds pointed at the little cream velvet sofa and he sat down carefully with his dirty trainers on his knees. Mrs Reynolds herself wore white leather loafers with immaculate soles.

"I like to keep the carpet nice," she explained, and Jack thought of all the coffee he'd splashed and the red wine he'd thrown and the food he'd trodden into countless carpets during the past year. Carpets that he now imagined had belonged to people like Mrs Reynolds, who had not ratted on him to Marvel, even though her son was a policeman.

He felt shame warm his cheeks. None of it had brought back what he'd lost.

"Are you a burglar?" said Mrs Reynolds, surprising Jack with her bluntness.

He took in a breath to lie about it. Then said, "I was."

"But not any more," said Mrs Reynolds, and dusted her hands briskly together, as if *her* decision was made and so *his* was just a formality. Then she got up and went to the mantelpiece, which held an eclectic collection of small china figurines. There were posh ladies and shepherds with flutes and harlequins and bullfighters and . . .

Jack thought of his hammer. Of the powder they'd make.

Mrs Reynolds picked up one of the figurines and handed it to him. "This is for your sister," she said.

It was a clown. Four inches tall and sad-faced, wearing a big yellow flower and baggy checked trousers, and with a bunch of balloons on thick china string.

Jack looked up but Mrs Reynolds was already walking to the front door. He followed her, slipping the clown into his pocket in the hallway so he could put his shoes back on.

"I think you should go out the front in case someone's waiting for you in your house, don't you?"

He hadn't thought of that. But she was right. "Yes," he nodded.

"How many newspapers will your father be burning?"

Jack widened his eyes at Mrs Reynolds' and said, "A *lot*."

She pursed her lips and said, "*Hmff*."

Then she opened the door, peered outside to make sure the coast was clear, and showed Jack out on to the street.

He turned to say thank you — but Mrs Reynolds had already shut the door in his face.

"Why didn't you tell me you'd been married before?"

Adam had brought home a toy horse on wheels. He'd knocked and Catherine had opened the door to find it there, by itself. Then he'd neighed from round the corner and come out laughing, and kissed her as if he'd been gone for a year, and kissed the baby via the top of her tummy, and then wheeled the horse through to the kitchen, doubled over it like an enormous hunchbacked child, talking nineteen to the dozen.

"Got it from a Blue Circle rep. Last year's marketing, apparently. Isn't it great? He'll be galloping about on it for years. Or she will. We should get riding lessons, too. But later, of course. But this will be a great way to start, won't it? And it was free! I couldn't turn it down, could I?"

Catherine had followed him.

Cold.

Silent.

She'd practised the line so she wouldn't falter, and took a deep breath so she'd get to the end of it without wobbling.

"Why didn't you tell me you'd been married before?"

"What?" He didn't look at her; he spoke to the horse.

"Why didn't you tell me you'd been married before?"

Slowly Adam straightened up and met her eyes.

If he said *To protect you* — or if he tried to deny it — she'd kill him.

But he said, "I don't know."

Then he looked at the garden through the window and shook his head and said, "I really don't know."

Catherine did falter then — but not for the reason she'd thought she might. Suddenly she was sad, rather than angry, and had to resist the urge to throw her arms around him and tell him she loved him and it didn't matter.

But she had to go on, because it *did* matter and she needed to know.

"Angela," she said, hating the name.

"Yes," he said. "How did you find out?"

"A policeman was here."

He blinked in surprise. "About the burglary?"

"No," she said. "About Eileen Bright."

Adam shrunk. Before her very eyes, everything about him seemed to grow smaller and weaker. Paler. Everything . . . *diminished*.

He bent and leaned his elbows on the kitchen counter and rubbed his face as if he were very, very tired.

"I was too scared to tell you," he finally sighed.

"Scared of what?" said Catherine.

"That you'd leave me."

"I'd *leave* you?"

He straightened up. "*She* did. Angela left me afterwards."

"After what?"

"After I was questioned."

"But you hadn't done anything wrong!"

He shrugged. "She left me anyway."

Then he told her about it. About stopping in a lay-by one parched day. About being put into the back of a police car — embarrassed and apologetic. About the six worst, longest hours of his life, where he'd gone from confused to affronted to angry to scared, to scared, and scared again.

"I can't tell you how frightening it was, Cath," Adam said softly, looking away and swallowing a lump in his throat. He picked up an orange from the bowl on the counter and squeezed it like a stress toy.

"I mean, I'd stopped for a pee in a lay-by and suddenly I'm a suspect in a murder case! At first it was like a joke, then a stupid mistake, and then I realized they weren't kidding, and they really thought I might have had something to do with killing a person. A woman. A *pregnant* woman. I mean, for *fuck's sake!*"

He looked at Catherine and she saw on his face the same shock and outrage that he must have felt then — it had been right there just under the surface, ready to relive at a moment's notice, despite the years that had passed. And now tears threatened to spill from his eyes.

"Adam . . ." she murmured.

He wiped his sleeve across his face.

"I wanted to die. I swear to you, Cath — at that moment, I would rather have died than sit there and have those people try to make me say I'd done that thing. That *sick, vicious* thing!"

Catherine nodded. Her own vague memory of the murder made her shiver even now.

"And then, when it's *finally over*, I come home and she's left me. Just gone! Just packed her stuff and gone, and my marriage is over, just like that, and I lost everything I'd ever had. If it weren't for my dad bailing me out, I'd have lost the house, too. As it was, I had to borrow money from him to pay Angie off. That's why I had all that debt when we first met. Why it's been so hard to —"

Catherine interrupted, "But I don't understand. You mean your marriage was fine up until then?"

"Absolutely!"

"Then why would she leave you over that?"

"Ask *her!*" he said angrily. "I guess she was stupid enough to believe it. After all, the police are questioning me, so I *must* be guilty, right? Even though I've never committed a crime in my *life*. You know me, Cath! You know I could never do anything like that!"

Catherine said nothing. She *wanted* to be on Adam's side. But he'd lied to her. He'd been married. He'd been questioned about a murder. He'd *lied* to her . . .

"Cath," he said urgently. "It's just like you said about the burglary. You made one bad choice — not to tell me. And after that it all got much harder."

She nodded slowly. She'd lied to him, too.

"If I'd told you I'd been married, you'd have wanted to know more. Wanted to know what happened, and if I'd told you the truth then maybe you'd have left me too! Why wouldn't you? That bitch did! Because there's no smoke without fire, right? And fuck that *innocent until proven guilty* shit, because — trust me — nobody believes that. Specially not the HR bastards at the place where I used to earn three times what I'm bringing in now. *Shit!* I have a degree in Geography, Cath! You think I want to drive a van and sell horse feed to farmers? I used to be a surveyor. Managed a whole office in Weston. But suddenly HR think it's a bad idea to employ a man who's been questioned about a *murder*. Not arrested, not charged, not tried and fucking convicted! Just *questioned* and then released.

"It was a mistake!" he shouted. "Not *my* mistake — *their* mistake. But they're not the ones who suffered for it. That was all me."

Adam's jaw worked angrily at the memories.

"So I lost my wife and my job, and I was in debt and I thought my life was over . . ."

He took her hand and spoke calmly. "Until I met you, Cath. You saved me, you really did. You gave me the strength to pick myself up. You gave me the chance to start all over again, and now we're creating a whole new life together and all I want is to love you and the baby and to work *so hard* to give you everything you both deserve, because I'm *so lucky* to have you and to have another chance to get this *right* . . ."

Adam shook his head in wonder. Then his voice became bitter again.

310

"And then this little *shit* breaks into our home, and suddenly I'm scared all over again in case the same thing happens. He makes threats and allegations. He lies to you. He says he's Eileen Bright's son, but is he *really*? We have no proof! Maybe he found something with my name on it and recognized it and hatched some kind of plan to blackmail us. Or maybe he's just crazy. Who knows what's next? Will he threaten to tell your friends? My boss? Put signs up on lampposts? I've been through that shit, Cath, and I wouldn't wish it on my worst enemy. The looks, the whispers, the conversations that stop when you come into the room ... my God! If it started all over again — and to *you*, as well — who could blame you if you left?

"So *that's* why I didn't tell you — because I was so scared of losing you and the baby. If it happened again, it would just fucking *kill* me ..."

He stopped, breathless with talk and emotion, squeezing her hand as if it were all that attached him to sanity.

But Catherine didn't feel sane. Catherine was in turmoil. It was all too much to take in at once. The man she loved was baring his soul to her about a great trauma in his life. A great injustice. But instead of overwhelming love and support for him, she felt only a low, rumbling panic. She remembered earthquake survivors saying that the ground under their feet had turned to liquid and rolled in great waves. That was how she felt. As if she'd built something on solid ground that had suddenly turned to ocean. And now here she was — bracing herself in a doorway, not knowing whether to stay here and ride it out, or leave the only thing that protected her and swim for it across a cold dark sea with no land in sight.

Mum never liked him.

Catherine almost laughed at the random thought. She had always dismissed that dislike as jealousy, thinking that her mother just couldn't come to terms with no longer being the most important person in her only daughter's life.

Or did her mother's prejudice come from another place? A place of experience? Of gut instinct?

Catherine just didn't know. Couldn't tell. Had lost all objectivity.

Before the fat policeman had come round, she'd thought she knew most things. Now she didn't know *anything*, and felt she might never again.

"Cath?" begged Adam. "Please say something. Please talk to me."

But Catherine didn't know what to say.

Slowly she withdrew her hand from his. She couldn't think clearly while they were connected.

Then she thought of the baby inside her.

And remembered that she and Adam were connected whether he was touching her or not.

For the rest of their lives.

Marvel had called an eight a.m. meeting in the interview room. Reynolds was there by seven forty-five. While he waited, he picked nervously at the scab of horrible coincidence . . .

Something going on next door . . . the boy looks all of twelve . . . She'll break my fence and then who'll pay? Not the scruffy brother, that's for sure!

The scruffy brother was Goldilocks!

Reynolds felt sick at how he had missed it. Where *missed* was a euphemism for "wilfully overlooked". Because a modicum of curiosity, a grain of suspicion, a *smidgen* of effort, would have uncovered the truth. And then he'd have been a hero. A lucky hero, indeed, but a hero nonetheless.

Now he couldn't be a hero. All he could hope for now was that nobody ever found out. The fact that Marvel had *spoken* to his mother and yet appeared not to have added two and two together to make four, was an almost miraculous escape. He was suspicious that it might be too good to be true, and was fidgety with dread.

He also wished that he hadn't been *quite* so chipper in his notebook about his solo apprehension of the arch criminal, Goldilocks.

Silently I pounced on the suspect . . .

At the time it had felt like the truth, but now he went hot at the thought of anyone finding out that, in fact, he could have pounced on the suspect over his mother's garden fence any time he fancied since she'd moved in.

Reynolds sighed and ran a hand through his hair.

He was doing that all the time now, like a tic. Running his fingers through it seemed easier, as if it were just that bit thinner. At night he woke from dreams of baldness and touched his head frantically for reassurance.

Rice and Parrott came in just before eight. Rice was eating the sandwich she'd bought yesterday for Jack Bright. It was cheese and onion and Reynolds could smell it from here.

Marvel came in a few minutes after eight and slapped the Goldilocks file down on the little Formica table.

"Right. Yesterday was a disaster from beginning to end. The only good bit was that Jack Bright escaped from custody and spared us all the embarrassment of having to release him on a technicality . . ." He paused just long enough to make Reynolds brace himself, before going on, "Which gives us the opportunity to do it *properly* next time."

Reynolds' phone vibrated on the table and he glanced at the screen.

Mr Passmore.

Jesus. As if he needed to be reminded of something else he'd screwed up!

"Take it if you want," shrugged Marvel. "We'll wait."

Reynolds got up and stepped into the corridor — acutely aware that they were waiting in silence, listening. He walked further down the corridor into reception and sat on one of the three plastic chairs as he answered the phone.

Mr Passmore's insurance company had refused to pay out on his claim and the man was apoplectic. He demanded that Reynolds intervene. He demanded he come and reinvestigate the scene. He demanded *justice*, goddammit! And a replacement TV.

Reynolds opened his mouth to tell him they'd caught Goldilocks and it wasn't him who had trashed his house, but Passmore was so illogically angry that he chickened out. Instead he fobbed the man off, then hung up and sat for a moment with his elbows on his knees, staring at his very shiny shoes. He hardly noticed the door opening and two people walking in with a pushchair. It was only when one of them stopped on his way to the desk and stood right in front of him and said, "Hi," that Reynolds looked up at Jack Bright.

"*Hur!*" Reynolds shouted in incoherent surprise. He leapt to his feet and grabbed the boy's arm in an iron grip, although Jack didn't try to pull away from him.

"Jack Bright!" he cried loudly, looking around for back-up — or an audience — but the desk officer was nowhere to be seen. "Jack Bright, I'm arresting you on suspicion of burglary! You do not have to say anything, but it may harm your defence if you do not mention when questioned something you later rely on in court!"

He stopped and took a breath, his heart pounding. Bright waited politely for him to finish. "Anything you *do* say may be used in evidence. Do you understand these rights?"

"Yes," said the boy.

Then the other person spoke. The one pushing the buggy. Reynolds looked at him for the first time. He was a young man wearing cargo shorts, with hairless legs and no eyebrows.

He looked at Jack and said, "Are you *sure* you understand, mate? Whatever they try to tell you, you're going inside."

Reynolds immediately bristled. "Who are you?"

"This is my friend," said Jack. "He knows all about knives."

"Good for him," said Reynolds. Then he saw that the policewoman with the cider nose had reappeared behind the desk. "Get the duty solicitor down here for a juvenile. Urgently!"

Then he turned to Jack Bright and said, "Come with me," and led him down the corridor to the interview room with a new spring in his step.

Screw Marvel! he thought. He *had* caught Goldilocks twice — and was getting better at it each time.

Smooth Louis Bridge picked up the evidence bag containing the murder weapon.

"Can I take it out?"

"No," said Marvel.

Louis sighed and hunched more closely over it, pressing the plastic against the knife, the better to examine it.

Unconsciously, they all leaned forward. Baz stood on Jack's knees with his chubby hands splayed on the Formica, watching as intently as anyone.

The only sound in the room was the photocopier sucking electricity out of the wall to keep its little green light running.

Finally Louis put down the bag.

"That's a VC knife."

"What's that?" said Marvel.

Louis picked the bag up again quickly, as if he'd made a mistake in letting it go. He turned it slowly over and over in his hands as he spoke, barely looking up.

"VC is one of the top three or four makers in the whole world. I mean, there's him and Jay Fisher and Gil Hibben. Maybe Buster Warenski, although he mostly does art knives nowadays. Gold and jewels. Stuff like that."

He glanced up to meet blank stares all round.

"Never heard of 'em," said Marvel.

Louis went on enthusiastically, still talking to the knife. "They're knife rock stars. These are all handmade, custom knives, with no limit on time, materials or money. And VC is top of the top. You're talking James Bond stuff. The stealth bomber of knives."

There was an impressed silence. Then Reynolds cleared his throat. "What are your credentials?"

"My credentials?"

"Yes. What makes you an expert?"

"I know what credentials are," said Louis coolly. "My credentials are that I know about this shit and you don't."

There was a spiky silence. Baz looked around the room, wide-eyed, then whispered, "Daddy said *shit*."

Marvel laughed and Louis said, "Yeah. Sorry, mate. Daddy's naughty."

From a new position of moral superiority, Baz said, "Porridge!"

"In a minute, mate."

"So where do we find VC?" said Marvel.

Louis grinned at his naivety. "You don't," he said. "Nobody even knows who he is. He's totally off the radar. Never goes to conventions; never does interviews. Just stays home and makes knives. Serious knives, for serious people with serious money."

"Where's home? In this country?"

"Who knows?" shrugged Louis.

"What kind of money are we talking about?" said Reynolds.

"Well . . . I knew a bloke once who had a VC. He used it to pay off a four-grand debt."

"*Four grand?*" said Marvel.

Baz copied his astonished face and said, "*Four grand?*" and Louis laughed.

"That's right, Baz. Four grand. And that's not new or personalized. I've never even seen a VC knife for real, only pictures, so this is amazing." He shook his head at the knife in the bag as if he hardly believed he was seeing it.

"Me see," said Baz, but Louis held it beyond him, turning the bag this way and that, peering and squinting to get the best view, stroking the knife through the plastic, trying to grip the handle.

"That blade's titanium. That's why it's so light, see? And it won't corrode. And the handle is most likely abalone."

"What's that?" said Marvel.

"It's a kind of mother of pearl, but incredibly strong. Mother of pearl isn't expensive, you know, so VC would use abalone for strength, not value. This knife was built to last."

"You know a lot about knives," said Marvel suspiciously.

Louis shrugged. "Everybody knows a lot about *something*," he said. "My something is knives."

He placed the knife reverently on the table, and a wistful note crept into his voice. "You know, they say that actually holding a VC is like . . ." He shook his head. "I dunno. Magical."

He laughed self-consciously, and ran a thumb along his jaw, as if *daring* a bit of stubble to show its head.

The stubble knew better.

Baz sighed and shook his head. "Four grand," he said again — then he made a sneaky grab for the knife and Louis made a grab for him, laughing and lifting him off Jack's knees and on to his own lap for a cuddle.

Marvel sat back in his flimsy chair and appraised Louis carefully. "You sure about all this?"

"As I can be," said Louis. "The diamond on the thumb stop is the VC trademark. Not to say someone else might not have copied it. It's a bit hard to tell through the plastic, but the quality is what confirms it. The materials used are top notch, and the clearances look . . . just *mad*."

He paused, then added, "But I'd have to hold it to know for sure . . ."

Marvel smiled and shook his head. "Sorry."

Louis shrugged and smiled back, but his eyes kept returning to the knife.

"What does VC stand for?" said Marvel.

"Initials, I'm assuming."

"Would he be working out of a commercial premises? Like a factory?"

Louis shook his head. "Nope. This is small-scale, big-margin stuff. I mean, Buster Warenski's been working on one single knife for five years! The tools you need are bulky and heavy but none of it takes up a lot of space. This bloke could be working out of his garden shed."

Marvel nodded, readjusting, reimagining . . . He picked up the bag with noticeably more care than he'd previously shown. "So this knife isn't one of thousands?"

Louis laughed and shook his head vehemently. "One of *one*, mate. One of effing *one*."

"Porridge!" whined Baz.

"All right, piggy. Give Dad a kiss and let's go home for brekkie, yeah?"

Baz obliged and Louis got up and popped him back in his buggy to go.

"Thanks for coming, mate," said Jack quietly.

Louis turned and smiled at Jack as if it were just the two of them in the room. Like they were on the bench by the canal with the kingfisher flashing and Baz feeding the ducks.

"I'm sorry about before, mate. Good luck." He held out his hand and Jack shook it. "You tell your old man he can have a job at the yard any time he wants. It's all above board with tax and that, so it's long hours and the pay's rubbish, but he's welcome to it."

Jack nodded. Could only whisper "thanks" as Louis and Baz left.

A long silence was finally broken by Marvel.

"Interesting bloke. How do you know him?"

Jack only shrugged.

Marvel toyed with the bag.

"What now, sir?" said Parrott, from his post beside the mop.

Marvel leaned back in his rickety chair.

"I think it's time to see the whites of Adam While's eyes."

DCI Marvel knocked on the Whiles' front door for the second time in two days. While he and Rice waited, he prepared to be businesslike with Mrs While. If she brought up his behaviour at their last meeting, he was ready to slap her down fast. He wasn't going to let her build up a head of steam, or start talking about her "rights". If she did, he would remind her, in no uncertain terms, that she had assaulted a police officer in the commission of his duties and that to take an accusatory stance could be very much worse for *her* than it might be for *him*. Pregnant or not bloody pregnant. The law made no allowance for hysteria.

Still, when he saw a shape approaching behind the pebbled glass of the door, his palms itched with sweat.

But it wasn't Catherine While. It was her husband, unshaven and hollow-eyed.

"Mr While?"

"Yes?"

Marvel held up his ID. "DCI Marvel. This is DC Rice. Can we come in?"

"What's it about?"

"Eileen Bright."

A look of such desperation passed across Adam While's face that for a moment Marvel thought the man was going to make a run for it — or pull a gun.

"Jesus Christ!" he snapped. "What do you want from me now that you couldn't get three bloody years ago? One piss in a lay-by and I'm Jack the bloody Ripper!"

"Calm down, Mr While," said Marvel — but only because it was usually guaranteed to wind a person up. Marvel was always up for a fight and liked to needle people he thought might be suspects.

Or just people.

But on this occasion, Adam While did calm down a bit. He sighed and opened the door and turned away — and Marvel and Rice followed him into the plummy front room. He turned to face them when they joined him. "Sorry," he said, running his fingers through his hair. "Just having a bad day."

"Sorry to hear that, Mr While," Rice said sympathetically. "Anything in particular?"

He flapped a vague hand and sighed. "Car trouble. Work trouble. Wife trouble. You name it."

No wonder, thought Marvel. He guessed that Adam While had got it in the neck from his wife over his secret past.

Good.

"Life, eh?" said Rice with a sigh. "It's a rollercoaster."

"You can say that again," While said, and even gave her a little smile, as if her corny platitude had actually helped him gain some perspective.

Marvel was suddenly pleased to have a woman officer with him. He could see their value in this kind of interaction.

And she'd bought a bottle opener for the capture house.

"Where's your wife, Mr While?" said Marvel.

"Gone to see her mother."

"Live nearby, does she?"

"Withypool."

Marvel paused, then said, "I have no idea where that is."

"On Exmoor," said Rice, and he nodded as if he knew where *that* was.

"We missed you when we came round yesterday," he said. Marvel liked to say "we" when his own behaviour might be called into question. It made it easier to blame another — fictional — colleague.

Then he cut straight to the chase. "We've come about your VC knife."

He'd hoped for an unguarded reaction he could work off. There was none.

"What about it?" said While.

"Can I see it?"

"Sure," he said, and reached into his pocket.

If that knife was in the house, it was in his pocket. Angela While's words rushed back at Marvel.

He held out his hand. "May I?"

While hesitated, as if he were being asked to hand over his first-born to a fox.

Then he gave it to him.

Marvel looked down at the knife. Jack Bright was right. It *was* the same.

But this knife was not blurred by plastic — and it was a thing of utter beauty . . .

The abalone was a turbulent storm cloud, captured and tamed by the smooth, warm handle that fitted his palm like magic. He touched his thumb to the diamond stud and the knife seemed to open itself! Seemed to *know* that he *wanted* it open, and obliged before he'd exerted any noticeable pressure. No hesitation. No notches. No friction. The blade sprang open like a living thing, alert to his every wish. Serrated on one edge, curved on the other to a cruel point.

It *was* the same.

And it *was* . . . magical.

Marvel was almost embarrassed by how magical it felt. He felt so connected to it! And he wanted to *use* it. Wanted to see what it could do. Wanted to cut and to stab and to slice. To carve his name in something.

Anything!

He gingerly touched his thumb to the blade. It kissed a thin line of blood there that made him shiver.

"Sir!" said Rice, and broke the spell.

Marvel breathed again.

"You've cut yourself, sir."

Marvel nodded. He held his bloody thumb away from the handle so as not to sully the shell. His regretful forefinger decreed that the knife must close, and the blade obeyed and bowed down into its pearly sheath without a murmur.

He cleared his throat and handed the knife back to While. "I see why they're so expensive. Where did you get it?"

"It was a gift from my father."

"I hear they're thousands of pounds. That's some gift."

"Yes," he nodded. "But it was for my twenty-first."

"Where did he get it?"

"What do you mean?"

"I mean, did he get it in a shop?"

While frowned at the knife, then wiped it clean of Marvel's touch on the tail of his untucked shirt, and slid it back into his pocket. "I don't know, to be honest."

"Or direct from the maker?"

He shrugged. "I wouldn't know."

"But he'd remember, wouldn't he?"

"Unfortunately, he's dead."

"Oh that is sad," said Marvel without sounding at all sad. "When did he die?"

"Last year," said While. "Cancer."

"The big C," said Marvel.

"Yeah."

"There are worse ways to go," he mused.

"I suppose so," said While.

"No suppose about it," said Marvel. "Some of the things you see in this job . . ."

He didn't finish the thought. Just stared at Adam While until even Rice looked nervous.

Then he said, "Well, thank you for your time, Mr While."

"He's lying," said Marvel as they drove away from the house.

"About what?"

"I don't know."

"Then how do you know he's lying, sir?" said Rice.

"A biiiiiiig hunch," said Marvel. "Tell me," he went on, "if two homicide cops turned up on your doorstep and asked to see your knife, wouldn't you want to know why?"

"I would," she said.

"Me too," said Marvel. "But he didn't. Even though the news of the murder weapon being found was never released to the public. So he should have *no idea* why his knife would be of any interest to anyone investigating the death of Eileen Bright."

Rice nodded. "Unless he knows his knife matches the murder weapon."

"That's right."

Rice sighed. "But it's *not* the murder weapon, is it?" she said.

Marvel nodded and his jaw set in frustration. "The one thing that links Adam While to the crime is the one thing that exonerates him."

They drove the rest of the way back to the police station in silence.

There was a website.

VC KNIVES: THE POINT IS PERFECTION

The site was ugly and text-heavy, with a lot of it in bold caps of red and blue, punctuated by exclamation marks, underlined sections and bizarre, angry headlines like TEN REASONS NOT TO BUY A VC KNIFE! and DON'T ASK ME WHEN YOUR VC KNIFE WILL BE READY BECAUSE <u>I!</u> <u>DON'T!! KNOW!!!!!</u>

Reasons not to buy a VC knife included SHOWING OFF!, CRIME! and OPENING LETTERS!

IF YOU DON'T HAVE A GOOD REASON TO OWN A VC KNIFE, the page raged at potential customers, DON'T BUY A VC KNIFE! And to customers who were even *thinking* of enquiring as to the progress of their custom-made knives, VC had a very special message indeed:

Every time I have to reply to a query about the status of your knife, you stop me working and risk delay or even damage to a knife — possibly YOURS!!!

Marvel was not, by nature, a friendly, easygoing man. But even he felt the tone of the VC Knives page was a bit . . . *brisk*. The point of the site seemed to be to put people off buying a VC knife.

He whistled low through his teeth. "What a nut."

"Indeed," said Reynolds. "No crime! What does he think people are going to do with a four-thousand-pound hunting knife? Peel fruit?"

Now and then there was a photograph of a knife. And, while the maker of the website — whom Marvel strongly suspected to be VC himself — had lavished no expense on its construction, the photos of knives had been taken with an obsessiveness that was almost pornographic. Lights were perfectly positioned, angles carefully arranged, accessories lovingly displayed. Each knife was laid out against an appropriate backdrop — a survival knife reclined on a camouflage net beside a snared rabbit; a combat dagger was clipped to a carefully mud-spattered paratrooper's boot; and a black carbon-fibre stiletto lay in a puddle of candlelight on a Victorian desk beside a chalice of wine and — in the shadows — a human skull. Fantasy tableaux of the powers that might magically be bestowed upon the owner of a VC knife — if only they could survive the obstacle course of purchase.

And on that last point, there were no clues as to price. Apparently VC operated on the basis of *If you have to ask, you can't afford it.*

Finally Reynolds found the only contact information. Right at the bottom of the last page — in tiny type, sandwiched between "Est: 1988" and a stern notice about photographic copyright ('THEY'RE MINE!!!!') — was a mobile phone number.

330

"That's a UK number," said Reynolds. "At least we know he's in this country."

Marvel rang the number twice. Both times it went directly to voicemail, where there was no message — only a fifteen-second silence and then a beep.

He didn't leave a message.

Instead he called Taunton and got them to run a reverse directory search on the mobile number.

Then he and Rice and Parrott stood and watched Reynolds scroll aimlessly through the website, desperately looking for clues in the photographs, in the small print, in the syntax, that might shed light on VC's identity or whereabouts.

"Hold on," said Marvel suddenly. "What date was VC established?"

"Nineteen eighty-eight, sir," said Reynolds, double checking.

Marvel flicked through the Eileen Bright file that Stourbridge had copied for him.

"Three years ago, in nineteen *ninety-eight* when While was picked up at the murder scene, he was thirty-five years old."

They all looked at him.

He went on, his intensity growing slowly as he worked things out, "An hour ago, Adam While told us that his father gave him the knife for his twenty-first birthday."

He turned to Rice, who nodded her agreement.

"But he must have turned twenty-one in nineteen eighty-four. According to this site, that's four years *before* VC Knives started trading."

"But what does that mean?" asked Parrott.

"It means his father didn't give him the knife," said Rice.

"Does it matter *who* gave him the knife?" asked Reynolds.

"No, but it matters that he lied about it," said Marvel. "Why would he lie about anything if he had nothing to hide? I *knew* he was lying!"

Rice's face broke into a broad grin. "Sometimes feelings *are* facts!"

Reynolds arched his eyebrows. "Sir, I do think this rather smacks of the no-smoke-without-fire school of policing."

"Too right," said Marvel. "When I like someone for murder, I'm usually right."

Reynolds closed his eyes briefly and realized there was nothing else he could say right now to convince Marvel otherwise.

"What about the boy, sir?" he said. "We really need to charge him or let him go."

Before Marvel could say anything, Taunton rang back, and he snorted as he wrote the address on a yellow Post-it note.

Then he got up with a great scrape of his chair.

"Get the kid," he said. "We're going to London."

It wasn't really London; it was Bromley. But it was close enough to London to make Marvel start dropping his aitches.

In the back seat, Jack Bright looked around him with interest as the buildings grew taller, the cars newer and the people more colourful.

As they crawled along the busy streets, Marvel got a wave of nostalgia for kebabs and diesel fumes and pavements spotted with chewing gum. Not far from here, his final case in the Met had ended in failure so abject that he'd known his time there was over.

A child lost, a child dead, a child found.

One out of three ain't good enough.

He hadn't said goodbye to anybody and nobody had said goodbye to him.

But he'd go back tomorrow if things could be the way they were before . . .

"How do you want to do this?" said Reynolds.

They hadn't discussed it on the way. That had been three hours of silence, punctuated by blunt directions and grunted decisions about where to pee.

At Membury Services, Marvel had bought a bargain bucket of KFC because it was the food of the gods, but the kid said he wasn't hungry.

Reynolds had had a hummus wrap and bottled water. The man was averse to living.

"How do you want to do this?" said Reynolds again.

Marvel would love to have told him they were going to kick the front door down and pin VC to the floor with his own knives until he admitted he'd sold the murder weapon to Adam While.

"Dead straight, for starters," he said instead. "You never know when you're going to get lucky."

They drove out of the town centre and into the residential areas — more green and with a mix of grand old homes, flats and ugly 1960s boxes, a legacy of wartime bombing.

VC's house on Cumberland Road was one of those brick boxes, with an overgrown front garden.

Reynolds swung the car around the corner and took ages to parallel park in a small space behind a lorry.

"You wait here," said Marvel, and Jack nodded.

"You sure that's a good idea, sir?" said Reynolds warily.

Marvel knew Jack Bright wasn't going anywhere. He wanted to catch his mother's killer more than any of them. If they failed to do that, *then* he'd worry about the kid doing a runner to avoid charges in the Goldilocks case. But until then, Marvel was confident Jack Bright would stay put.

He didn't bother reassuring Reynolds on this point. He went to university. Let him work it out for himself.

"Can I listen to the radio?" said Jack.

"No," said Reynolds, and looked defensively at Marvel. "I'm not leaving him the *keys*, sir!"

Even Marvel agreed that that would be tempting fate, and they left Jack sitting in the car as they walked back around the corner and turned into the short driveway.

"I'm uncomfortable bringing the boy, sir," said Reynolds. "He's been questioned without a legal guardian, locked up without charge and now he's here with us and I'm not sure why . . ."

Marvel shrugged. "He might come in useful."

"Useful *how?*" said Reynolds.

"Everybody has their uses, Reynolds. It's all about context. If it turns out he isn't useful, we'll take him back down the M5, charge him with the Goldilocks crimes and no harm done."

"He hasn't even seen a solicitor yet, sir."

"Well, we haven't formally interviewed him."

"It's almost twenty-four hours! We need to charge him or let him go."

"Calm down, Reynolds," said Marvel. "Don't forget *he* came to *us*. He insisted on talking even when we told him not to. Wanted to make a deal. And, thanks to your joke arrest, he wasn't even in legal custody for most of it."

Reynolds pressed his lips together and said no more as they turned into the property.

The ragged lawn was home to a brightly painted gnome pointing a camera at them. Marvel glanced up and saw the black CCTV under the eaves. A TO LET sign leaned against the inside of the haywire hedge.

Reynolds knocked and they both got out their ID. Through the obscured-glass door a figure approached and Marvel braced himself.

But the door was opened by a small, frumpy woman in her late fifties. She had thick spectacles, a mumsy grey bob, and a cat chasing a ball of wool across her jumper.

"Hello?" she said warily.

"Hello," said Marvel. "Detective Chief Inspector Marvel and Detective Sergeant Reynolds." Marvel held his ID up for her to see and she peered at it. "We're here about VC Knives."

"Oh," said the woman. "It's my son you want. He's not here."

"And what's your son's name, ma'am?" said Reynolds.

"Christopher."

"Surname?"

"Creed," she said. "Christopher Creed."

Marvel frowned. "We assumed VC were the initials of the knife-maker."

"I think it's for Victoria Cross," she said. "Like the medal. But you can ask him when he gets home."

"Great," said Marvel. "When will that be?"

"Tuesday," she said. "He's gone to Lanzarote."

"Shit," said Marvel. It was Friday.

Reynolds smiled smoothly. "Could we call him?"

"Call Christopher?" said Mrs Creed, looking surprised. "I wouldn't know *how* to!"

"Doesn't he have a mobile phone?"

She looked unsure for a moment, then said, "Well, he has one, but I don't know whether he'd have it with him on *holiday*."

Probably the phone they'd already called, thought Marvel. "Do you know which hotel he's at?"

"No," she said regretfully. "He didn't say which hotel. But Lanzarote's very small, isn't it? You can hardly see it on the map! Couldn't you just phone the island and ask where he's staying?"

Old people, thought Marvel. *No fucking clue.*

He shook his head and blew out a lungful of air in frustration. Here in this house — or in some shed out the back — one of the world's finest knife-makers apparently plied his trade to the wealthy and — more likely than not — the criminal. He was intrigued to meet him, if only to fix in his head an accurate mental image of Christopher Creed. Was he a square-jawed ex-marine, milling titanium with battle-scarred fingers and the zeal of the righteous? Or some fat, lazy man-child, eating crisps in his underpants, whose metal-work skills had started with a *Lord of the Rings* obsession, and been honed to perfection only because he never left his bedroom?

It could be either, or neither, or anything in between.

They'd come all this way! He didn't want to leave empty-handed.

"Could we come in for a moment, Mrs Creed?"

"Of course," she said. "I don't often get visitors! Would you like some tea?"

"Thank you."

Mrs Creed showed Marvel and Reynolds into the front room and went to make tea.

The house smelled funny. Metallic? Acidic? Marvel didn't know about the processes of knife-making but maybe that was part of it.

There was a fading photograph of a boy on the mantelpiece — Christopher, he assumed — but it gave no real clues as to the adult.

Other than that, the room was all about cats.

China cats, wooden cats, knitted cats, felt cats, cat door stop, cat air freshener, cat-shaped vases, cat lampshades, cat curtains, cat couch, cats, cats, cats.

Mrs Creed brought in tea on a tray. She poured it from a china pot, and covered it with a cat cosy, then put the cat cups down on cat coasters.

"You like cats?" said Marvel.

"Oh I *love* cats!" she cried, and fixed him with a magnified stare that was both eager and strangely off-putting. "Do you?"

"I do," said Marvel.

He hated cats. Couldn't bear the hoity-toity little fuckers. But he was a whore for information.

She beamed at him. "They're like little furry children," she nodded dreamily.

"Talking of children, you must be very proud of Christopher," said Reynolds. "I understand he has quite a reputation in his field."

"I suppose so," sighed Mrs Creed. "And I know he's very good at what he does, but I do wish it wasn't *knives*. They're so . . ." she searched long and hard for the perfect word, and finally settled on "*sharp*".

Marvel nodded sagely and agreed, "Yes. Knives are sharp."

"I always worry he'll cut himself, you see?" said Mrs Creed.

"I'm sure he takes every precaution," said Reynolds reassuringly. "He's a professional, after all."

Mrs Creed gave him a very small smile. "I hope you're right, Mr Reynolds. Would you like a biscuit?"

Marvel took a bourbon, Reynolds a custard cream. Old-people biscuits.

"Maybe you can help us," Marvel said, although he doubted it.

Mrs Creed sipped her tea, then put the cup back on its saucer and said, "Of course, if I can."

"It's a simple thing," said Marvel. "We just need to find out whether Christopher ever sold a knife to a particular customer. If you could show us his records, I'm sure we'd be able to find it in a moment."

"Oh dear," said Mrs Creed. "I can't get into Christopher's room when he's away. He locks it, you see?"

"You don't have a spare key to the door?" asked Marvel.

"Oh no!" Mrs Creed shook her head. "Even if I did, I think he'd be very annoyed with me if I went in there without him. You know how boys are about their *things*."

Marvel itched with frustration. A flimsy bedroom door was all that stood between him and the information he wanted. He could probably knock it clear off its hinges — or get Reynolds to do it. Now he'd have to go away and come back! And even then he would need a warrant. He didn't have probable cause to search the house without one, and unearthing probable cause could take weeks.

Marvel made a huge effort not to let his frustration show. Mrs Creed was not her son, and her son was not a criminal. *Yet.* So he couldn't treat *her* like a criminal, however much he'd like to. He'd already tried to cuff the wrong pregnant woman this week — he wasn't going to add to his tally of shame with an old lady in a cat jumper.

"Is there a problem with the knife?" said Mrs Creed. "Because Christopher's never had a complaint of any kind about a knife. I'm sure he'd be very concerned to hear there was a problem with a knife."

She looked genuinely anxious.

"It's not about the knife," Marvel reassured her. "We're investigating the owner of a VC knife."

He took the knife from inside his jacket and laid it on the coffee table next to the biscuits. Mrs Creed peered at it through the plastic evidence bag. "Well, isn't that pretty?" she said. "Are you sure you're looking for a man?"

"We assume so," said Marvel.

Mrs Creed smiled moonily at him. "To assume makes an ass out of u and me . . ."

"So my mother always says," said Reynolds. "But in the case of knives, it's a pretty fair assumption."

"Well, Mr Marvel, I do hope it wasn't used in the commission of a crime?"

"I'm afraid it was," said Marvel. "A very serious crime. That dark substance at the base of the blade? That's blood."

Mrs Creed peered through the plastic. "It's very black," she said.

"It's very old," countered Marvel.

"Oh dear," Mrs Creed said. "I can't believe Christopher would sell a knife to a *criminal*. He's very specific on his website that his knives are not to be used in crimes."

Marvel stared at her in case she was being ironic.

Apparently she wasn't. Apparently she actually believed that it was possible to tell people not to commit a crime and expect them to simply obey!

"Well," he said, "it's very difficult to know *what* people will do with things once they *have* them, isn't it?"

"I suppose so," she said.

"So you wouldn't know who bought this knife from Christopher?"

"Oh no," she said. "But he has a very exclusive customer base. I'm sure he could tell you without even looking in his book!"

"On Tuesday," said Marvel.

"On Tuesday," she agreed.

Marvel nodded and pursed his lips. It was a dead end. Christopher Creed was in Lanzarote, and wishing he were not would not bring him home.

With a sigh, he took his card from his wallet and handed it to her.

"That's my number," he said. "Please call if you think of anything that could help, or if Christopher calls, please do pass on my number."

"Of course," she said.

They had finished their tea. They should leave.

Marvel hated to go. He felt *so close* to the information he needed.

He glanced at Reynolds in case he could pull this out of the fire.

"I'd love to see more of his knives," Reynolds said suddenly. "We've heard so much about them."

Good thinking, Reynolds! Marvel nodded at him approvingly. Every mother he'd ever met thought their kids were special — even if they hadn't been *born* yet! So why not appeal to Mrs Creed's pride in her son? Why not get her to show off his work, like a crappy bit of Lego or a finger-painting on a fridge?

"Well," she frowned, "everything's in his room — I'm very strict about him not leaving knives lying around the house, you see? — but he did make me a little penknife a few years ago for my birthday. Would you like to see that?"

"Please," said Marvel, and to his surprise she immediately took it from the patchwork pocket of her corduroy skirt.

It was unremarkable at first sight. A few inches long, with a very flat, black handle. Slightly curved, with a tiny diamond on the thumb stud. Mrs Creed opened the blade with the merest flick of her thumbnail. The blade was less than three inches long — the legal maximum carry.

342

Marvel was disappointed.

"Very nice," he said.

"Very pretty," said Reynolds.

"No, no, no," said Mrs Creed. "You don't understand."

That surprised Marvel. The woman was looking at him a little disapprovingly through her thick spectacles, like one of his old teachers.

"You have to *hold* it . . ." Mrs Creed closed the knife and pressed it into his hand and wrapped his fingers around it.

Marvel felt a shudder go through him — a physical response that started in his hand and ran up his arm to his head. It wasn't pleasant. For a second he felt almost sick, and licked his lips like a dog.

Then he opened the knife, and — once again — he felt transported by something so odd, so indefinable, so *dark* that he felt exposed and laid bare.

"It has ceramic pivot bearings," Mrs Creed said. "That's why it runs so smoothly on the track, you see?"

Marvel nodded mutely. He closed it, then opened it again. He'd been here before. Captured. Enthralled.

It was magical.

"That's a titanium blade," said Mrs Creed. "And the handle and stop are carbon fibre. And see the diamond? That's Christopher's trademark. He gets his diamonds from a funny little man in Amsterdam. I think it's very stylish, don't you?"

She smiled and Marvel smiled too. It *was* stylish. The little diamond sparkled brilliantly in the black carbon fibre thumb stud.

He opened it and closed it, opened it and closed it. Opened it again.

"And look at the clearance on the blade. That's two-thousandths of an inch."

She must have read ignorance in his eyes because she explained, "The best makers in the world would be happy with twenty!"

Marvel closed the blade more slowly. Watched it disappear into the handle by an invisible whisker. When folded, the spine of the knife looked like one solid piece of metal. Only turning it to the light revealed the hairline clues to the blade hidden within.

"Very clever," he said, and meant it.

"Yes, and not easy to make," Mrs Creed went on. "Titanium dust is so flammable you can't let it build up. So you have to grind the blade very, very slowly. And the dust has to go straight into a bucket of water to stop the whole room bursting into flames!"

She laughed at the very idea.

Marvel laughed back, and wondered whether her home insurers knew about the titanium dust and the bucket.

Then Mrs Creed held out her hand and Marvel placed the knife reluctantly in her palm, feeling like a little kid who has to give back the drum at the end of a music lesson.

"Thank you," he said.

"Christopher does make a lovely knife," she sighed with obvious pride. "You come back on Tuesday, Mr Marvel, and I'm sure he'd be very happy to help you with your inquiries."

344

Marvel picked up the abalone knife in the plastic evidence bag. "Thank you for your help."

"You're very welcome, Mr Marvel," she said. "Mr Reynolds."

They walked back to the car and got in.

Jack Bright was still there. Just as Marvel knew he would be.

"What happened?" he said. "Did you see him?"

"He wasn't there," said Marvel. "We spoke to his mother, but she couldn't give us any information."

They got in and sat for a moment — Reynolds with the keys in his hand, held loose on one thigh. He shivered — a full-body shudder, a goose on his grave — and then laughed in embarrassment.

"What's wrong with *you*?"

"Just a bit nippy," said Reynolds. But still he didn't start the car.

They sat in silence.

Marvel felt oddly as if he'd woken from a dream. All those fucking cats! That sick shudder that turned his stomach. And the blade revealing itself as smoothly as obedient butter.

Had it even been real?

The whole encounter seemed like something from a fairy story. Enchanted — but in a dark and scary way.

Foolishness!

Foolishness?

He tried to shake off the feeling. Then he held the abalone knife up to the window so he could see it better. He was a hair's breadth from opening the sealed bag and taking it out, just to recapture the buzz . . .

"I'm not cold," said Reynolds suddenly. "I'm . . . creeped out." He shot an embarrassed glance at Marvel. "Something about the house. Or her. Or the *smell*. Did you notice?"

Marvel nodded. He'd noticed it all.

Reynolds went on, "It felt as if someone we didn't even know was there was *watching us*."

"Besides the gnome?" said Marvel wryly.

"Besides the gnome," said Reynolds, and Marvel nodded.

It was the first time they'd ever agreed on anything. Marvel doubted it would happen again.

"You think Creed *was* there?" said Reynolds.

Marvel pursed his lips. "I think it's entirely possible. There's a CCTV camera outside, he might have cameras everywhere. A knife nut. A security nut. Watching everything."

"Doesn't even let his mother in his room," Reynolds nodded. "Sounds like the paranoid sort." He looked nervously over his shoulder, as if he expected Christopher Creed to be standing beside the car — sudden as a ghost and brandishing a VC knife . . .

"It would all make her a very smooth liar," he said.

"She's obsessed with cats," shrugged Marvel. "Who knows *what* she's capable of?"

Reynolds laughed.

"But she *was* creepy," said Marvel carefully. "When she handed me the knife, she touched my hand. Made

346

me feel almost sick. I thought it was the KFC, but now . . ."

"You think we should stake it out?" said Reynolds suddenly.

Marvel grunted. "Just us?"

"And me!" said Jack.

They both ignored him.

Reynolds shrugged. "We could book into a place overnight, get a couple of hours' sleep now, and then come back when it's dark and see who's in the house when the lights are on."

"I think we should do that!" said Jack.

They both ignored him some more.

Reynolds went on, "I know it's a long shot. But if she lied and Christopher Creed really *is* at home, it would give us a reason to return with a search warrant. And all we need is one bit of paperwork with Adam While's name on it . . ."

Marvel nodded. Any record of While ever having been a customer of VC Knives, and the case would start to move inexorably in the right direction.

The direction of murder.

Bromley was not a tourist destination and John Hurt was doing something at the Churchill Theatre, so rooms were hard to come by, and two rooms in the same place at such short notice turned out to be impossible.

It was four o'clock before Reynolds managed to find a twin room in a B&B on Pickhurst Lane, where the owner agreed to put a folding bed in the room for an extra tenner. As they were going to spend most of the night in the Ford Focus, Marvel deemed it acceptable.

The B&B was supposed to be run by a couple called the Copples, who looked very happy and welcoming in their brochure in the hallway. But Mrs Copple seemed to have left, and Mr Copple could hardly have been less interested in running a B&B by himself.

He pointed out their room from the bottom of the stairs, and then handed them each an unfolded towel, like a PE teacher.

"Breakfast's at eight," he said. "There's no bacon."

Then, as he headed back to the lounge to finish watching the football they'd interrupted, he stopped, dug in his trouser pocket, and gave each of them a rather fluffy Murray Mint.

"For your pillows," he said, and closed the lounge door.

Reynolds searched to see if there was a kettle and tea tray, and by the time he'd established there was not, Marvel had turned on the TV, peed loudly in the toilet with the door open, bounced heavily on both beds, toed off his shoes, and was propped up against his chosen headboard, channel surfing.

Reynolds sat on the rumpled bed Marvel had left for him and frowned at the DCI's feet. He had always felt a little uncomfortable in the presence of another man's socks.

"You mind if I draw the curtains?" he said.

Marvel did not.

Reynolds did that and lay on the bed. If he'd been alone he'd have got into it — even fully clothed — but somehow that didn't seem *manly*, so he lay on top of the covers instead.

Jack had assumed correctly that he'd be on the folding bed. He lay down on it and went to sleep immediately.

He didn't even flinch when Reynolds' phone rang.

It was *Mrs* Passmore. The old reverse panda herself. She shouted at Reynolds for five minutes while he tried to speak — first to offer advice, then to remonstrate, and finally to tell her that the conversation was at an end. But she hung up before he could get to any of those points, and he was left with his phone buzzing in his ear, feeling like an idiot.

"Trouble in paradise?" said Marvel.

"Mr Passmore's been arrested for insurance fraud," said Reynolds, and braced himself for *I told you so*.

But instead Marvel nodded and said, "It's good you didn't get involved," as if it had been Reynolds' own good judgement that had saved him from humiliation.

"Indeed," said Reynolds. He plumped his pillow and lay down again. People were always surprising him.

Even Marvel!

Turned out the man wasn't so bad after all.

Reynolds folded his arms awkwardly, and wished he had the guts to get under the covers.

For a few minutes, Marvel carried on flicking through channels, his chin on his chest and his eyes glazed.

Then — just as Reynolds' eyelids were drooping — Marvel said, "I told you so."

Jack found his mother.

She was on the hard shoulder, walking to the phone, and he was following her with Merry heavy and sweaty in his arms.

His mother kept looking back at him, but the sun was behind her and he couldn't see her face — only the shimmer of her golden hair like a halo around her head.

He was tired and wanted to stop and put Merry down for a bit.

Mum? he kept saying. *Mum?*

But she didn't stop, just kept walking, and he started to fall behind. He hoisted Merry up and hurried, but as soon as he stopped hurrying, he fell behind again. Further each time, until his mother was fifty yards ahead of him. A hundred.

He hoisted Merry up again.

And his mother disappeared.

There was nowhere for her to disappear *to*; she had just gone.

Jack stopped and stood in the heat.

The road was all there was left. Beyond the crash barriers on either side, the world had disappeared into a yellow-grey haze, as far as the eye could see. The fields, the grass, the hedges. All were gone. Only the road was left. And the —

Small bugs

Small bugs

Merry wriggled and twisted, and reached out beyond his shoulder —

Mama! Mama!

Jack turned to see his mother, but too slow, too late — and the knife slit him from navel to neck.

He woke with a gasp in the dark and knew he was not alone.

He sat up, panting, one hand clutching the place where the knife had entered his belly as if he might still stop the blood.

It felt so *real*!

He looked around the room, slowly remembering where he was.

The TV was still on and by its light he could see that Marvel and Reynolds were both asleep. Reynolds was curled on his side with his back to the room, Marvel slumped against the headboard, his tie loosened and the remote control on his chest along with his chin.

Carefully, carefully, Jack got off the bed and stood in the middle of the room.

He'd done all he could. The police were on the case. His father was home. Merry and Joy were safe. He could go now and not even have to buy a train ticket to London. No charges, no court case, no detention.

Start at the beginning again.

He didn't even have to pull on his shoes, because he'd slept in them, the same way he'd slept in them every night for a year.

Always ready to run.

He walked soundlessly across the carpet. The door handle was cold round brass, and made a small squeak as he turned it. Marvel stirred and Jack held his breath. He watched the big man roll and resettle into a more comfortable position on his side, facing him.

Jack opened the door, and thought of Goldilocks creeping into the Three Bears' home, eating their porridge and sleeping in their beds.

Fuck Goldilocks, he thought, and then grinned at the memory of Marvel's words.

Fuck Goldilocks.

Marvel was a copper and a dick — not necessarily in that order. He'd told Jack straight that he didn't want to get involved with his case, and Jack had wanted to punch him.

But then he *had* got involved, and they'd made a deal. And now Marvel was doing all he could to keep his side of the bargain.

Marvel had surprised him. And — more than that — Marvel had revived something inside Jack that he thought he'd lost.

Hope.

The hope of justice.

Of an ending, and of a new, better beginning.

Of sleeping without dreaming.

Marvel was on the case, and didn't need him any more, just as Joy and Merry didn't need him any more.

Nobody needed him any more.

Jack was free to go.

And yet he did not move. He just stood, silhouetted in the doorway.

He couldn't leave.

Not when his best hope for justice was right here in this room — lying in a lumpy bed, with the light from the TV flickering across his face and a Murray Mint stuck to his cheek.

Quietly, Jack shut the door.

They went back to the house at eleven. There were no lights on.

They parked across the street and Reynolds squinted into the night.

"The TO LET sign's back up. It had fallen down."

Marvel chewed over that for half a minute. "I assumed she'd just moved in. She didn't look like someone who was planning to move out. And, trust me, those cats were there to *stay*."

Reynolds nodded.

They all stared at the house.

"Can you see the gnome?" said Marvel.

"What gnome?" said Jack.

"No," said Reynolds.

Marvel focused his binoculars on the lawn. "It's gone."

"Strange," said Reynolds.

Marvel handed him the binoculars and took out his phone. "Read me the number on that TO LET sign."

Reynolds did, and Marvel rang it.

He could hear the ring-tone change as the call was patched through — he guessed from the closed letting office to some on-call person.

"Hello?" The on-call person sounded quite cross to have been called.

Marvel told him who he was and asked about the tenant in the Cumberland Road property.

"There's no tenant in there," said the young-sounding man. "That's why it's to let."

"I spoke to the tenant at the house this afternoon," said Marvel. "So check your records again, please."

"I know the house," said the agent snottily. "Sixties brick. Cumberland Road. It's been empty for months."

"When were you last there?" said Marvel.

The man hesitated. "A while ago."

"OK," said Marvel, and hung up. It wasn't his business to run a letting agency.

He turned to Reynolds. "They're bloody squatters!"

They got out of the car.

"Can I come?" said Jack, and they both said "No!" as one.

Reynolds went round the back, while Marvel walked down the side of the driveway in the shadow of the neighbour's hedge, where the neighbour's large-sounding dog barked angrily at him. Then across the front of the house, his shoulder brushing the brickwork, trying to cheat the CCTV.

At the front window he cupped his hands around his torch and looked in.

Everything was the same. The cats were all present and as correct as cats could be. The tea tray was still on the table.

Marvel wondered if Mrs Creed was all right. She didn't strike him as the kind of person who would leave dirty cups in the living room. A teapot getting stained by old bags. That used to drive Debbie mad when they lived together. One of the many things. So he was a little concerned. It was only a niggle, but definitely there.

What if Christopher Creed *had* been watching them? What if he was furious with his mother for letting them in? What if they'd had a row? The dumpy little woman versus her ex-marine, underpants-wearing, spoiled-baby son with the knife obsession? What if he'd killed her in a fit of anger? It might sound far-fetched to the uninitiated, but Marvel had seen far worse things with his own eyes.

Marvel joined Reynolds at the back of the house.

"Anything?" he said quietly.

"Nothing. Can't see anything. Too dark."

Marvel nodded. "I think we should go in."

"On what grounds?" said Reynolds. "We can't break into a house just because we fancy a nose about."

Marvel ignored him and tried the back door, but it was locked.

They walked around the house, but the front door was locked too.

"Shit," said Marvel.

Then they just stood there while the dog went mad next door.

Finally Marvel said, "Go get the kid."

Reynolds was aghast. "Sir, *we* barely have probable cause to enter the house, let alone a known felon!"

"I'm concerned for the safety of Mrs Creed," said Marvel grandly. "I could break down her back door, but the least intrusive way of gaining access and making sure she is all right is to send the boy in."

"But what if he gets injured? Or even killed? Christopher Creed makes *knives*, and one of them has been used to commit murder. He has a vested interest in not being caught!"

"If Creed is there, he's hiding. Hiding is not an aggressive act."

"Hiding from *us*, maybe! He's not going to take on two police officers on lawful business," hissed Reynolds. "But a boy alone in a dark house? Anything could happen!"

"Jack Bright can take care of himself," said Marvel. "And we're right here if he needs us. Go get him."

"I don't like this, sir," said Reynolds stiffly. "Not one bit."

"Noted," said Marvel.

Reynolds went to the car and came back with Jack.

"There's no answer," Marvel explained to the boy. "We are concerned that Mrs Creed might be injured or unwell. We'd like you to break in to make sure she's safe."

"OK."

"Do you understand?"

"Yeah," he said. "See if she's all right."

"And if you happen to see any relevant paperwork . . ."

357

"It's an illegal search," said Reynolds. "Anything he finds is inadmissible."

"He's not going to *search* for anything," snapped Marvel. "He's going to go in and see if Mrs Creed is all right. If he happens to see any documentation with Adam While's name on it, in drawers or filing cabinets . . ." — he nodded at Jack — "well, that's just a lucky accident."

"I won't be any part of this," said Reynolds, and turned away from both of them.

Marvel rolled his eyes, and Jack couldn't help grinning.

"Do your thing," said Marvel.

He followed Jack Bright round to the back of the house. Despite his grand declaration, Reynolds did remain a small part of it by trailing behind them, muttering.

Jack walked ten feet down the back garden to assess the guttering and drains. There were always more at the back of a house, where the soil pipes ran.

His burglar's eye quickly found the weak point — a small window over the garden shed. He glanced about the patio and picked up a trowel that had been dug into a planter full of dead daisies. Then he put a patio chair next to the shed, scrambled quickly to the apex of the roof, and easily scaled a downpipe to reach the window. Once there, he worked the trowel into the wooden window frame until it cracked and popped open, then slid silently through the window and disappeared from view.

358

The whole operation had taken less than two minutes.

"Impressive," said Marvel.

"Appalling," said Reynolds.

Jack dropped into a box room. Even empty, it looked too small for a bed.

He crept across the carpet, treading gingerly in case of creaks, but the house was not so old that the nails had shrunk in their holes, and his step was comfortingly silent.

He opened the door on to a narrow landing, off which there were only closed doors.

Jack took a shaky breath. He never broke into houses where he thought there were people. Catherine While had been a mistake. Shawn had fucked up, and it had been a horrible shock to suddenly realize that he wasn't alone in the house.

But here, he *knew* he wasn't alone, and he was nervous as hell.

He opened the first door.

It was dark, but he could see it was a bathroom. Empty. Not even toilet paper.

He took a few paces down the thick pale carpet that lined the hallway. The next door opened on to an empty bedroom. No bed, no wardrobe. Only more carpet.

And a smell he couldn't place.

Industrial. That was as close as he could get to it.

Another bathroom. This time Jack stood in the doorway long enough to see that there were no towels. No toothbrushes. No toilet paper. Again.

Odd.

There were only two more doors. One on his right and the other straight ahead at the end of the landing. For some reason he went past the door on his right and headed to the one facing him, and turned the handle slowly.

It was the master bedroom. Jack could see that from the light of the streetlamp outside. And it, too, was empty of everything but carpet.

He frowned in the dark, then quietly shut the door.

The last door. He was expecting more of the same, but resisted the feeling of complacency. He hadn't got away with 117 burglaries by being complacent.

There could be anything behind the final door.

Anything.

He turned the handle slowly and pushed open the door.

Nothing.

Jack stood for a moment, unsure of his next move. Then he remembered that Marvel said they had spoken to an *old* lady. Maybe she couldn't get up the stairs. Maybe there were more bedrooms downstairs.

He took a moment to regain the required caution, then crept down the stairs and searched methodically.

Every room was empty. The kitchen did not even have a kettle. Jack opened the fridge and the kitchen cabinets. Empty.

Everywhere.

Except the one room that was entirely filled with cats.

It was the weirdest thing he'd ever seen.

Jack walked to the back door to let Marvel and Reynolds in. But as he reached for the bolts, a woman's voice demanded, "Can I help you?"

The longer Jack was in the house, the more tense Marvel got.

He'd hoped the boy would be inside for a few minutes at the most, and would come back out the way he'd gone in, telling them that Mrs Creed was asleep in her bed, and — hopefully — clutching an invoice addressed to Adam While.

Now he really *did* begin to wonder whether Mrs Creed was OK.

Maybe sending a fourteen-year-old boy into the house to find out hadn't been such a great idea, after all. What had Ralph Stourbridge said?

Not my finest hour.

Marvel hoped he wouldn't look back on this hour and think the same thing. Even if Jack were safe, he wouldn't want the kid finding a body. Marvel had found his share of bodies during his years in homicide, but you never got used to that initial shock, even if you were expecting it. It was like a balloon you were blowing up bursting in your face.

Reynolds was looking through the kitchen window, his hands cupped around his eyes, and Marvel stepped alongside him and peered into the darkness himself.

"Can I help you?"

They both flinched and turned to see a middle-aged woman. She was wearing a yellow towelling dressing gown and green wellington boots, and had a large black dog on a lead.

"Hello," said Marvel.

"What are you doing here?" she demanded.

"Police," said Marvel, and held up his ID. "What are *you* doing here?"

"Oh!" said the woman, visibly relieved. "I live next door. Bobby was barking and I wanted to make sure everything was all right."

"You're a friend of Mrs Creed's?"

"Not really, just a neighbour. She's only been here for a few months. Keeps herself to herself."

"She doesn't seem to be at home."

"No, she left," said the woman.

"When?"

"This afternoon. Around four."

The men exchanged glances. Mrs Creed had left shortly after they had. That felt suspicious — as if their visit had prompted her departure.

"Do you know when she'll be back?" asked Marvel.

"No."

"What kind of car does she drive?"

"She doesn't have a car," said the woman. "She has a lorry."

"A big blue lorry?" said Reynolds, glancing at Marvel. "Parked round the corner?"

"Yes. Bloody great thing. She parked it there three months ago and never budged it once, even when Mrs Chandra in the bungalow asked her nicely because it was blocking her light."

Marvel and Reynolds exchanged sick looks. They'd parked right behind the getaway vehicle.

"She never moved it until today?" said Marvel.

"That's right. She often got *into* it, as if she *was* going to move it, but she never actually did. Mrs Chandra thought she was taunting her, but she doesn't seem like that kind of person to me."

"Was her son with her when she left?" said Marvel.

"Her son?"

"Christopher."

"I never saw a son," she said. "But then, I'm not nosy."

Again Marvel and Reynolds exchanged confused looks.

Reynolds asked the next question: "What's Mrs Creed's first name, do you know?"

"Veronica, I think."

"Veronica?" said Marvel.

"Veronica Creed," said Reynolds slowly. "VC."

"Shit," said Marvel. "*She*'s the maker!"

"Jesus," muttered Reynolds. "Jesus!"

"What's this all about?" asked the neighbour, but suddenly Marvel wanted her out of there, not witnessing their failure.

"Police business," he said brusquely. "Thank you for your help, Mrs . . .?"

"*Mizz* Flowers."

"Thank you for your help, Ms Flowers, but I'm going to ask you to go home now while we continue our inquiries."

Ms Flowers looked disgruntled. "What? So I come over here and give you a whole load of useful information and you're not going to give me any back?"

"That's right," said Marvel, and ushered her and her dog into the night.

Marvel, Reynolds and Jack Bright stood in the cat room with the lights on.

The photograph of Christopher Creed — or whoever the hell he was — was gone, and in its place a Chinese lucky cat waved its mocking golden fist up and down, leaving them in no doubt as to what it thought of them.

"She even asked if we were sure we were looking for a man," groaned Marvel. "She made an ass out of u and me."

"It's not our fault, sir! She lied!"

"They all lie!" Marvel snapped. "It's our job to remember that! But we had our witness in our effective custody. Our witness made us *tea*. And then we let our witness go because we *assumed* that the knife-maker must be a man."

"Well, yes," said Reynolds. "Maybe a little bit our fault."

Veronica Creed had toyed with them. Dropped a big fat clue in front of them and then watched them ignore it as they stumbled around blindly, trying to pin the tail on their own prejudices.

They'd been outwitted by an old lady in a cat jumper.

"She must work in the lorry," Reynolds went on. "Why else would she have a vehicle that big?

Knife-making requires some heavy-duty milling and grinding equipment, so keeping everything in her lorry — and nothing in the house — means she can just up and leave at a moment's notice."

"So this isn't even her house?" said Jack.

"No," said Marvel. "She probably squats in one place so she can set up things like phone accounts and credit cards, and then, if things get a bit warm, she moves on."

"So all this," Jack waved an arm around the cat room, "it's really just a *capture house.*"

Marvel and Reynolds exchanged embarrassed looks and Jack laughed.

"So what happens now?" he said. "How are you going to catch her?"

"God knows," said Marvel morosely. "How many other clues did she give us that we didn't even *notice* because of the cats and the custard fucking creams?"

"Or because she's an unattractive middle-aged woman," said Reynolds.

"All right, Germaine Greer," snapped Marvel. "It's not like she wasn't trying to deceive us. If she was trying to make it *easy* she would have just given us Adam While's bloody invoice."

The two of them glared at their notebooks. The only sound was the tiny click of the cat's golden paw waving back and forth.

"Can't you just find the lorry?" said Jack.

"Good thinking," snapped Marvel. "I'll put out an alert. Big blue lorry. Somewhere in London. Should do the trick."

"I thought you could trace the number plate."

"Well, if we had it, we could."

"X250 TBB," said Jack.

The both looked at him and he shrugged. "Well, you were gone *ages* and there was nothing else to do."

With the help of three force control rooms, they finally found the lorry three hours later on a blunt spur of tarmac that was a small excuse for a car park overlooking a Sussex beach.

Marvel parked the Ford Focus fifty yards away, next to a bin overflowing with chip paper and plastic bottles. On the side was a notice that said *Keep Pevensey Bay Beautiful*.

In the dark they couldn't see whether Pevensey Bay was beautiful or not. Couldn't see the caravans or the little boats corralled by wire, or even the ocean — although they could hear the waves breaking on to the beach below, each one dashing pebbles on to the shingle, then sucking them out to sea again in hissing, clicking foam.

It was a warm, still night and with only the stars and the sound of the waves, it made Jack think they could be in Bali.

"What now?" he yawned. It was the first thing he'd said since they'd left Bromley.

Marvel said nothing. Jack wondered if he'd heard him, so said again, "What now?"

"Don't keep going *on*," said Marvel rattily.

Jack shut up. He didn't really mind being sidelined. It was nice not to have to make any decisions. To have them made for him and take no responsibility for the outcome.

"William the Conqueror landed here, you know," mused Reynolds. "Ten sixty-six."

Jack looked down the beach and imagined men with bows and arrows and pikes and maces, slipping and sliding up the shingle. The roar they would make. The way their blood would run between the pebbles and disappear into the land below.

"What else did you nick of mine?" said Reynolds.

"What?"

"From the capture house. Besides my suit and tie."

Jack glowered at him. They'd been having a nice time! They were a team! And now he had to bring *that* up.

He folded his arms and said nothing.

"We need to get her out of the lorry," said Marvel. "So we can have a look inside."

"We can't search the lorry without a warrant, sir," said Reynolds.

"We're not going to," agreed Marvel.

They both turned to look at Jack.

"OK." Jack unfolded his arms, and his heart started to pick up its pace. He'd never broken into a lorry but already knew how to. While he'd been waiting for Marvel and Reynolds with no radio to distract him, he'd studied the back of this very vehicle — his practised eye idly working out how the latches operated, and seeking the weak link in the mechanism. Planning a break-in was a habit. A dirty little habit of which he was ashamed and proud in equal measure. He'd never imagined he'd put this particular bit of knowledge to practical use, but if it would keep the investigation on track, he was more than willing to have a bash.

"Another illegal search," said Reynolds, tight-lipped.

"And where would we be without the first one?" Marvel shot back. "Anyway, Veronica Creed upped and moved within hours of us asking her about the knife used to kill Eileen Bright. I think that gives us probable cause."

"For a warrant, possibly. Not to just bowl in and search! And to send in a *burglar* to turn the place over . . . I don't think any judge in the land would sign *that* order, sir! It's contributing to the delinquency of a minor, at the very least!"

"That bird has fucking *flown!*" laughed Marvel. "And I'm not sending him into the Tower after the Crown bloody Jewels — just the back of a lorry to look for a bit of paper that could help us catch the man who killed his mother!"

Reynolds looked unconvinced.

"And anyway," Marvel went on, "who's going to tell?"

"Not me!" said Jack.

Marvel turned to Reynolds, who shook his head and said, "I feel very uncomfortable about this, sir."

"Well," said Marvel, getting out his phone, "you can feel uncomfortable for both of us while Jack and me catch a killer."

"Jack and I," said Reynolds.

"Oh good," said Marvel. "Then we're all agreed."

Jack rummaged through the toolbox in the boot while Marvel spoke to the local police, and within ten minutes a marked patrol car crunched slowly past them and pulled up beside the lorry.

As soon as it had, Jack slipped quietly into the night — embraced by the darkness that tanged of salt and wild adventure.

As he skirted the shadows of the lorry, a copper in a hi-vis jacket knocked on the door of the cab.

Once.

And then again.

And a third time.

"Police. Open up, please."

The door opened. Low voices. Then the sound of somebody climbing down from the cab, and they led the woman away to speak to her, just like Marvel had asked. She was dressed in a heavy coat and boots.

Using the wheel brace from the Focus, Jack wrestled with the padlock. It was a good lock, and the brace was not long, but leverage and grunting won out, and the lock popped with a click. It was then a simple matter to lift the catch on the door. It creaked open, and Jack vaulted inside.

They watched Jack Bright spring easily into the back of the lorry.

"Whatever happens with this," said Marvel suddenly, "I don't think we should charge him."

"*What?*" said Reynolds. "But he's Goldilocks! He's admitted it!"

Marvel stared steadily at the back of the lorry. "In three years, two police forces have failed to find his mother's killer. I don't want to charge him for crimes he committed because of our failure. I don't feel *comfortable* about it."

Reynolds pursed his lips. "Whatever the reason, sir, the fact is, he's burgled and vandalized more than a hundred houses. Even *he* accepts now that a custodial sentence is inevitable!"

Marvel nodded and was silent for a short while. Then he said, "It's not, though, is it?"

"Not what?"

"Not inevitable."

Reynolds frowned. "What do you mean?"

"Not if we're . . . *flexible*."

Reynolds didn't like the sound of that. In his experience, flexibility was a very overrated quality.

"There's no way around the law, sir."

Marvel barked a laugh. "We both know *that*'s not true!"

"I don't know that at all," said Reynolds stiffly. "After all, I arrested Jack Bright myself! Twice!"

"Did you?" said Marvel.

"You know I did," grumbled Reynolds. "Read him his rights, the whole nine yards. Especially the second time!"

"I didn't see the arrest myself," said Marvel. "Do you have witnesses?"

"*Witnesses?*" said Reynolds. "To the *arrest?*"

"Yes," said Marvel.

"The arrest in the *police station*?"

"Yes."

"No," said Reynolds.

"Hm," said Marvel.

"What's *that* supposed to mean?" said Reynolds, getting aerated.

"I mean, if you have no witnesses to the arrest, then it's his word against yours."

Reynolds looked at the DCI in utter astonishment. "You mean the word of a boy who's a liar and a thief against the word of a serving police officer with an impeccable record?"

"A serving police officer who screwed up the first arrest," said Marvel. "And who has no witnesses to the second *alleged* arrest of an unaccompanied and un-represented minor — a boy whose mother was brutally murdered, and who was let down by the police and then by everybody who should have helped him. From his own father to all those people who should have noticed three little kids not going to school and living alone in that shithole of a house. *That* boy, Reynolds?"

Reynolds glared at the lorry. "It was a lawful arrest," he said. "You know it, and I know it."

He didn't say *sir* and he didn't care.

The sea air was replaced inside the lorry by a flat, metallic taste that sat badly in the back of Jack's throat.

Jack stood still for a moment; he could hear the woman and the policemen talking outside. He had to find the evidence they needed fast, and get out.

372

He used the torch on his phone to pan around the room. Louis was right — the machines used to make knives would have fitted in a shed. Packed closely together at the far end of the container, there was even room left over for a little fridge, a hotplate and a microwave oven. Everything had been fastened to a metal framework welded to the interior walls of the lorry, so that nothing could budge while in transit.

Even a plastic bucket had been clipped to the wall.

But there was no filing cabinet. No cupboard. No safe. Nowhere the records of a business might be kept. He even checked the fridge and the microwave.

Nothing.

"Shit," he murmured.

He examined the tools. They were big, oven-sized blocks with gleaming shafts and blades and calibrations. The base of one of them opened out in a door that he'd missed the first time around, and inside it were sliding metal drawers of segmented trays — compartments of various sizes, each with a hinged, clear lid so he could see at a glance the array of hand tools, and drill bits and half-tooled knife blades and mouldings for handles and indeterminate pieces of metal and wood and stone and leather.

Four slim drawers. Scores of compartments.

But only one with diamonds.

Jack held his breath as, slowly, he lifted the lid.

This compartment alone was lined with black velvet, so that the dozens of brilliant stones glittered like a distant galaxy in a dark new world.

Jack breathed out. Then in again. Then quickly he folded the velvet over the diamonds, scooped them out and stuffed them deep into the pocket of his jeans.

He was a burglar, after all.

But he had not come for diamonds.

The voices outside rose slightly. Thank-yous and goodbyes.

Shit!

Jack looked around desperately. The records weren't here. The sliding drawers were the obvious place for them and they weren't there. With a plummeting heart, he realized the logical place for important business records would not be in the back of the lorry at all, but in the cab! Up front, where VC would have them at her fingertips.

He was in the wrong place and there was no time to get to the right one.

He forced himself to stand still and listen.

He heard the police car crunching away, and the woman's footsteps cross the gritty tarmac towards him. He glanced at the back door. It was open, but only a bit. If she checked it, he was screwed. He had nowhere to go. Nowhere to hide.

She didn't check.

He breathed a sigh of relief as he heard *and felt* her climb back into the cab, the vibrations of her movement travelling through the metal and his feet. And if he could feel her movement, she would feel his. Jack knew that any move he made now would have to be made with extraordinary caution. He put his torch off and took a careful step towards the door.

The engine started.

For some reason, Jack hadn't expected that. He'd thought VC would just get into her cab and go back to sleep.

But VC wasn't sleeping. She was moving on. Getting away.

With him!

Sound of car driving off.

Panic gripped Jack. He had to get out! Now!

But before he could move, the hydraulic brakes hissed and the lorry jerked backwards, throwing him to his hands and knees. He got up but then stumbled again as the vehicle lurched forward, and grabbed the edge of the fridge for support.

Then the vehicle turned sharply and Jack rolled across the floor with a grunt. The door of the fridge swung open behind him, illuminating the scene. As the lorry swayed he grabbed it again and hauled himself back to his knees, now at eye level with a narrow freezer compartment he'd missed before.

He yanked it open as if looking for a snack.

Inside was a bag of frozen peas, and — under that — a plastic bag containing something large and flat. Something that had no more place in a freezer than a knife does in a boot . . .

Reynolds was going to have a heart attack.

It was bad enough to be told that his arrest of Jack Bright would be called into question once they were back in Tiverton, without having to watch the same little thief sneak across the car park and break into private property — all with the blessing of the Senior Investigating Officer.

And to have to sit and wait and not know what the *hell* was going on inside the back of the lorry was a rare torture.

There might be booby traps. Armed guards. A tiger in a cage!

He tensed unbearably as Veronica Creed — cutler to kings and killers — finished up her conversation and headed back to the cab.

And then she started the engine . . .

Reynolds went cold. He hadn't expected that.

And neither had Marvel, who grunted his surprise.

"Sir?" said Reynolds nervously.

"Give him a minute," said Marvel.

Reynolds gave him ten seconds, then said "Sir?" again, more forcefully. But Marvel stood his ground.

The lorry backed up. Then went forward. Then reversed again in an arc. Now they couldn't see the back door any more. Didn't know what was happening inside the lorry *even more* than they hadn't known what was happening a minute ago.

The brakes hissed and Reynolds saw the big front wheels turning to make the final sweep out of the car park.

"*Sir!*" he squeaked.

"Give him a minute," said Marvel.

Reynolds imagined the disciplinary hearing — maybe the trial. How he'd bear witness to Marvel's cold, uncaring tone as the child he'd sent out to steal evidence for him was injured or killed or kidnapped and never seen again. A fat, selfish Fagin. While *he* was —

Reynolds' imagination hit PAUSE. What *was* he? What would *he* be in all of this if Jack Bright came to harm?

"Shit!" he yelled, and finally flung open his door to put a stop to this madness, just as the big blue lorry rumbled past them in the darkness.

"Shit!" he yelled again, and threw himself back in his seat and slammed the door shut and shouted, "Go! Go! Go!" like a bank robber.

But Marvel didn't go. Didn't even start the getaway car.

"SIR!" Reynolds yelled at him, but Marvel was grinning.

Grinning and pointing.

At Jack Bright, on his hands and knees, alone in the middle of the car park.

"I told you to give him a minute," he said.

Reynolds watched in amazement as the skinny boy rose gingerly from the tarmac, looked around to get his bearings, and then jogged towards them unevenly, clutching something large and flat to his chest.

He yanked open the back door and fell on to the seat, gasping for air.

"Did you get it?" said Marvel in the mirror.

"I got *something*," said the boy, and held it out.

"Why's it cold?" said Marvel. He switched on the interior light. Inside the clear plastic bag they could see a black leather ledger.

And embossed in gold on the cover:
BOOK OF KNIVES.

The book was all in code.

Every entry was a series of seemingly unrelated numbers and letters in short bursts, annotated here or there by a symbol and a footnote that was also unintelligible.

Marvel had grumbled and bumbled over it in the car park for a while and hadn't made an iota of progress.

"Mumbo fucking jumbo," he'd finally said — then closed the book with a petulant clap, handed it to Reynolds, and started the car.

As they left Pevensey Bay, Reynolds opened the Book of Knives on his knees.

He relished the task. At school he'd been good at maths — could spot patterns and anomalies more quickly than his classmates. And he liked crosswords, too. The Times, the Telegraph. Cryptic stuff. He was sure his talents would help him now.

First he scanned each lined page without much focus — just letting his eyes drift down the entries, which were written in a hand that was so tight and precise that it hardly seemed human. He turned the pages with an easy rhythm, his eyes gliding smoothly over the entries until the writing ran out.

There were ten entries on each page and a little over nine pages had been filled. If he assumed (even though he winced at the very thought) that each entry related to a single knife, it would mean that VC had made an average of fewer than ten knives a year. It didn't seem a lot.

Or it did.

Reynolds realized he had no frame of reference so any speculation was pointless.

In the back, Jack Bright said something. He turned to look at the boy, but he was asleep, frowning against the upholstery, his fist balled over his ear.

"What did he say?" said Marvel.

"Didn't catch it, sir," said Reynolds. "He's asleep."

He paged through the book again, more slowly this time.

He assumed that the entries had been made in chronological order. With that his only focus, dates made themselves known to him. Days were in figures, months represented by a letter or two, the year in figures again. Just the two that counted.

Once that small triumph had been silently celebrated, there was little else in which to rejoice. Every entry was a jumble of numbers and upper- and lower-case letters, broken into batches as if they were words, except they were not. Every entry had a single full stop. Other than that, each was a string of unintelligible nonsense.

His eyes burning with lack of sleep, DS Reynolds stared at a random entry, *willing* it to miraculously rearrange itself into sense.

22AP98S7433t 334546anPK3gWC e0.3CTN133500
It meant nothing to him.
14JL98G7869r 667897aST7vAGC e0.7CCF72s6500
Neither did the next one.
12OC98W799h 223988iFH5lABT e0.5CTA1110250R
And then they were out of ninety-eight. Still no sense.
19MR99H7224a 775888yPK3deWT n0.2CBR173250
"Any luck?" said Marvel quietly.

Reynolds sighed. "Not really, sir, although I can see they're listed by date, so I assume each entry relates to the sale of a knife, but that's about it. It's not a code based on mathematics or language, but on the unique attributes of knives and the business dealings of their maker — to which we are not privy."

Marvel drummed his fingers on the steering wheel. "Surely it can't be that different from any other sales ledger. What would she have wanted to record about each sale? Date, item, price, purchaser. What else?"

"Ummm . . . address? Quality? Special features?"

Marvel nodded. "That's about it, isn't it? So even if she was thorough, we're still only talking about half a dozen things she'd record. So, as long as that's a sales ledger and not her attempts to communicate with Martians, we *do* have a guide to decoding it. We just need to relate each element to a knife or purchaser and so on."

"But we don't know anything about the knives or the purchasers."

"We know about one knife and one possible purchaser," said Marvel. "Start there."

"Well, after the date," said Reynolds, "every entry has a letter and a seven." He read random entries. "*W7991, L7634, P7220* . . . it goes on."

"And what comes after that?"

Reynolds took a moment to check several entries before answering.

"Another letter. Seemingly random. So, a random letter, a random four-figure number starting with a seven, and another random letter . . ."

"And then?"

Again Reynolds checked several entries. "And then a six-figure number. Again, seemingly random. There's a full stop in each entry."

"Where?"

"About two-thirds along in each case. Oh, and with a zero in front of it. As if it's zero point five, zero point two, etc."

He read out an entry. "*19MY00H7224a 775888yPK3de-WTn0.2CBR173250.*"

Silence.

"What comes before the full stop?"

"A zero, sir. In every case. And after it a number and the letter C."

"In every case?"

Reynolds checked and nodded. "Looks like it."

Marvel gave a precautionary yank on his nasal hairs while Reynolds stared stupidly at the book on his lap. And all the time the convergent white lines of the M4 motorway rushed at them out of the darkness and flickered away under the car.

Jack Bright woke and stretched and then hung between the front seats, peering at the book too, as if he might help.

"Why's that one got R at the end?"

Another ten miles of black road hissed under them.

"Could C be for carat?" said Marvel. "Could that be the size of the diamond?"

Reynolds frowned and ran his finger down the entries. "Yes!" he exclaimed. "Sir, I think that's right! In every case it's a similar value — from zero point two to zero point seven-five, followed by a C."

He beamed at Marvel, who nodded grimly. "We're not there yet."

"I know, I know." But Reynolds was enthused all over again. They knew dates. And now they knew for sure that each string of numbers and letters somehow resolved into details of the knife as well — most probably the price and the buyer. It was only a matter of time.

They pulled into Reading services and all got out for a pee and some coffee, then headed west again.

Jack curled up on the back seat and fell asleep again almost immediately.

In the front seat, DS Reynolds opened the Book of Knives with new determination. He was sure that cracking the code that could link Adam While to the murder weapon was only a matter of time.

Reynolds frowned, and flicked through the pages to check. "Jack's right," he said suddenly, glancing at Marvel. "Only one entry ends with a letter."

"Yeah? Which one?"

Reynolds bent over the book for the hundredth time, flicking pages, his finger seeking, eyes checking . . .

12OC98W799h 223988iFH5lABT e0.5CTA1110250R

"The knife sold in October 1998."

"That's two months *after* Eileen was murdered," said Marvel quietly. "Adam While had his knife for years before that."

"But what if he had *both*?" said Reynolds. "What if he had the knife before *and* afterwards? What if he murdered Eileen with a knife he'd bought or been given years earlier? And then he panicked and threw it away at the scene? He went back to the lay-by to try to find it, but it was only when he was picked up that he realized the police had already found it."

Marvel nodded. "He was one of a small handful of people who knew the police had found the murder weapon."

"Exactly! For all he knew, they'd be releasing pictures of it to the press and someone like his wife might see it and start asking questions about *his* knife. So he needed to get another one as soon as possible because, after all, how could the police have *his* knife if *he* still had it? It was watertight."

Marvel joined in. "The problem was, he couldn't just buy an identical knife off the shelf, because it's not one of thousands, it's one of one."

"Or, in this case," said Reynolds, "one of *two*."

"So R is for replica," said Marvel.

Reynolds nodded. "Or replacement. Or re-order. Or re-issue. But all of them mean the same thing — Adam

While had to commission a new VC knife to cover his back. Ordered at the end of August and finished in October."

Reynolds grinned like a fool. He couldn't remember the last time he'd felt so good. Marvel glanced at him with a look in his eye that he'd never seen before, so it took him a moment to realize it was respect. And although DS Reynolds thought that DCI Marvel was an arse, he still felt proud.

"Once she'd made a replacement in a rush, Veronica Creed must have known he was guilty of *something*," said Marvel. "That's probably why she took off so fast after our little visit."

"Exactly," said Reynolds, and bent back over the book.

Now he focused on that single entry. He took out his notebook and wrote out the code so he could break it down and play about with it, like an anagram. All the letters, all the numbers. Where he knew the first six characters were the date, and the 0.5C was a half-carat diamond, and R stood for replica. Or replacement. Or re-order, or re-issue, or rush . . .

After that, it was only a matter of time.

Near Swindon, he took the knife out of the glove compartment and measured it and put it away again with a proud click.

"Got it!" he shouted.

Jack woke up and yawned and rubbed his eyes and hung over Reynolds' shoulder to hear what he had to say.

"All the information we need is right here! All she's done is break it up and mix it up so it looks like gibberish, but once you crack it, it's *easy* to read!"

He showed them. With Marvel glancing across as he drove, and Jack Bright breathing hard in his ear, Reynolds broke the code down for them, drawing lines to show breaks, and circling letters . . .

12OC98W799h 223988iFH5lABT e0.5CTA1110250R

"The first six characters are the date. We already know that. Then comes a random capital letter. Then a number always starting with seven. All mobile phone numbers in this country start with zero-seven. You see? She's just removed the zero to make it less recognizable, and broken the number into two parts, with what looks like a random letter either side!" He beamed at Marvel, who nodded.

"So now we know those numbers make up a phone number. Then there's another two letters — two capitals and a number, followed by a lower-case letter and three capitals. *FH5lABT*. Given this comes just before the size of the diamond, this *must* be a description of the product. The knife. So I imagine it's something like Folding Handle or Hunting, and five is the length of the blade in inches. Then the lower-case letter, and then ABT, which probably stands for something else about the knife . . ."

"Titanium," said Marvel. "Titanium blade."

"Yes, of course!" said Reynolds. "And Abalone handle! That's AB for Abalone and T for Titanium! And then another lower-case letter before the carat value, followed by more capital letters, but I don't know what they mean. *TA1110250R.*"

Marvel took it slowly. "What else was it that we said any manufacturer would want to record about a sale? Product, price, date, customer name and address —"

"Address!" said Reynolds. "TA is the postcode for Taunton."

"While was living in Taunton at the time of the murder."

"So, TA1 or TA11, which means this last number is the price, which would make that . . ." Reynolds paused, and glanced at Marvel. "Ten thousand, two hundred and fifty pounds."

Marvel whistled softly through his teeth. "She knew," he said grimly.

"You haven't seen the best bit yet," said Reynolds. "All these leftover letters scattered about that help to confuse the other information? Look at them . . ."

He held the notebook up so that Jack could see it more easily.

"W —" started Jack. Then he stopped and swallowed a lump in his throat. "While," he said. "They spell *While.*"

They got back to the Tiverton police station just after nine in the morning, with Marvel and Reynolds in rare matching good moods, and with Jack trailing a little way behind them, as if even Reynolds knew that he wasn't going to run now.

Jack sat down on one of the cheap plastic chairs near the door and stuck his hands deep into the pockets of his hoodie to await what came next, with a feeling of calm in his belly that was unfamiliar but welcome.

"Adam While's our man," Marvel said. "We've got so much on him he's never going to wriggle out of it now."

Parrott and Rice both broke into broad grins. Parrott gave them a little solo round of applause, while Elizabeth Rice came over and gave Jack's narrow shoulder a motherly squeeze.

"Parrott, get a patrol car. We'll go and pick him up now."

"Yes, sir," he nodded and hurried outside.

"Rice, you'll have to stay here, unless you can get anyone to relieve you?"

"I'll try," she said.

Marvel turned to Jack. "You can wait here if you want, but you're free to go."

Jack looked at Marvel in surprise.

"Sir!" protested Reynolds.

"A deal is a deal," shrugged Marvel. "You want me to lock him up until we actually drag While into the nick in handcuffs?"

The look on Reynolds' face said that was exactly what he wanted.

Marvel turned to Rice. "You don't have any objection, do you, Rice?"

"Absolutely not, sir," she said. "A deal is a deal."

Jack stood up tentatively, unsure of whether he was allowed to go or not.

"I made a lawful arrest," insisted Reynolds.

Neither Marvel nor Rice said anything.

"A hundred homes burgled and vandalized! What about *those* victims?"

His words hung in the silence and Jack didn't know what to do. Reynolds *had* arrested him — but a deal *was* a deal . . .

Inside his hoodie pockets, his fists tightened nervously — one around his phone, the other around the little figurine Mrs Reynolds had given him.

Mrs Reynolds.

Embarrassingly late, Jack put two and two together and made a startling — a *wonderful* — four!

Slowly he pulled the clown from his pocket and held it loosely in his hand, while looking DS Reynolds straight in the eye.

Reynolds saw it and flushed. "Where did you get that?" he demanded.

"My *next-door* neighbour gave it to me," said Jack carefully. "For fixing her lawnmower."

Reynolds opened his mouth and then closed it again.

Tentatively, Jack reached out and gripped the door handle. Nobody stopped him. Not even Reynolds.

"Thanks," said Jack, then grinned at them all. "Thanks for everything!"

And he walked out of the police station.

Jack wanted *so badly* to be home. Wanted to check Joy was OK and to give Merry the clown. Wanted to walk through the front door and find his father had restored the house to a home. *Somehow . . .*

With his spirits lifting in hope, he hurried past the benches and broke into a jog across the Tesco car park.

A car screeched and bounced to a halt at his hip and Jack slapped an angry hand on the bonnet and glared through the windscreen.

The driver was Catherine While.

"Jack!" she said through the open window. "Please help me!"

For a moment Jack didn't move. He was so disorientated.

What's your emergency?

Catherine While had been crying. Her eyes were red, and tears had led mascara down her face in ragged streaks. Her hair was a mess and she appeared to be wearing a nightdress.

"What's wrong?" he said.

"Jack," she said, and then had to stop and start again. "I think you might be right," she went on haltingly. "I think maybe Adam —"

She couldn't finish, but Jack's breath caught in his throat.

Time seemed to slow right down. He looked away from Mrs While, across the metal roofs of the cars glinting in the sun.

Was this really happening? *Here?* In a supermarket car park, three years later? Was he going to find out exactly what had happened to his mother *right here? Right now?*

"Can we talk?" she said.

He looked at her, dazed. "How did you find me?" he said.

"This is the only place I've seen you before," she said. And then she repeated, "Can we talk? Please?"

He nodded dumbly.

She waited. She waited. She was waiting.

For him, he finally realized. To get in the car. So they could talk.

Jack walked slowly around the front of the Volvo, opened the passenger door and got in.

It was hot inside. *Baking* hot. Even with the windows down.

Mrs While was squeezed behind the wheel so tight that it pressed against her big belly.

"Thank you," she said with a wavering voice. Then she wiped her eyes and took a deep breath, and released the handbrake, and they drove slowly out of the car park.

Jack wondered if they'd talk in the car, or drive somewhere else. Not her home, he thought. *He* might be there.

They passed the showroom full of cars nobody could afford, and then they passed Jack's house. He willed Mrs While to stop.

She didn't stop, and they left his home behind.

He kept looking at her but she didn't look at him. She was pale and her hands trembled on the wheel.

"Are you OK?" he asked, even though she was the grown-up and he was the child.

She nodded, but her mouth wobbled and she kept wiping her eyes, so he knew she wasn't OK.

She drove to the dual carriageway, and headed north.

"Where are we going?" he asked.

She shook her head mutely and Jack felt a cold stone of unease settle in his belly.

"Where are we *going*?" he insisted.

A sob escaped Catherine While like a big bubble of fear and Jack turned too slow, too late, too stupid.

A bump in his back, a dark blur in his eye, and a knife at his throat.

Abalone.

Nobody answered the door at the While home.

"Shit," said Marvel. Just his luck!

Reynolds and Parrott went round the back to see if anything looked out of place.

Across the road, a man washed an already very shiny car. Marvel went over to him and showed him his ID. The neighbour's name was Norman Kent.

"We're looking for Adam While," said Marvel.

"I saw him this morning," said the neighbour. "I heard him leave around seven."

"Did you see him?"

"No, I just know the sound of his van."

"What kind of van?"

"White, with a horse on the side and a red rosette on the back doors."

"Easy to spot," said Marvel, and Mr Kent nodded and smiled.

"And what about Mrs While?"

"She has a green Volvo."

"Have you seen her today?"

"No, I haven't seen her for a few days," said Mr Kent. He paused and then said, "Do you think she's all right?"

Marvel looked at him sharply. "Why would she not be?"

"No real reason," said Mr Kent. "It's only that she hasn't been herself lately. Usually she's full of smiles and waves. But in the past few weeks she's looked a bit anxious. I wondered if there was a problem with the baby, but you can't just ask about stuff like that, can you?"

"God, no," said Marvel.

"And I heard them fighting."

"The Whiles? When?"

"I can't remember," he said. "Four or five days ago? Adam came home late, I know that. I assumed he'd been drinking because he hadn't taken his van, and I noticed him coming in on foot around one in the morning."

"That's a long time after last orders."

Mr Kent shrugged. "Anyway, I heard her shouting at him when he went in."

"Did you see Catherine again after that?"

Mr Kent squeezed his sponge like an aide-memoire and took a long time to say, "No."

"Do you have a spare key to their house?"

"Afraid not," said Mr Kent.

"Thanks for your help," said Marvel.

He rejoined Parrott and Reynolds at the Whiles' front door.

"Anything?"

"Nothing, sir."

"Neighbour says he heard them fighting four or five days ago. Hasn't seen Catherine While since."

Marvel's phone rang. He answered and only listened, looking increasingly grim.

"What time?" was all he said, before hanging up.

"That was Rice," he said. "Catherine While's mother just reported her missing. Apparently she'd been staying there for a few days, went downstairs at seven this morning to make tea, and never came back."

As one, they all looked at the front door.

"We should get a warrant," said Reynolds.

"Or a brick," said Marvel, and picked one out of the path, and smashed the glass in the front door. "Don't give me the stink-eye, Reynolds. I've reasonable grounds to believe a crime's been committed here and that Catherine While's life may be in danger."

They searched the house.

And found nothing.

"Shut up!" said Adam While. "*Shut up!*"

But Jack hadn't said anything.

Maybe it was for his wife, who was now choking on sobs and red in the face.

"*Shut up!*"

The angrier he got, the worse she drove.

Jack stayed out of it. He tried to think. To plan . . . as best he could with his head pushed to one side and the point of a knife pricking his neck.

Catherine While drove erratically — now on the accelerator, now on the brake — and the knife pricked him often. He could feel blood trickling down his throat and over his collarbone.

If he moved, if he spoke, While would kill him. He had no doubt.

How could he stop him? Jack didn't know. He had no weapon, he had no skills, and Adam While was behind him. He'd have to turn to face him, and by the time he did, his vein would be slit, blood gushing out, even if it was only by accident.

They neared the end of the dual carriageway. He knew there was a roundabout ahead that led to the

M5. Maybe he could jump out if they slowed down enough.

He thought of his mother. Had she planned like this? Had she tried to jump from Adam While's car? Had she seen him and Joy and Merry on the hard shoulder? Waved frantically? Hoped for help. Watched him turn away from her?

Scared.

Stupid.

Watched them grow smaller instead of bigger?

Tears fizzed up Jack's nose but furiously he willed them away. Crying never got anybody anything. He had to think about other things right now.

Like staying alive.

He tensed. He slid his eyes sideways and looked at the door handle. He imagined how it would feel in his hand, how it would open, how he'd roll sideways — away from the blade — how he'd hit the tarmac and try to stay loose as a drunk, and hope he wasn't hit by a truck . . .

Catherine dithered on to the roundabout. "Where —"

"North!" While shouted. "North!"

"Which way is north?" Catherine turned to look at her husband — her lips red and swollen with bawling, her red eyes rimmed with black that ran rivers down her face. She looked like a clown.

A sad clown.

"Left!" shouted While, and leaned between the seats to yank the wheel. "Left!"

The car lurched one way, While lurched the other, and Jack twisted and smashed the china clown into the bridge of his nose. It shattered in his hand and blood ran through his knuckles, although he didn't know whose it was.

Catherine screamed as her husband fell behind the passenger seat, his left hand protecting his face, the knife in his right stabbing at air.

Jack leapt into the back in a single movement. He landed on While knees-first, snatching the knife from his hand even as he ground the shards of clown into the man's eyes. While shouted and grabbed his wrist, and Jack slashed at his hand and arm until he let go.

Horns blared. Catherine screamed again and the car veered the other way, and Jack fell on to his back behind the driver's seat.

While flailed blindly for something to pull himself upright. He struggled into a sitting position on the floor of the car, and Jack kicked him in the face. He was only wearing trainers but a kick in the face is a kick in the face, and While slammed against the door, crying out through a bloody mask. Even his teeth were red. Then he doubled over in the footwell behind the passenger seat, dripping blood into his hands, howling like a mourner.

"*My eyes! My eyes!*"

Jack slithered into the front seat and groped for the recline lever. He found it and threw himself backwards, and While cried out again as the seat hit him in the back of the head, doubled him over, and trapped him on the floor.

"*Adam!*" screamed Catherine.

"Keep driving!" shouted Jack. "Just keep driving!" He would make her drive to a town. Somewhere big enough for a police station.

Adam While tried to force the seat upward. It bucked under Jack and he jumped on it hard with his knees.

"You little fucker! I'm blind! I can't see!"

Jack turned around and sat on the seat-back to give it extra weight. There was blood all over the back seat and the windows. His left hand was bleeding, but not enough to have made so much mess. He winced at the needle-like shards of china still stuck in his palm. The handle of the knife was slippery with blood. He wiped it on his sleeve.

"I'm so sorry," said Catherine. "I'm so sorry! I didn't know ..." She choked on her tears, then got back enough control to go on: "He said he only wanted to talk to you."

"You don't talk with a knife," said Jack angrily. "Nobody talks with a knife."

He focused on the road ahead. They were on the motorway. He didn't know where. He'd lost his bearings.

"Where are we?" he said.

"M5 south," she said.

"*Fuck!*" shouted While. "Fuck, fuck, *fuck!*" Then he whimpered, "Cath, help me! My eyes are bleeding. I can't see! I think I'm blind!"

"Shut up," said Jack, without energy. He stared at the knife in his lap. Wiped more blood off it.

One of two.

Catherine started to cry again.

Adam While said "*Catherine*" once, but she didn't answer him.

Jack squinted into the fast-lowering sun. A big blue signpost said Exeter was straight ahead. Exeter was good. There was a big police station there. They would go to Ex —

"Stop!" he cried.

"What?"

"Stop right here!"

Catherine swung the car over as others hooted and swerved around her. They crunched to a halt on the hard shoulder, close to a short line of conifers.

"Turn it off."

She switched off the ignition. And for a long moment the only sound was Adam While, snuffling and moaning in the footwell. Then a car sped past them, and made them shake. And another.

Too dangerous.

Jack stared at the road ahead, memory making him shiver in the heat.

"This is where it started," he whispered.

"What?" sniffed Catherine. "Where what started?"

"This is the last place I saw my mother."

Catherine blinked at him, wide-eyed.

"The car stopped right here," he said, and pointed up ahead with the knife. "And she walked up the road to find a phone."

Catherine looked up ahead. There was no phone in sight, and then a wide bend hid everything.

"We waited for an hour," Jack went on. "I had a watch for my birthday. It was so hot it smelled like the

400

car was melting. We played 'I Spy'. Me and Joy. But we waited too long to go after her . . ."

He cleared his throat. "*I* waited too long."

Catherine stared at him questioningly, but Jack went on, his eyes distant and his voice soft, as if remembering a dream.

"We walked and we walked. We were thirsty and scared and nobody stopped to help us and I had to carry Merry because she wouldn't walk." He glanced at Catherine and gave a brief smile. "She was such a brat!"

Then he sighed and looked up the road again. "So I carried her, and all the time I kept thinking, someone will stop. Someone will stop and help us. But nobody did. Nobody helped us. And when we got there, Mum was gone. The phone was just dangling."

"What happened?" said Catherine, her voice low with horror.

"Lies!" cried Adam. "He's telling you *lies*!"

But Catherine's eyes never left Jack, transfixed by his story.

"Somebody *did* stop to help her. She *thought* he'd stopped to help her, you know? But he didn't stop to help her. He stopped to kill her."

Jack wiped his nose on his bloody arm, and stared at the sun turning orange in the sky.

Catherine was shaking so hard that Jack could feel it through the seats.

"Adam?" she asked. "Adam?"

There was a long, stretched silence.

"Adam?" she said again, and her voice was tremulous with fear.

"One bad choice, Cathy," he whispered hoarsely. "I only snapped once. I'd never do it again . . ."

Catherine While started to cry big, gasping sobs of horrible understanding.

Jack felt strange. For years, he had imagined this moment. The moment he would hear someone confess to killing his mother. He had always thought that when it came he would rage and rant and slash and burn. That the anger and loss he'd kept inside him for so long would explode like a sun, and consume the whole planet in a fiery rampage of hatred and vengeance.

But he heard Adam While's confession now with dull disinterest.

It meant nothing.

It changed nothing.

He didn't even want to know why.

It was just . . . over.

He got out of the car.

"Where are you going?" said Catherine.

The boy shrugged and stared at the horizon. "I don't know," he said. "I'm just going to walk."

Then he looked at her intently.

"Will you be OK?"

Catherine opened her mouth to say *NO!* but instead she said, "Yes, I'll be OK."

Jack Bright paused, then nodded — then turned and walked away without another word.

402

Catherine While felt some part of her leave with him. Some part that didn't want to be her any more. Wanted a different life, a different future from the one where her pregnant belly was pressed against the steering wheel of the pea-green Volvo, with blood on the seats and her husband — her murderous husband — trapped and bleeding to death in the rear footwell.

"Cath?" he whined. "Can you take me to a hospital?"

Catherine thought about it. She could take him to a hospital.

Or she could not.

"Catherine?" he said. "I'm bleeding a lot. I think he cut a vein in my arm. And I'm blind. And I can't breathe so well, bent over like this. I can't move! I can't fucking move! Can you put the seat up? So I can breathe? Please? . . . Catherine? Please?"

"Be quiet," she said. "I'm thinking."

One bad choice, she was thinking. *One bad choice.* She must be careful not to make another. Here. Now. On the hard shoulder.

She stared up the road. The boy was almost at the bend already. A small figure, getting smaller, and indistinct against the fields backlit by the orange sun.

Adam started to cry again. Weaker now.

Her heart barely heard him.

Finally she turned the key.

"*Catherine!*" he wept.

But Catherine didn't answer him. She checked her mirrors, signalled, and manoeuvred the pea-green Volvo with Side Impact Protection System and automatic child locks out into traffic.

By the time she passed Jack Bright, she was doing seventy. She had a full tank of petrol. She could drive all night if she wanted to. Maybe she'd do that.

Things would be clearer in the morning.

Jack was on the hard shoulder.

Small bugs whirred through the motionless air, and cars that passed kicked up little dust devils on the verge, where long yellow grass grew to his hip.

But cars passed less frequently now, and the rolling hills to the west made for a tall horizon. Dusk was on its way, and the heat was starting to leave the day.

There was a scrubby little tree up ahead. Wild red apples scrunched softly underfoot as Jack approached. He sat down and picked one of them up.

It was small but perfect, like an apple for an elf.

He remembered Joy biting into one; spitting out the sour chunk. He remembered putting Merry down in the dirt among the fruit. He remembered hiding the baby bag . . .

Slowly he got up, and wiped his bloody, dusty hands on his jeans, still wincing at the splinters.

The apple tree leaned on the barrier like a weary spectator. Jack reached over the warm metal, his hand groping blindly in the narrow gap between the two. Expecting nothing, but touching something.

Something plastic. Soft. Familiar.

Carefully he tugged the bag free of the place where he'd left it three years ago, when he'd been another boy and Joy had been Joy, and Merry had been no more to him than a hot, awkward weight on his shoulder. And his mother had only been gone a long time, and wasn't yet dead . . .

The bag was squashed and a bit grubby, but still easily recognizable — zippered pink plastic, with the Mothercare logo.

Jack sat down cross-legged under the tree once more, and unzipped the bag.

The smell of it alone was like time travel. Warm plastic, and that weird baby-bottle smell.

The bottle was the first thing he took out. He held it up and squinted. There were still a few drops of water in the bottom. Then the nappies. Two of them in a plastic sachet that held three. Joy had taken one so their mother could change Merry when they found her. Which they never had, of course. Jack tried to remember when someone had next changed Merry, but he couldn't.

There was loads more stuff in the bag. Wipes and a flannel, and a little wooden dog on wheels with a spring for a tail, and three plastic pots of food — withered carrot sticks, dry, black apple slices, and immortal jelly babies.

Jack cleaned the blood off his hands with the wipes and ate the jelly babies.

At the very bottom of the bag was an old red leather purse.

Jack raised it slowly to his nose and memories went off in his head like fireworks. His mother's smile at the school gate; standing bored beside her at the supermarket checkout; her hand on his back as he bent over his homework . . .

He opened the purse. There was money inside. Not much. A few quid. A credit card. He ran his thumb over the raised letters of her name.

MRS EILEEN BRIGHT

There was a loyalty card and two coupons for teabags. *50p OFF!*

Jack opened the soft leather folds wide so he wouldn't miss anything. There were a few coins. And a piece of stiff paper.

Jack's heart beat faster.

A secret! Something wonderful that only his mother knew . . . Please, please, please . . . Please don't let it be a shopping list. Please let it be some precious thing . . .

Jack held his breath as he withdrew the paper from the purse.

It was blank. He turned it over.

It was the photo.

The photo he remembered. The photo he'd thought was lost or imagined. The photo that had a stolen frame waiting for it at home.

They weren't doing anything special. They were just laughing together on the blustery cliff, with their hair in their eyes, and blissfully ignorant of their own futures. His father had Merry in his big strong arms, Joy wore that jumper she never took off, while he made bunny ears behind her head. His mother had one hand on his shoulder, but was bent a little, as if speaking to him.

He couldn't remember what she had said to him, but from the look on her face he knew it was *I love you.*

Anger left Jack like a balloon, and even through his tears he felt so dizzy with joy that he wondered why he had held on to its cruel string for *so long.*

It doesn't matter, he thought. It was late, but it wasn't never.

Jack stared at the photo for so long that when he looked up again, it was night. The cars that passed him now had their lights on. Nearby, an owl called, and the dry scrub around the apple tree was suddenly silent. Then slowly, slowly, it came alive again with scraping and rustling and creeping and crawling . . .

Small bugs

He put the purse back in the nappy bag along with all the other stuff. He put the VC knife in there too.

He didn't want it, but he knew the police would. And after that, maybe Louis . . .

He didn't put the photo back in the bag though. That, he slid deep into his pocket so he could look at it at a moment's notice. He would show it to Joy and Merry when he got back home. Because back home was where he'd be going. Back home to his family. Back home to Marmite and sparklers.

It was a long walk. He wouldn't make it tonight, and wasn't going to try, but the west was gorgeous with red, and it wasn't going to rain.

So he lay down on the hard shoulder, with the baby bag for a pillow.

Tomorrow, a police car would find Jack Bright stretched out among the apples, already covered by a fine sheen of road dust, and so still that they'd think he was dead.

Tomorrow a policeman would shake him awake, as if for school.

But tonight he slept under the brand-new stars, with one pocket full of diamonds and the other full of love.

He didn't dream.

Acknowledgements

Catherine While paid cold hard cash for the right to appear as a character of my choosing in *Snap*. She was the highest bidder in the annual CLIC Sargent Get In Character auction for children and young people with cancer. Thanks to Catherine, and to all the under-bidders who forced her to be so generous!

Many thanks to my publishers and translators all over the world, but particularly to my editors, Sarah Adams, Amy Hundley and Stephanie Glencross, for their patience, enthusiasm and insight.

And a special mention to Sarah, who first imagined a knife beside her bed . . .

Other titles published by Ulverscroft:

THE BEAUTIFUL DEAD

Belinda Bauer

Crime reporter Eve Singer's career is in a slump when a spate of bizarre murders, each carefully orchestrated and advertised like performance art, occurs in her territory. Covering these very public crimes revives her byline; and when the killer contacts her himself, she is suddenly on the inside of the biggest murder investigation of the decade. Eve welcomes the chance to tantalize her ghoulish audience with the news from every gory scene. But as the killer becomes increasingly obsessed with her, she realizes there's a thin line between inside information and becoming an accomplice to murder — possibly her own . . .

THE SHUT EYE

Belinda Bauer

When James Buck pops out to buy fireworks, leaving the front door of his flat open, his little son, Daniel, wanders outside and goes missing. Now James struggles to cope with his guilt, while his wife Anna spends her days guarding the small footprints her son made in the forecourt near her door. A flyer advertising a psychic, Richard Latham, offers Anna hope at last . . . DCI John Marvel knows Latham from another case of a missing child — that of twelve-year-old Edie Evans — but he was of no help. With two children missing, Marvel is astounded when his boss asks him to find his wife's missing poodle. He must also make a decision about Latham. Is he a visionary? A shut eye? Or a cruel fake, preying on the vulnerable?